DEFENDING ALLYE

DISCOVER OTHER TITLES BY SUSAN STOKER

Ace Security Series

Claiming Grace

Claiming Alexis

Claiming Bailey

Claiming Felicity

Mountain Mercenaries Series

Defending Allye

Defending Chloe (December 2018)

More titles to come!

Delta Force Heroes Series

Rescuing Rayne

Assisting Aimee (novella) *loosely tied to Delta Force*

Rescuing Emily

Rescuing Harley

Marrying Emily

Rescuing Kassie

Rescuing Bryn

Rescuing Casey

Rescuing Sadie

Rescuing Wendy

Rescuing Mary

Badge of Honor: Texas Heroes Series

Justice for Mackenzie

Justice for Mickie

Justice for Corrie

Justice for Laine (novella)

Shelter for Elizabeth

Justice for Boone

Shelter for Adeline

Shelter for Sophie

Justice for Erin

Shelter for Blythe

Justice for Hope

Shelter for Quinn (TBA)

Shelter for Koren (TBA)

Shelter for Penelope (TBA)

SEAL of Protection Series

Protecting Caroline

Protecting Alabama

Protecting Fiona

Marrying Caroline (novella)

Protecting Summer

Protecting Cheyenne

Protecting Jessyka

Protecting Julie (novella)

Protecting Melody

Protecting the Future

Protecting Alabama's Kids (novella)

Protecting Kiera (novella)

Protecting Dakota

Beyond Reality Series

Outback Hearts

Flaming Hearts

Frozen Hearts

Stand-Alone Novels

The Guardian Mist

A Princess for Cale

A Moment in Time

Writing as Annie George

Stepbrother Virgin (erotic novella)

DEFENDING ALLYE

Mountain Mercenaries, Book 1

Susan Stoker

This is a work of fiction. Names, characters, organizations, places, events, and incidents are either products of the author's imagination or are used fictitiously.

Published by Montlake Romance, Seattle

www.apub.com

ISBN-13: 9781503949904
ISBN-10: 1503949907

Cover design by Eileen Carey

Printed in the United States of America

DEFENDING ALLYE

Chapter One

"So I'll see you back at the rendezvous point, right?" Black asked.

"Absolutely," Gray told his friend and partner as he readied himself to slip over the side of the fiberglass boat into the Pacific Ocean. It was an easy mile swim to his target, especially since he was a former Navy SEAL.

Rex, their handler, had gotten word that an exchange would be taking place tonight. Their job was to intercept a money drop, which was payment for a sex slave. Gray's part of the mission involved swimming to the boat that was waiting to receive the money and subduing those on board, and Black would intercept the boat that was dropping off the cash. The people on both boats would be interrogated to find out more information about how the major sex-trafficking ring worked, who the key players were, and how to find them.

Gray had no idea how Rex got the information he did. All he knew was that the man had rarely ever been wrong.

Their handler himself was an enigma to the men of Mountain Mercenaries. No one had ever met him. Rex was their boss, and one of the smartest men they'd ever known, but he communicated only via phone, using some sort of device to change his voice as well. He was secretive and slightly paranoid, but no one who worked for him could deny that he was passionate about what he did. And Gray trusted Rex simply because he had never let him or the team down. His intelligence was almost always one hundred percent accurate, and in their line of work, that was literally a matter of life and death. He relayed information to the team, and they'd go make sure another asshole got what was coming to him.

Gray had no problem killing people who thought it was all right to kidnap women and children and force them to have sex with whoever was willing to pay for the privilege. He'd gladly spend the rest of his life fighting to wipe the assholes off the face of the earth.

Today's mission had been called in on very short notice. Thus, only he and Black were on it, having been the only two available. The rest of the guys—Meat, Arrow, Ball, and Ro—were busy gearing up to head to Mexico on their own mission.

Rex had informed them that a woman, Allye Martin, had recently been reported missing by the owner of the Dance Theatre of San Francisco. She was one of the dancers, and she hadn't shown up for rehearsal. Since that area had been rife with disappearances of young women lately, Rex was monitoring activity in the city. His network of informants had done their thing, reporting back with intel that the missing dancer's name was heard in connection with the notorious Gage Nightingale.

Nightingale was the leader of an underground group that bought and sold women all over the world. If someone had the right connections, all they had to do was contact Nightingale, let him know who they wanted, and voilà! The woman would be delivered to the person on a silver platter. It wasn't cheap, but assholes powerful enough to have any woman they wanted taken against their will seldom cared about price.

Hopefully, by interrupting the flow of money from the buyer to the supplier, they would get enough information to shut down the operation once and for all . . . and of course, find out where the woman was being kept. Gray was prepared to get the information from the captain by any means necessary—or kill him, if he attempted to get a message back to whoever had bought the woman or to warn Nightingale that the operation was in jeopardy.

They'd gotten GPS coordinates of where the pick-up boat was supposed to be waiting to receive the money for the dancer. After Black headed off the other boat, their plan was to meet back at another prearranged set of coordinates.

Gray nodded at Black and slipped into the waters. It was late, and he could see the lights of San Francisco in the distance but knew they were miles away.

As he swam toward the coordinates, Gray briefly reflected on the days when he used to do this sort of thing for his country. He had always loved the water. His mother said that he'd loved baths from his very first one, when he was just two days old. He'd been on his high school swim team and had earned a swimming scholarship to the US Naval Academy. It was almost inevitable that he'd become a Navy SEAL. But after they'd gotten fraudulent intel and his entire team had been killed, he'd become jaded. He'd taken out his anger over losing his team on anyone and everyone around him.

Thank God Rex had offered him the job with Mountain Mercenaries. Gray had no idea how the man had found him, and frankly, he didn't really care. He enjoyed what he did and honestly felt like he was making a difference in the world. There would always be those who took advantage of others, but maybe, just maybe, he and the rest of the group were making a dent in the numbers.

The slightly choppy ocean waves didn't bother him as he continued to stroke through the water. He took the time to go over the plan in his head once more. He thought about what he wanted to ask the courier and what information Rex needed about Gage Nightingale so they could shut down his massive operation once and for all. It was risky driving the boat to the rendezvous, because it probably wasn't registered, and the last thing Gray wanted was to be caught by the Coast Guard and questioned. Ball was a former Coastie, but since he wasn't here,

Gray couldn't rely on him to smooth things over, if necessary. But he'd deal with any trouble later, if it came to that.

Lifting his head as he swam, Gray saw the large form of the fishing vessel bobbing in the water ahead of him. He smiled—he'd made good time. He switched from a freestyle stroke to a breaststroke, so his movements wouldn't be seen from the vessel if anyone was watching the dark waters. He knifed through the waves as easily and stealthily as an eel.

When he arrived at the boat, Gray reached down and slipped off his flippers, and they quickly sank below the surface.

The boat was bigger than he'd expected. It was black and white, with quite a bit of rust marring its sides. It was also run-down, not cared for in the way someone who actually fished for a living would be sure to look after it. Using his upper-body strength, Gray pulled himself up far enough to see over the side to check things out. The wheelhouse was located toward the front of the vessel, and there was a door that led belowdecks. There were nets hanging here and there on the back of the boat, as well as at least a dozen fishing poles. Miscellaneous crates and tubs were also strewn about the deck.

Seeing no one, Gray silently pulled himself up and over the back of the boat, landing without a sound on the crowded back deck. Ducking behind a crate, then a barrel, he made his way to the door to the lower deck of the vessel. He didn't want someone coming up behind him while he was interrogating the captain. There was only supposed to be one man on the boat, but Gray never assumed anything.

Gray was wearing a black dry suit equipped with several strategic pockets for things like knives, identification for the authorities in case they got involved, and other essentials. The dry suit was imperative for swimming in the Pacific. The water was way too cold for a simple wet suit. Wet suits allowed for the easy flow of water in and out of the material, whereas a dry suit kept water out. Gray wasn't planning on being in the water for an extended period of time, but he'd be a poor excuse for a SEAL if he didn't prepare for everything that could go wrong.

After extracting the small wedge of wood he carried for exactly this purpose, Gray shoved it under the tight bottom gap of the door. If someone tried to push it open from below the deck, they'd be unable to manage it without a lot of noise—thus alerting Gray to anyone else's presence on the vessel.

Finally, he turned his attention to the wheelhouse. There was a man inside the small room, looking down at a handheld GPS, oblivious to the presence of anyone else on the boat. Gray smiled at how easy this was going to be.

Without a sound, he made his way over to the man and had him in a headlock before the guy even knew someone was standing behind him.

"Hello," Gray greeted casually, as if they were old buddies.

The man immediately began to struggle, but it was no use, as Gray had him totally under his control.

"Here's how things are going to go," Gray said in a low, even tone. "You're going to answer all my questions. If you lie to me, I'll know, and you'll lose one of your fingers. If you lie again? I'll take another. We'll keep at it until your hands are nothing but useless nubs. And if you *still* lie to me, then I'll start on your toes. Got it?"

"Fuck you," the man sneered. "I'm not saying shit."

As quick as a flash, Gray had his KA-BAR knife out of its sheath, and he grabbed hold of the man's hand. Without mercy or fanfare, he sliced the razor-sharp blade across the base of the man's thumb.

The digit fell to the wood boards at their feet with a light thud.

The man immediately clutched his bleeding hand to his chest and began to scream.

Gray smirked and let him go, knowing he wouldn't be a threat to him at the moment, not when he was more concerned about the pain in his hand.

"Here's my first question: How do you get information about where to meet for the money drops?"

"You cut off my thumb, you asshole!" the man exclaimed, not looking up at Gray. "Fucking *fuck*, that hurts!"

"You want me to take another finger? Answer the question," Gray said harshly, looming over the bleeding thug with his arms crossed.

"I get a text," the man said quickly.

"From who?"

"I don't know. It's an unknown number. Gives me the coordinates. I drive the boat to where I'm told, get the money or merchandise, then go where I'm told to deliver it."

Gray practically growled at the offensive word the man used. "Women aren't *merchandise*," he spat.

The man shrugged. "I need the money. I don't ask no questions, and all's well that ends well."

Oh, this man was pissing Gray off. He leaned down and grabbed the man's other hand.

Within seconds, his other thumb was lying on the deck next to the first.

The man started screaming again, but Gray ignored him. He put the tip of the knife under the man's throat and said, "All's well that ends well? Tell that to the children whose mothers disappear. Tell that to the women who are raped day after day. Tell that to the families who never get any closure when their loved ones disappear. Women are *not* property. And there are consequences for assholes like you who think you can turn your head and pretend you're not taking money so women can be debased and abused for the rest of their lives. How did you get into the courier business?"

The man answered without hesitation this time, as if he knew Gray was one second away from slitting his throat. "Through a buddy. I pretend to be a fisherman, and no one looks twice when I take my boat out at odd hours."

"What's this buddy's name?" Gray asked, pressing the knife a little harder against the man's throat.

"Screw you!"

Gray opened his mouth to say something else—when there was an explosion below their feet. It rocked the boat, and he had to throw out a hand to keep his balance.

Gray looked in disbelief at the scared-out-of-his-mind captain. "There's someone else on board? Who?"

"I don't know his name! He said he was an escort for the merchan—er . . . the woman. The buyer didn't want anything to happen to her in the transfer."

"Fuck," Gray swore, knowing the mission had just been FUBARed—fucked up beyond all repair. There wasn't supposed to be anyone else on board the small boat. Not only that, but if the dancer had an escort, someone had to be *very* interested in getting his hands on her.

The boat lurched then and began to tilt slightly downward.

Knowing he didn't have a lot of time, Gray mercilessly slit the man's throat from ear to ear, making sure to cut into his jugular vein. He turned his back on the man and was exiting the wheelhouse even before the captain fell to the deck.

Already feeling the subtle tilt of the boat, Gray returned to the door that he'd jammed earlier, leading down into the living quarters of the vessel. Removing the wedge, he leaped down the stairs, past a door that probably led to a bedroom, and went straight to the engine room, where the explosion had to have come from. He threw open the door—and barely had time to dodge the large pipe that would've slammed right into his head if he hadn't moved.

Without thought, Gray brought up a leg and kicked at the man who had tried to kill him. He looked older than Gray's thirty-six years, but he was still deadly. The other man took another swing, which Gray easily dodged. Water swirled around their feet, growing deeper with every second. The man had obviously sabotaged the boat, and it was sinking incredibly fast.

"If you want to live, tell me why the dancer is so important," Gray ordered as he lashed out and sliced the man's thigh when he got too close.

"Fuck you," was the man's response.

"We don't have time for this," Gray growled. "Who bought the girl?"

"I'm not telling you shit," the other man said, throwing a wrench at Gray's head.

He ducked and tackled the man as he tried to slip past him out the door of the engine room.

They struggled for a moment, but Gray quickly got the upper hand. He was straddling the other man, his hands around his throat. The water was lapping at the man's chin, and his eyes were huge in his face as he stared defiantly up at Gray.

"Who wants the girl?" Gray asked again.

"It doesn't matter if you kill me. He'll still get the girl one way or another. He always gets what he wants."

Frustrated, Gray forced the man's head under the water for a beat, then hauled him above the waterline. "Where were you going to take her?"

The man grinned then. A sinister smile that made the hair on the back of Gray's neck stand straight up. "It doesn't matter where or who. He wants her. *Bad.* Even if you get her off this boat, he'll come for her. And you can't stop him."

Gray blinked. *What the fuck?*

The boat tilted then, and both men slid across the deck toward the engine. Knowing he was seriously out of time and options, Gray got nose to nose with the man.

"I'm not only going to stop him, I'm going to kill him," he vowed.

The other man opened his mouth to respond, but Gray didn't give him the chance. He hauled him upward and turned him in his arms as if he were a five-year-old child. Within seconds, he'd broken his neck.

Drowning him would've taken too much time. Time he didn't have, if the height of the ever-deepening water was any indication.

Throwing the dead body aside, Gray started for the door. He'd wanted to take his time and torture the man, using the threat of drowning as a very real motivator, but with eight words, the man had sealed his fate.

Even if you get her off this boat . . .

There wasn't supposed to be anyone on the boat other than the captain.

There wasn't supposed to be an escort.

And the dancer certainly wasn't supposed to be on the frickin' boat. This was supposed to be a money drop, not a transfer.

Sloshing through shin-deep water now, Gray went back through the engine room door toward the only other place anyone could be.

He forced the other door in the hallway open—and stared in disbelief at what he saw.

Chapter Two

Allye Martin frantically yanked at the handcuff on her wrist. The explosion had scared the shit out of her, but the water that had begun to seep in under the door of her prison scared her even more. And she hadn't thought she could be any more frightened than she'd been in the last forty-eight hours.

But nothing was more terrifying than knowing death was imminent. Being snatched off the street was bad. Facing the reality that someone had specifically targeted her hadn't been her best moment. Seeing the water get deeper and deeper around the bed she was sitting on, knowing there was no way she could get free, to get out of the room and have a fighting chance, was horrifying.

Drowning wasn't her idea of the best way to die. Bullet to the head—nice and quick. Head-on collision . . . hopefully immediate. Shanked? Not ideal, but if the knife cut her just right, it might not be so bad. Holding her breath until she couldn't hold it anymore, knowing that when she instinctively gasped for air, she'd fill her lungs with water? Absolutely horrendous.

She tugged at her wrist for the one hundred and forty-seventh time, hoping against hope that either her wrist had magically shrunk and would now fit through the cuff, or the metal would somehow come loose from the headboard it was attached to. But neither happened.

Just as she was trying to decide if she should take in a huge breath of water as soon as it was high enough to make her death faster, or if she should somehow try to prolong the inevitable, the door to her prison was pushed open. She had no doubt it would've banged against the wood behind it if the water hadn't slowed its movements.

Allye expected to see either the man who had cuffed her to the bed in the first place or the scruffy fisherman who'd tried to pretend he couldn't hear her yelling for help when she was dragged below deck.

But it wasn't either of those men. It was someone she'd never seen before, and she knew she would have definitely remembered seeing *this* man.

He was huge. Both muscular *and* tall. In fact, he couldn't stand up straight in the room because of the low ceiling. She wasn't short, but Allye knew without a doubt standing next to this behemoth of a man, she'd feel tiny. His jaw was square, and his lips were pressed together in a tight line.

He had short, dark hair and dark eyes. Eyes that were piercing in their intensity. He was wearing something that looked similar to a wet suit, except it seemed to have pockets that were bulging in places. His face had some sort of black paint or something smeared on it, which made it hard to really make out his features in the dim room.

They stared at each other for what seemed like an eternity before Allye remembered where they were and what was happening. She had no idea if he was a good guy or a bad guy, but at the moment, it hardly seemed to matter. Not if he could get her out of there. She held up her arm, the handcuff making a jarring noise as it scraped against the headboard.

"I'm stuck."

The words sounded silly in her head, but *he* didn't seem to think so. He reached into a small pocket at his hip and pulled out what looked to her like a handcuff key.

He sloshed his way to the bed and leaned over her arm. Allye saw that it was, indeed, a handcuff key.

"Do you always carry handcuff keys when you're lurking about in the ocean?" She winced at the question. She had a bad habit of blurting out whatever she was thinking, whether it was appropriate or not.

"Yup."

She blinked.

One word. He'd said only one word, but it was enough for her to fall in love with his voice. It was low and raspy, and she knew if he recited the telephone book she'd gladly listen all damn day.

"Well . . . good. Then today's my lucky day that you just happened to find me here in need of one. You know . . . 'cause the boat is sinking and all. The boat *is* sinking, right?"

"Yeah."

"Right. Um . . . I hate to bother you, but you didn't by any chance see a really scary guy out there? He's a little taller than me, black hair. Wearing jeans and a white button-up shirt? I know, totally inappropriate for the time and place, but that's what he had on."

When her rescuer just looked at her, she continued. "I'm only asking because, well, I don't think he really wants me to leave, and I don't want to run into him. And we will, you know, because this boat isn't that big. So I just wanted to know if you'd seen him . . ."

Her voice trailed off, and she felt stupid as the big man just continued to stare at her for a second. Finally, he said, "You don't have to worry about us running into him."

She sighed in relief. She figured this man had probably taken care of the asshole who'd gotten great joy out of telling her what awaited her, but she'd had to check. "Awesome."

"Come on, let's get out of here."

Still not knowing if she was jumping out of the frying pan into the fire or not, Allye scrambled off the bed. She winced when her feet landed in the water. She wasn't wearing shoes, they'd been taken from her, but she still had on her jeans and T-shirt, and the water was absolutely freezing.

The man turned and waded his way to the door, still slightly crouched so he wouldn't hit his head on the low ceiling, and Allye followed.

At the last second, she turned back and headed for the small desk in the room.

"What the fuck? Come on, lady! You said it yourself, the boat is sinking. We have to get out of here," her maybe-rescuer, maybe-sex-slaver said impatiently.

Without a word, Allye palmed what she'd detoured to get and turned back to the man. "I know. I'm coming."

When he turned his back once more, secure in the knowledge she really was following him this time, Allye slipped the flash drive she'd taken from the laptop computer on the desk into the zippered pocket of her shirt. Her kidnapper had left it in the room when he'd abruptly disappeared just before the explosion.

Content that even if the boat *did* sink to the bottom of the ocean, she'd still have something to show the cops to prove that she'd been kidnapped, Allye followed the giant out of the room toward the upper deck.

He'd gotten to her in the nick of time, it seemed, because as soon as they stepped topside, the boat shifted again. The man threw out an arm to push Allye out of the way of various crap that had been lying on the deck as it came barreling toward them. Allye was thrown against the wall of the wheelhouse hard enough to make her grunt. But almost as soon as she hit, the man was there, holding her arm to help steady and steer her around the crates and fishing poles that were now scattered everywhere.

"Thanks," she murmured.

He didn't answer, but kept hold of her as they made their way upward, assisting her toward the back of the boat. He stopped to grab something black from a crate that had spilled open with the force of the boat's movement. The deck was now tilting fairly alarmingly, à la *Titanic*, the light from the wheelhouse looking almost like a strobe as the boat pitched.

Allye glanced around, expecting to see another vessel, but when she saw nothing, she blurted out, "Where's your boat?"

"Don't have one."

Allye stared at him in disbelief. If he didn't have a boat, how in the world were they going to get back to the city? She opened her mouth to ask just that when he stopped at the back of the deck and crouched, pulling her down with him.

"Take off your pants," he said brusquely, not looking at her. He was scanning the surface of the water. For what, Allye had no idea. She couldn't see anything in the darkness all around them, and he'd said he didn't have a boat. But she certainly wasn't going to take off her jeans. No way. Screw that.

"Um . . . shouldn't we be finding the emergency raft? Or the life jackets?"

He turned and looked at her then, his eyes raking over her hair, her face, then down her body, before coming back up to meet her gaze.

"In case you haven't noticed, kitten, we're sinking. Even if we did have time, we wouldn't find either."

Allye blinked. "But . . . it's against the law not to have personal flotation devices."

He stared at her for another second, then grinned.

Allye's breath caught in her throat. Boy oh boy, when he smiled, it completely changed his entire countenance. He looked almost friendly. Almost.

"I'm thinking the fact that the owner of the boat was illegally transporting a kidnapped woman he was delivering to someone to be some sort of sex slave means that he wasn't too concerned about making sure he had the proper equipment onboard."

"True," she mumbled, feeling kind of stupid. Then she looked around. "Where *is* the driver guy and that other asshole, anyway?"

"You really do need to get those jeans off," the man next to her said without answering her question. "And you need to slip this on. We're most likely gonna be in the water for a bit, and the second we go overboard, you're gonna feel like you've got anchors attached to your hips if you don't lose the denim."

"But the water's cold," Allye protested, sounding ridiculous even to her own ears as she reached for the button of her jeans. She realized the black thing he'd scooped up from the deck and was now holding out to her was a wet suit. The thought of going into the ocean scared the hell out of her.

She was a good swimmer, though there was no way she'd make it long, not with the temperature of the water. But the boat was sinking faster and faster. Suddenly, putting on the wet suit seemed like a great idea. Even though it wouldn't keep the water away from her skin, it would keep her warmer than if she were wearing only her T-shirt and panties.

All things considered, taking off her pants in front of this stranger was the least of her worries. Her only thought was getting the wet suit on before the boat disappeared beneath them.

"The water *is* cold," the man said, and Allye realized he was responding to her asinine statement.

She waited for him to elaborate. He didn't. She had a million more questions and wasn't sure she should trust this stranger. He'd appeared out of nowhere. With a handcuff key. And she hadn't seen the other two men in a long time. Had he killed them?

Of course he had. Why else wouldn't they be trying to stop them by now? Unless this man was a part of whatever this was? Maybe he was trying to make her think he was a good guy so she'd do whatever he said. She'd be easier to control that way, for sure.

"Maybe—"

"Get out of your head," the man ordered, interrupting her before she could finish her thought. He squeezed her arm to get her attention. "I'm not one of them. I'm on your side. I'm gonna get you home. Trust me."

"How'd you know what I was thinking?" Allye asked as she pulled the cold material of the wet suit up and over her arms. It was snug, luckily. If it had been too big, it wouldn't keep her as warm. The events of the last forty-eight hours pressed down on her like a ten-ton weight, and she felt exhausted all of a sudden.

"Because it's what I'd be thinking if I were in your shoes."

"I'm not wearing any," she said inanely, holding up one of her legs, indicating her bare foot.

He didn't reply, but she thought she saw the corners of his mouth tip up before he controlled his reaction and wiped the emotion from his face.

Allye heard water lapping all around her, but kept her eyes on the man's. She swallowed hard. "Are we really about to jump off this boat into the ocean without any life jackets? And you think what? We can just swim to shore?"

"Piece of cake," the man said, smiling again.

"Maybe it won't sink," she said hopefully.

"Oh, she's gonna sink," her rescuer said with conviction.

The boat shifted just then, as if proving his words correct, tilting upward a bit more, forcing them to hold tight to the side. The ocean was closer now. He was right. All hopes of being able to cling to the bobbing boat until the Coast Guard or some other fisherman found them disappeared.

Closing her eyes, Allye took a deep breath. When she opened them, the man was still right there next to her, looking at her so intently it made her nervous.

"Ready to go, kitten?"

"Why are you calling me that?"

"Because you have two different-colored eyes. I had a kitten like that once. You remind me of her. Wide-eyed and innocent, but every now and then, she'd let me know she wasn't to be messed with by scratching me with her claws."

Allye rolled her eyes. "Great. I guess it's better than you saying I'm possessed by the devil. Between my eyes and this white streak in my hair, you can't imagine how many people have tried to 'save me.'"

The boat made a loud groaning sound, and, without a word, the man next to her twisted and put his hands around her waist. Before she knew what he had planned, she was flying through the air and hurtling toward the churning ocean.

Gray felt bad for a split second, but when he saw the entire front end of the boat disappear, he simply reacted, wanting to get the woman he'd nicknamed "kitten" out of the way of danger. He didn't want to be sitting on the end of the boat when it went under.

He knew even if he was sucked down with the boat, he could easily break free and kick to the surface, but the same likely couldn't be said for Allye. He preferred to get her clear of the boat once and for all, rather than risk her being in danger.

Sparing a precious second to glance at his watch, noting it was a little past nine, Gray dove off the back of the boat without waiting to see if the woman's head emerged between the waves. He hoped Black realized early that Gray wasn't going to make it to their rendezvous point so they'd have to spend less time in the cold Pacific. He could take it, but he wasn't sure about Allye Martin.

He didn't give a second thought to the two men who would disappear forever along with the vessel. Their burial ground would be the bottom of the ocean, but their souls had most certainly already been sucked down to hell.

Gray immediately began swimming toward where Allye had landed, waiting for her head to pop up and for her to give him shit for throwing her without warning.

Several seconds went by, and with each, Gray got more and more tense. Fuck, had she been hurt when she landed? He hadn't even bothered to ask if she could swim. He'd simply reacted instinctively.

Just when he was about ready to dive below the surface and blindly search, he saw her. She was about twenty feet farther out from where she'd landed. He was stroking toward her even as he was wondering how she'd gotten there so quickly.

When he reached her, he didn't worry about keeping his distance. He swam right up to her and put an arm around her waist, pulling her into his side and easily keeping them both above the waves.

"Are you hurt?" he asked brusquely.

The woman reached up and wiped her hair back from her face, the white streak visible amid her dark-brown locks. It truly was unusual . . . and interesting.

"No, but a little warning might've been nice."

Gray relaxed a fraction. The last thing he wanted or needed was her getting shitty with him. He knew Black would come looking for him when he didn't show up with the boat at the rendezvous point, but it was going to take a while.

He hoped Black had been able to locate and intercept the other boat. They needed more intel. Whoever was in the other boat might be the person who'd dropped her off. Lord knew he hadn't gotten anything out of the owner of the fishing vessel, or the surprise asshole who'd been escorting the lady to whoever had bought her.

He hadn't found what he'd expected when he entered the bedroom on the small boat either. He'd expected a freaked-out, scared-out-of-her-mind kidnapping victim. Instead, he'd found a calm and somewhat amusing woman who, so far, had done what was necessary to survive. Not only that, but she was attractive.

Allye Martin wasn't an in-your-face beautiful woman, but she was pretty. She had a cute nose that turned up a bit at the end, and even though he hadn't seen her outright smile yet, he'd spotted a dimple in one of her cheeks. Her lips were plump, and her dramatic cheekbones gave her face interesting angles. But her eyes . . .

Her right eye was a dark-blue color, like a stormy sea. Gray had a feeling in different light, it would change hues. And the left was a hazel brown. The effect was somewhat startling, but didn't detract from her beauty at all. Her eyes were wide set, with extremely long lashes. Her cheeks were currently flushed despite the cold water, and he could tell she was stressed to the max.

When dry, her hair had been a rich chestnut color, except for a streak of white that was about an inch wide and ran from the top of her scalp down the right side of her head. It went all the way to the end of her hair, which hung past her shoulders. Like her gaze, it was unusual and eye-catching. And it fit her. Gray didn't know how he knew that, but he did.

Her body was lithe under his hand. She was muscular and in shape, as any professional dancer would be.

The casual way she'd asked if he had a handcuff key had amused him. He'd expected her to be hysterical. At the very least crying, but she'd seemed to be holding up extremely well. Everything he'd seen so far had attracted him . . . but he wasn't here to pick up a date. Not even close.

Disgusted with himself, Gray mentally shook his head. He needed to concentrate on getting them as close to the rendezvous point as possible. If necessary, Gray probably could've made it all the way to shore, since he had on the dry suit and was somewhat used to the freezing ocean temperature, but he highly doubted the kitten in his arms could.

Keeping her mind occupied so she didn't panic was his focus right now.

"Sorry," Gray apologized, remembering her earlier statement about wanting some warning before being flung through the air as if she were a child rather than a full-grown woman. "I saw the boat sinking out of the corner of my eye and just reacted."

She sighed and said through chattering teeth. "It's okay."

"How'd you get all the way over here so quickly?" He could feel her legs brushing against his as they treaded water. Thoughts of their legs tangling in a different way shot through his brain, but he pushed the image aside. Not the time, and definitely not the place.

She shrugged. "I realized even before I landed what was probably happening, and visions of the *Titanic* flashed through my brain. I didn't want to be sucked down with the boat, so I swam underwater for as long as I could hold my breath."

"Smart," Gray murmured.

Her eyebrows rose.

"What?" he asked.

"A man—a macho, obviously badass man—admitting that something a woman did was smart?"

He couldn't help but chuckle. "I'm more than capable of telling you when you've done something right," he defended.

She looked at him warily. "But . . ." She let the word trail off.

"But I'm also capable of telling you when you've done something stupid. And going back for a piece of jewelry, or whatever it was you felt you couldn't leave that bedroom without, was just plain stupid. If the boat had gone under when we were still in that room, more than likely, we'd be headed for the bottom, along with the two goons that were on board with you."

She stared at him for a moment before sighing and turning her head away. "It only took about three seconds, but you're right. Sorry."

The apology was appropriate for the situation, but the tone wasn't. She sounded disappointed. In him. And that irked him.

Gray knew something was wrong, but then again, lots of things were wrong right about now. He wanted to demand she tell him what was so damn important she'd been willing to die for it . . . but he didn't. They had a rough ordeal ahead of them, and he wanted to stay on her good side. The last thing he needed was for her to get upset with him and become even more difficult.

"What's your name?" he asked, even though he already knew. Keeping her talking was paramount. It would keep her mind occupied and allow him to assess her physical state.

"Allye. Like the space between two buildings, but the *y* comes before the *e*."

He chuckled. "You sound like you've made that explanation a lot."

She shrugged. "I have."

"And your last name?"

"Martin. Allye Martin. And you?"

"Grayson Rogers." He didn't have any problem telling her his real name. It wasn't like she could google him and discover he was with the Mountain Mercenaries. When he wasn't being sent around the world by Rex to take care of horrible human beings who deserved whatever they got, he was an accountant. A damn good one at that.

"Nice to meet you, Grayson," Allye said.

Gray couldn't help it. He laughed.

Her eyes narrowed. "What's so funny?"

"You, kitten. Here we are, in the middle of the ocean, no boat, no life jackets, and you're acting as if we're in the middle of an eighteenth-century parlor or something."

She pushed at him, and he let her go. He needed to assess her swimming skills anyway, and this seemed as good a time as any.

"Would you rather I start screaming and crying? Is that it? Acting like a helpless victim? I've never been a victim in my life, and I'm not about to start now. And I don't cry, so you can forget that too."

"Ever?"

"What?"

"You don't cry ever?"

She shrugged, but continued to glare at him. "No."

"Why not?"

Her eyes widened. "Can we not talk about this?"

"Why not?" he asked again.

"Shit, you sound like a two-year-old. Why, why, why?" she complained.

He chuckled. Damn if this wasn't almost fun. "It's not like we have anything else to do at the moment," he said. "I mean, while we're hanging out, we might as well get to know each other. Why don't you cry?"

She said something under her breath that he didn't catch, but sounded a lot like, "Save me from macho men," then turned to face him. "Because it doesn't do any good. All crying does is make others uncomfortable and make *you* miserable."

"Crying doesn't make me uncomfortable," he told her.

She rolled her eyes. "Of course it doesn't."

"Crying is a good way to release emotion. If I'm around a kid, and he or she is crying, it tells me that they're hurting, physically or mentally."

"And if a woman cries?" Allye asked.

"Then I have to figure out who I need to beat the shit out of or kill."

Gray hadn't thought about what he was saying before the words were already out of his mouth. He inwardly cringed. He hadn't meant to remind her of what she'd just escaped. He knew what she was going to ask before she even opened her mouth.

"You killed them, didn't you?"

He didn't have to ask who "them" was. Sighing, and deciding to go with the truth and hopefully continue to gain her trust, he simply said, "Yes."

"Good."

Her answer was short and succinct, and threw Gray for a loop. It wasn't as if he was feeling remorse for what he'd done, but it had been a long time since a civilian had been as bluntly appreciative of his actions as Allye seemed to be.

When he didn't say anything, she got defensive. "I mean, it's not like they were pillars of San Francisco society or something. I begged the one guy to help me escape, but he acted like I wasn't even there. He knew I wasn't on that boat of my own free will, and he didn't care. And that other guy . . ."

Gray saw her visibly shudder.

"He may as well have been Satan's brother. He was so cold."

Gray flexed his arms and floated closer to Allye. The moon was bright in the dark sky, giving enough light that he could see her face. He didn't touch her, but he was right in front of her, so he could make out her facial expression as he asked his next question. "Did he rape you?"

Allye blinked at his frank words. "No," she answered without hesitation. "But he sure took pleasure in telling me all about the man who had bought me, and how I was to call him Master, and how *he* was going to enjoy every inch of my body . . . after he 'trained' me. As if. I'm not a fucking dog to be brought to heel."

"Do you know who bought you?" Gray hated even saying the words. It sounded so wrong to say *bought you*, as if she were truly a slave.

But they weren't exactly in a situation where they should, or could, beat around the bush.

Allye shook her head. "No. The guy never told me his name. But he said that my new master has been watching me for a while now, and that he's obsessed with me . . . hence sending someone to escort me. He wanted to make sure nothing happened to his property."

Gray was thoroughly confused. If the person who'd bought her had been watching her, it was likely he lived or worked in or around San Francisco. And if he lived in the same city as Allye . . . why all the subterfuge? Why not just have the escort bring her straight to him? The boats made no sense.

Making a note to discuss that with Rex, he asked, "You're a dancer, yeah?"

She nodded. "Uh-huh. With the Dance Theatre of San Francisco."

"Ballet?"

Allye rolled her eyes. "Why does everyone think every dancer does ballet? No. I mean, I *can* do ballet, but it's not my thing. I do pretty much every other type of dancing. Modern, jazz, ballroom, even some tap. I once spent three months on tour with Janet Jackson. Let me tell you, that was so much harder than the nightly gigs I do with the theatre. She's a perfectionist, and if we screwed something up during a show, she didn't hesitate to let us know . . . *and* we had to practice an extra two hours before the next performance."

A wave came out of nowhere and crashed over both their heads. Gray shook off the water as if he had gills on either side of his neck, but Allye coughed and spluttered as she spit out salt water.

If Gray could've kicked his own ass at that moment, he would've. They needed to be heading toward safety, not treading water and shooting the shit. The more salt water she consumed, the worse off she would be. But that was the least of their worries. She'd die of hypothermia long before the salt in her system became an issue.

"When's the last time you had anything to eat or drink?" he asked, coming close again and grabbing hold of her biceps with his hand.

"I'm not sure. But not too long ago. Asshole guy made me eat and drink when we first got on board. Said that if he showed up with me sick or dehydrated, my *master* wouldn't be happy."

Gray felt unusually angry at hearing the reminder of what had nearly happened to the woman, but he shook it off. "Good. Here's the deal. Do whatever you can to not swallow the seawater."

She nodded. "I'm not an idiot. I've seen movies and TV shows where people are stranded in the ocean for days and go crazy after consuming all the salt."

"We aren't going to be in here for days," Gray informed her. He didn't add that if they were in the ocean for hours, let alone days, they'd be dead because of the water temperature. If she wasn't going to bring it up right now, neither was he.

"Uh-huh. I hate to break it to you, Grayson, but those lights are a lot farther away than they appear. Not to mention this isn't exactly the neighborhood backyard swimming pool. Creatures with teeth, lots of teeth, live in this ocean."

"Gray."

"What?"

"My name. It's Grayson, but everyone calls me Gray."

She stared at him for a second before rolling her eyes once more. "Fine. Whatever. Gray."

"You do that a lot," he told her.

"Do what?"

"Roll your eyes."

"That's because you're saying stuff that's so ridiculous I can't help it," she shot back.

Yeah, it was safe to say he liked her. Liked her spirit. Liked that she wasn't freaking out. Liked that she could still throw sass at him even though she'd just been through a horrific experience. "I'm a good swimmer," he informed her.

"So am I," she said immediately. "But that doesn't mean I can swim a million miles to shore before either freezing to death, dying of thirst, or being eaten by a shark."

Gray reached up and took her head in his hands, supporting both their weights in the water with the constant movement of his legs. "I'm going to get you home, kitten. Mark my words."

This time she didn't roll her eyes. She stared into his own with her mismatched ones and simply nodded.

Chapter Three

9:18 p.m.

"Can you tell me what happened? How you ended up on that boat?" Gray asked after they'd been swimming for a few minutes. He could already feel Allye shivering every time he brushed against her in the water. He'd gotten her into the wet suit, but it wasn't going to keep her alive if Black didn't hurry up and find them.

"I c-can't tell you much. I was on my way home and had gotten off the streetcar. There were vehicles parked all along the s-street, as usual, and just as I was approaching one, the back door opened, and someone jumped out. He grabbed me, and I was in the back seat before I could do more than squeak in s-surprise. I started screaming as soon as I could, but he'd already shut the door, the car was already m-moving, and he'd injected me with something."

"Injected you?" Gray asked, hating the way she was stuttering from the cold. He wasn't supposed to meet up with Black for nearly an hour. He wasn't sure Allye had that kind of time.

She nodded. "Yeah. Stuck a needle right in my thigh. Hurt like a m-mother. When I woke up, I was being carried onto the boat. I yelled at the c-captain that I was being kidnapped and to help me, but you already know he ignored me."

Gray was disappointed that she didn't know more, but wasn't surprised.

"Tell me about your f-family," Allye asked, obviously wanting to change the subject.

"I have a brother, Jackson, who's three years younger than me."

"Let me guess, he also spends his days rescuing damsels in d-distress."

"He's an elementary schoolteacher," Gray told her.

She was silent for a beat, then began to giggle.

The sound echoed in the water around them, and Gray couldn't help but smile in return. He could just imagine her rolling her eyes.

"Seriously?" she asked.

They were swimming side by side, doing a modified breaststroke with their heads above the waves so they could talk. They'd used the freestyle stroke for a while, but because it was dark, Gray wanted to be able to assess how she was doing by talking to her. It was also easier to make sure they weren't drifting apart in the darkness if they swam like this.

"Seriously," he confirmed. "Growing up, he wanted to be the usual things—fireman, policeman, cowboy—but in his senior year in high school, he was required to take a semester class called Occupations. They were exposed to all sorts of different jobs, and he said the day he spent volunteering in a third-grade class, something clicked."

"That's c-cool."

"It *is* cool. He's a damn good teacher too. He's won all sorts of awards, and his kids love him."

"I bet your parents are proud," Allye said.

Gray heard something in her tone, something he couldn't interpret. "Yeah, my mom has always liked him best," he quipped. "My dad died a while ago, but he would've also been as pleased as punch that his son is doing something he loves and making a difference in kids' lives."

Allye didn't respond.

"What about you?"

"What about me *what*?" she asked.

"What about your family?"

"I don't have one."

Gray blinked and tried to see her face in the darkness. He couldn't. "Everyone has a family."

"No, Gray, they don't. Some people just aren't meant to have a m-mom who loves them."

"Bullshit," Gray retorted.

He heard her choke a little, but she didn't rise to his bait.

"I don't care if it's an adoptive mother, a foster mom, or a biological one, every kid deserves to be the apple of a mom's eye."

"How'd you end up on that boat r-rescuing a damsel in distress, anyway?" Allye asked after a couple of minutes had gone by.

Gray wanted to know more about her mother. Wanted to know whose ass he needed to kick, but he allowed the change in conversation. "It's a long story," he warned.

She snorted, and once again, he could imagine her rolling her eyes. "It's not like we have anything else to do at the m-moment," she said sarcastically.

"True. Let's see . . . I'm not sure where to start."

"How about at the beginning?"

Gray grinned. He liked this woman. He was beginning to regret the fact that after Black found them, and they reached shore, he'd be leaving her behind. It had been a long time since a woman had snared his interest as thoroughly as Allye had.

"Right, the beginning. I got a swimming scholarship to the US Naval Academy, and once I graduated, immediately tried out for the SEALs. I thought I knew what to expect from the notorious Hell Week, but no one can ever be prepared for that."

"You were a SEAL. That explains a lot," she said with no sarcasm whatsoever. "I've seen some d-documentaries on the kinds of training you went through," Allye said as they continued to slowly swim through the water. "It looks miserable."

"It *is* miserable," Gray confirmed. "It's the worst thing I've ever been through in my entire life. I wanted to puke and quit every single second."

"Why didn't you? Quit, I mean," she asked.

"Because I was pissed at the instructors. I knew they were doing everything they could to get us to quit—me, especially—since I was an officer, and that made me all the more determined not to let them win."

"Hmmm."

Gray knew it was an impossible concept for anyone to grasp who hadn't been through the physical and mental torture. And it *had* been torture. But it had also been the best thing that had ever happened to him. He'd used what he'd learned from those hard-as-nails instructors several times over, and it had saved his life more than once.

"One of the things we had to do in training was a night swim. We all knew it was coming. It wasn't a secret that it was one of the tasks we had to complete. We'd only been sleeping for an hour when we were woken up and herded into a small room. We were exhausted from all the hell we'd been through already, and the instructors droned on and on about how we'd never make the swim. That there were sharks out there waiting to take a bite out of us. They got us good and freaked out, then showed us a documentary about shark attacks."

"Jeez, that's s-sadistic," Allye said.

"Yup. But it did what they wanted—two people quit right then and there. Which was their goal."

"I thought they *wanted* people to become SEALs?"

"They do. But only the toughest men, both physically and mentally."

"I'm not sure t-talking about sharks is the best idea right about now," she commented dryly.

Gray chuckled. "Anyway, they told us that if a shark does come around when you're swimming, all you have to do is bop it on the nose."

"Oh, good Lord. *That* was their advice?"

"Yup. And during the swim, they swam us through these kelp beds. The stuff would lightly brush against our legs and totally freak us out. Of course, they didn't tell us that sharks hate the stuff and won't swim in them because they get stuck. But three more men quit in the middle of the ocean as a result."

"I take it no one got eaten by a sh-shark," she said.

"Nope. And you know what else?"

"I'm scared to ask. What?"

"That was actually one of the best experiences I had during the entire Hell Week."

"Really? You're crazy."

He chuckled again. "They'd separated us, so we didn't have our buddies to help us through that part of the training. We were on our own. It was actually peaceful and boring. And trust me, boring was good."

"So you made it through and didn't quit," Allye prompted when he didn't continue.

"Yeah. Was a SEAL for a while, and after an incident, I got a phone call from a man who called himself Rex."

"The Latin word for *king*? Seems a bit c-conceited," Allye observed.

"Ha. Right? That's what I thought. But he told me he was forming a group who would do missions all over the country and world, similar to what I'd done for the Navy, except I'd be paid twice as much and wouldn't have to answer to Uncle Sam."

"S-Sounds s-sketchy."

Gray didn't miss the way her teeth seemed to be chattering more and more. "That's *also* what I thought. But I was disillusioned after my service to my country for various reasons, and he'd explained what the team would be doing in such a way that I was interested. He instructed me to go to a pool hall in Colorado Springs for my interview. The rest is history."

"Hmmm," she said. "Somehow I doubt it was that easy."

It wasn't, but Gray wouldn't go into more detail. They were only passing through each other's lives. He couldn't, and wouldn't, endanger the operation Rex had set up, even if he'd already told her more than he'd ever told anyone outside the group.

When she was silent for a long moment, Gray asked, "How're you holding up?"

"I'm okay," she answered immediately.

"Want to try again, and be honest this time?"

"I'm r-rolling my eyes," she informed him. "Just s-so you know."

"I figured as much."

"I'm t-tired. And scared. And cold. And I honestly have no idea how we're going to make it all the way to shore."

"We won't have to make it all the way to shore," Gray told her, hoping the confidence in his teammate was coming through loud and clear. "My friend will come for us. We just have to hang on until then." He knew they wouldn't be able to swim the entire way. But that wasn't the point. The point was to keep moving. Swimming would keep her warmer, and the promise of rescue would also hopefully give her a much-needed boost.

9:29 p.m.

Gray glanced at his watch. Time was moving extremely slowly, and he knew every minute that passed was one more minute that Allye didn't have. "How about a game of rapid-fire questions?" he prodded when she hadn't said anything in a short while.

"W-What's that?"

"I'll give you a choice of two things. You tell me which you prefer. Then you ask me a question. We'll go back and forth."

"You're trying to d-distract me," she guessed.

"Yup," Gray admitted freely. "Look, you've been amazing. I'm impressed with how well you're doing. I'm just trying to keep your mind occupied until my friend shows up."

She sighed loud enough that he actually heard it over the sound of the waves. "F-Fine."

"Great. Beach or mountains?"

"Right about now, I'd have to say m-mountains," she quipped.

"Can't say I blame you," Gray said. After a second, he prompted, "Your turn."

"Does it have t-to be a choice-type question?" she asked.

"No. Whatever comes to mind."

"How many times have you done th-this?"

"'This?'"

"Rescued a woman like m-me."

"None. There's never been someone like you," Gray said immediately.

She shook her head. Gray saw the white streak in her hair move back and forth. "No, I mean, how many m-missions have you been on where you rescued s-someone?"

"I don't know," he told her honestly. "I haven't kept count. But I can tell you that, fortunately, there have been more where I actually got to rescue women than when I had to recover a body, or bodies." He let that sink in for a moment, then added, "This wasn't supposed to be a rescue mission tonight. You were a surprise."

"Really?"

"Really. Our intel told us that there would be a transfer of money, and that the actual delivery of the package . . . er . . . *you* . . . wouldn't be until later. The goal was to find out as much as we could about a man who's been orchestrating a massive sex-slavery ring on the West Coast. A man named Gage Nightingale."

"But instead you f-found me," Allye said quietly.

"Instead I found you," he confirmed. Then added, "Thank God."

After a beat, she said, "Your turn."

"What made you decide to be a dancer?"

"I always loved to d-dance, and when I moved to San Francisco, I was w-working as a waitress. It wasn't exactly my d-dream job. I decided to take a dance class in my f-free time. The instructor recommended me to the lady who ran the d-dance theatre, and before I knew it, I was being offered a job there for way m-more than I was making at the restaurant. How old are you?"

"Thirty-six. You?"

"Twenty-nine. How tall are you? You almost hit your head in that r-room back on the b-boat."

He chuckled. "Six-five."

"Good grief. You're a giant."

He couldn't help but guffaw. He really liked how she didn't beat around the bush. "I'm not sure I would go that far. But yeah, I'm tall. You?"

"Five-seven. Personally, I think it's a perfect height. I'm not so tall that I tower over people when I wear heels, but I'm also not so sh-short that everyone has to look d-down at me all the time. Present company excluded."

He saw the flash of her teeth as she turned her head and smiled at him.

They continued with their game, asking nonthreatening questions back and forth. Getting to know each other. Creating a kind of bond that Gray never would've thought possible in so short a time. He knew it was a result of the situation they were in, but it still felt good.

Besides his mom and brother, he hadn't felt so close to another person, so quickly, as he did Allye. Not even the men he worked with, which made him uneasy . . . though not enough to stop answering or asking questions.

But eventually their queries began to trickle off. The time between each stretching farther and farther apart.

9:44 p.m.

"You okay?" Gray asked after glancing at this watch again.

He heard her take a deep breath, then she reached out, and her hand brushed against his back before grasping his biceps. He stopped swimming and started treading water, concerned.

"I'm tired," she said quietly. "And c-cold. I don't think I can m-make it."

"Bullshit," Gray said immediately. "You're going to make it."

"I feel as if I've been in a d-dance marathon for hours. My muscles are cramping, and I'm f-freezing. My mouth is like c-cotton, and I feel a little sick."

Gray didn't like any of that, but he refused to coddle her. If he did, she really *wouldn't* make it. But he also couldn't treat her as if she were a candidate in SEAL school. He'd prefer that she keep swimming, to keep her blood moving, but he didn't want to exhaust her either. It was a delicate balance, and he felt that no matter what he did, he was making the wrong decision when it came to her.

"Hold on to me," he told her after a moment, grasping her hand in his and bringing it down his body to one of the pockets at his waist. He wrapped her fingers around it. "You can lie on your back, and I'll tow you."

"That's not f-fair," she protested. "Besides, you have to be t-tired and cold too."

"I won't let you down," he told her. "Trust me. I know myself. I'm fine. I could probably move faster this way than if you continued to swim next to me, anyway."

"That's probably t-true," she murmured.

"If you relax enough, you could even take a catnap while I swim," he said.

"But I wouldn't be able to h-hold on."

"I won't let you drift away, kitten. Swear."

"Okay. But . . . this isn't like m-me. I'm usually the last to leave rehearsal."

Somehow, he knew she wasn't lying. She'd held up extremely well. He was impressed. "I know it's not. There's nothing wrong with asking for help."

"Everyone I've ever asked for help has l-let me down," she told him in a flat tone that he knew instinctively meant she wasn't exaggerating.

"Well, after we get picked up, you won't be able to say that anymore. Lie on your back, kitten," he ordered. He helped support her with a hand at the small of her back. He drifted closer to her and made sure she had a tight grip on his dry suit. "Ready?"

"S-Sure. I'll just lie here and nap."

He smiled. "You're rolling your eyes again, aren't you?"

"Yup. C-Carry on. Take us home."

Home. He liked the sound of that word coming from her lips, but he didn't respond. He simply set out toward the rendezvous coordinates once again. It took him a moment to find a stroke that wouldn't disturb her hold while allowing him maximum efficiency.

He fell into a smooth rhythm, and, interestingly enough, he didn't feel tired at all. There was something about being one hundred percent responsible for the woman at his side that made him get a second wind. He hated that she had been let down by everyone she knew. He vowed that he wouldn't be just another in a long line of those people.

Even if he was only in her life for this brief moment in time, it was important to him that she know he was reliable, trustworthy, and that he had her back.

For a second, he wished that he could be there for her for the rest of her life, but he pushed the thought back. It wasn't possible, and she wasn't his. Couldn't be.

But for now, here in the middle of the ocean, they may as well have been the only people on the planet. She *was* his. He'd fight any shark that dared show its face, and he'd kill any other sex traffickers who might show up. He'd stand between her and the evils in the world to keep her safe.

Chapter Four

9:58 p.m.

Allye lay on her back and allowed Gray to pull her along. She had no idea how long they'd been in the water, but it felt like hours. Being in the middle of the ocean in the dark was terrifying.

She had one arm above her head, fingers clinging to one of the pockets on Gray's dry-suit thing. He was swimming mostly on his side, using some sort of modified sidestroke to propel them through the water.

She hadn't wanted to be weak and let him tow her, but she was exhausted, thirsty, and freezing. She had known she wasn't going to last much longer trying to swim on her own. She'd been quaking with cold for a while, but now her shivering had tapered off, and even she knew that wasn't the best sign. Their game of questions had worked to keep her mind occupied for quite a while, however. She'd learned a lot about her rescuer, and everything she'd heard, she liked.

Besides, he really didn't seem to be tired at all. He didn't *sound* tired, and wasn't even breathing hard. She would've thought he was some sort of fake human, a prototype machine or something, except for the small grunts that escaped his mouth every now and then as he exerted energy to keep them moving through the water.

For some reason, when he'd vowed earlier that he was going to get her home, she'd believed him. It was stupid. She'd been kidnapped, thrown into a boat, and told all about how her new life was going to be spent locked up in a gilded cage under the guise of being "protected and revered." She'd been informed she would "get to" continue dancing, that her new master loved the way she danced and had created his own venue, solely for her. Just the thought made her want to throw up. There was no way she'd *ever* perform for someone who had kidnapped her. She wasn't going to be a circus sideshow. No way in hell.

Then, just when she'd thought she was going to drown, by some miracle, Gray had shown up and thrown her into the big, bad ocean. But he hadn't left her. No, he was right there by her side every step—er, stroke—of the way.

"Tell me something else about you," Gray said.

His words were muffled because her ears were underwater, but Allye still heard him. She tilted her head back to look at him as he propelled them forward. "W-What do you w-want to know? I thought we'd c-covered everything earlier."

"Anything you want to tell me," was his response.

Allye sighed. She usually hated personal questions, going out of her way to either give bullshit answers and completely lie, or give only bits and pieces of her past. But for some reason, she felt as if she owed it to Gray to be honest with him. She felt a connection with him. She knew it was because of their situation and because he'd rescued her, but it was a connection nevertheless.

Besides . . . what else were they going to talk about? It was pitch-dark, and she was bored. If *she* was bored, he *had* to be. She remembered him saying how tedious his night swim had been when he'd trained to be a SEAL. She didn't want him to be bored. She wanted him to be alert and ready to bop any shark that might appear out of nowhere to try to eat her. Maybe he'd asked because he was getting tired and wanted a distraction.

They had to talk about something. Might as well be her shitty life.

Keeping it from him seemed silly now, when they'd bonded so quickly and easily.

"Do you b-believe in k-karma?" she asked before she started telling him her life story.

"Absolutely," Gray said with conviction.

"I thought I d-did," Allye said, turning her head to look back up at the dark sky. "I m-mean, I thought if I was a good p-person and did good deeds, that surely my life would improve." She snorted, careful not to inhale seawater. "It's all b-bullshit."

"Tell me," Gray ordered.

Allye closed her eyes. "I was born to a woman who didn't want k-kids. But she thought if she had a baby, that would make the man she was with love her and want to be with her f-forever and ever. She told me that he left the week she b-brought me home from the hospital. She blamed me, of course. I cried all the time and was too d-demanding."

"Fucking bitch," Gray said, interrupting her.

Allye picked up her head again and looked at him in surprise. He sounded extremely pissed off . . . and she hadn't even started telling her story.

He caught her looking at him and said, "You were a baby. Crying and needing attention is what babies do."

"True. I guess sh-she didn't think it through," was all Allye could think to say. "Anyway, so yeah, having a k-kid didn't end up like she'd hoped. She barely tolerated having me around. I s-started school when I was four, simply because she didn't want me underfoot and didn't want to pay for childcare anymore. It was t-too early; I was the stupidest kid in my c-class."

"Don't say that," Gray said, pausing in his swimming and reaching over to squeeze her arm.

Allye shrugged. "It's true. I got b-bullied all the time because I was also smaller than everyone else. But that's because my m-mom never bothered to buy the good food."

"Good food?"

"Yeah. You know, the nutritious stuff. Oh, there was always shit like Oreos and ch-chips and hot dogs, but never fresh fruits and vegetables. I didn't really know I should've been eating that k-kind of food until I got older."

"I already don't like this story, but I have a feeling I'm *really* not going to like whatever you say next, am I?" Gray asked as he began swimming again.

Allye chuckled, but there was no humor in the sound. "I don't know you well enough to say whether you will or w-won't, but I can tell you that *I* don't like this s-story."

"Fucking hell. Go on."

She rolled her eyes even though she knew he couldn't see her. "You asked me to t-talk," she reminded him. "I can shut up, and we can just coexist in s-silence again if you want."

"Nope. Talk, kitten."

She was really starting to like Gray. He was down-to-earth and, so far, hadn't bullshitted her. And there was that whole "rescued her from a sinking ship and life as a sex slave to some freak who wanted to be called 'master'" thing. She also tolerated his nickname for her, though she'd refused to let even past boyfriends call her cutesy names.

"Right, so life went on like this for a while. I'd be sh-shoved out of the house at six thirty to go to the bus stop and wait for the bus, which wasn't coming until seven forty-five. Then I'd get home around four. The house was always empty. Mom was out doing whatever she did. She'd come home around eight and send me to my r-room."

"Did she abuse you?" Gray asked.

Allye hated that question. And because she was exhausted, thirsty, cold, and scared, for once, she didn't prevaricate. "If you m-mean did she hit me, then, no. But if you c-consider letting me eat chips for breakfast, never being at the house when I was there, and n-never once hugging me or telling me that she loved me 'abuse,' then, yes. Every d-damn day of my life."

"Fuck, I'm sorry, kitten. You're right, that is *absolutely* abuse. My question was out of line."

Damn, now *she* had to apologize. She forced herself to sit up in the water, almost choking on a wave that chose that moment to crash over her head. Gray was there immediately, putting his arm around her and holding her upright as she coughed.

When she'd caught her breath, she looked Gray in the eyes. They were close enough that she could see them in the bright light of the moon. "No, I'm s-sorry. That was uncalled for. Technically, I wasn't abused. My mom provided me with f-food and shelter. She sent me to school. But she never, not once, helped me with my homework. I had to c-clean the entire house by the time she got home in the evenings or there would be hell to p-pay. She treated me like a live-in servant rather than her k-kid most of the time. I can't ever remember her h-holding me when I was scared or upset, and she n-never read to me, or did anything else a real parent does for their kid."

"That sounds like abuse to me," Gray repeated dryly.

"Yeah, well . . . not to the s-state. I called them once," Allye admitted out loud for the first time ever.

"Who?"

"Child services. I r-reported my mom for abuse. They came to the house and investigated. But it was all b-bullshit. They saw the orderly house, the clean kid with no bruises. They c-called my school, and even though I was behind the other kids in my class intellectually, the teachers reported no s-suspicious b-behavior. They interviewed my m-mom, and apparently she snowed them as easily as she t-tricked everyone else. The case was closed."

Gray's mouth came down in a frown and he murmured, "Jesus."

"Yeah. My mom was p-pissed and tried for months to figure out who reported her. I never admitted it was m-me. But I realized then how useless it would be to do it again. Eventually she f-forgot about it. I really wish that I had been put into the f-foster-care system then, rather than later."

"What happened?"

"Can we keep going? I mean . . . if you're not too t-tired."

Gray eyed her for a long moment. "I'm not too tired, kitten. It's easier to talk about it if I'm not looking at you, isn't it?"

Surprised he'd figured her out, Allye simply nodded.

Without a word, he brought her hand back to the pocket she'd been holding on to earlier and motioned for her to lie back. She did, and felt his powerful legs kick them into motion once more.

"Maybe when I was s-six, I would've had a chance to be adopted. But at nine, there was no way. I was too old. No one w-wanted a weird kid who was a C student at best and p-preferred to sit in her room and read rather than socialize."

Allye sighed and told him about the most painful day of her life. "It was a Saturday, and Mom didn't want me hanging around the house, as usual, so she took me to the local m-mall. She did that all the time. Dropped me off in the morning and picked me up in the late afternoon. I have no idea what she d-did when I was at school or at the mall, but I'm guessing she was screwing men for m-money. Anyway, that day she never came to pick me up."

"Are you serious?" Gray asked.

"Yup. I went to where she usually met me, at the usual time, and she never sh-showed up. I hung around until eight at night, w-when one of the security guards spotted me and m-made me come inside with him. I gave him my mom's number, but s-she didn't answer. The cops came and drove me h-home. I tried to thank them and send them on their way, but I guess they weren't comfortable l-leaving a nine-year-old who hadn't been p-picked up by her mother without at least talking to an adult. I let them in the house . . . and that's the first time I knew k-karma was a big f-fat lie."

"What happened?"

"The house was empty. My mom had cleaned it out. P-Probably backed a moving van right up to the door and shoved everything inside. Even the s-stuff in my room was gone. All my clothes, my bed, all of it, just gone."

"Where'd she go?" Gray asked.

"No c-clue."

Gray stopped swimming again. "You mean you haven't talked to her since?"

Allye didn't sit up, just floated on her back next to him. "Nope. Never saw her again. Never *w-wanted* to see her again."

"Fucking bitch," Gray swore again as he resumed swimming.

"Yeah. So, I went into f-foster care. But it's not much fun as a preteen. Or a teenager. I didn't really have any horrible experiences. I mean, I wasn't b-beaten or anything like that, but I never felt like I truly belonged. The homes I lived in were okay, I guess, but my foster parents were always busy, and I never felt like they were truly parents . . . if that makes s-sense."

"Yeah, it does."

"Anyway, when I first went into the s-system, I was optimistic. I thought if I was super n-nice and always did what p-people told me to, that I'd get lucky and get adopted. Karma, you know. No such luck. It s-seemed as if the more I tried to do good, the worse luck I had. In one of the homes, there was this c-cat. I loved her. She was older than d-dirt, but super affectionate. She liked to sleep under the covers with me. I fell asleep more than one night with her p-purring against my chest. On my way home from school one day, I saw a s-stray cat meowing down into a storm drain. I looked and saw two k-kittens were stuck down there. I was small enough that I could shimmy into it. I r-rescued those kittens and reunited them with their mother. I was so proud of that good d-deed I did, but when I got home, I found out that my f-foster dad had accidentally run over the cat I'd loved so much."

She huffed out a breath. "So much for k-karma *that* day," she said, not able to hide her bitterness. "It's been like that my entire life. I do something good, and almost immediately, I find it turns around and b-bites me in the ass instead."

"Give me another example," Gray demanded.

"You m-mean the cat-and-kitten thing wasn't enough?"

"No."

She knew Gray wasn't being mean, he simply didn't believe her. "Okay, f-fine. So, one of the other dancers at w-work needed a place to stay because her boyfriend was knocking her around. I let her s-stay with me, thinking it was the nice thing to do. Well, her b-boyfriend found out where she was staying and s-started harassing her at my place too. It got so bad, my landlord evicted me for d-disturbing the rest of the residents."

"What? Jesus. What happened to your friend? Did her boyfriend get to her?"

"No. She m-moved out right before I was evicted and went home to South Carolina."

"So, your letting her move in saved her from her abusive boyfriend," Gray concluded.

"No."

"Yeah, kitten, it did."

"Whatever. Okay, how about this? Another d-dancer wanted to go out one night to this new club. It was her b-birthday, and she was so excited about going, but her friend bailed on her. So she asked me to go. I did, and it turns out the c-club wasn't a dance club, not like I was thinking. I thought we'd go and have a few drinks and d-dance all night, but instead it was a BDSM club. She had been w-wanting to try the lifestyle and didn't want to go by herself. So, I had to spend the n-night watching my friend get naked and t-tied to a cross while a man wearing leather pants got her off. Not only that, I had to fend off m-men all night who kept wanting to tie *me* up. It was awkward and embarrassing and *so* not my s-scene."

"I can see how that would be a shock," Gray said.

Allye swore she could hear the humor in his voice. She raised her head and glared at him.

He smiled, his white teeth looking impossibly bright in the moonlight. "What else?"

"It's not just isolated incidents, Gray," Allye said in defeat. "It's everything. I m-mean, look at me now. I got *k-kidnapped*, for God's sake. Then instead of being sold off or m-murdered, I'm unlucky enough to have been on a boat that the creepy asshole b-blew up! Now, I'm in the middle of the freaking ocean. Karma hates me."

"I'd say you're the luckiest woman I've ever met," Gray said calmly.

Allye sat upright again. "Did you just say that I'm *l-lucky*?" There were clouds rolling across the sky, and she realized when she sat up that they'd covered the moon, taking away any semblance of light. She'd also let go of Gray, and now she couldn't see or hear him anywhere near her.

"Gray? Fuck . . . Gray? Wh-Where are you?" Her words were panicked, and Allye felt her heart rate increase from the mellow beat it'd been as Gray was towing her through the water to a hysterical staccato.

"I'm here, kitten," he said into her ear.

Allye immediately relaxed when she heard his voice and felt his arm go around her waist. She dug her nails into his thigh, feeling the muscles there flexing as he moved his legs, keeping them afloat. "Don't leave me," she blurted out. "Please don't leave m-me alone out here."

"I'm not going anywhere. Promise," he told her, not sounding at all upset or freaked out by her outburst.

He put one of his large hands on her sternum and gently eased her onto her back. "I'm right here. I'm going to get you home. Swear."

Allye tried to relax, but found it almost impossible. She'd always liked to swim, but now she wanted nothing more than to be back on dry land. She brought her other hand up and used both to hold on to him as he once more began stroking through the water, presumably toward land.

He began speaking as if she hadn't just had a freak-out moment. "The way I look at it, Allye Martin, you're the luckiest woman I've ever met in my life, and karma is working just fine for you."

He paused as if waiting for her to disagree, but Allye didn't have it in her. All she could think about was everything that could go wrong. Sharks, or if Gray accidentally started swimming in the wrong direction, or if the man who wanted to buy her got impatient when she wasn't delivered and came looking for her himself.

"Let's just take today as an example, okay?" he said. "I could start back from when you were little, but I'd prefer to talk about things I know firsthand."

"Whatever," Allye mumbled.

"Yeah, you were kidnapped, which sucks. But you weren't assaulted. You weren't knocked around. You were fed and given water. Both of which are helping you now, whether you want to admit it or not. Instead of the money transaction going down, you happened to be on the boat I showed up on. You weren't supposed to be there, but you were. Then, instead of you sinking to the bottom with the boat, I happened to have a handcuff key on me, and I was able to get you free. And now you're also free of your captors and on your way home. That sounds like karma is working really well for you, kitten. Because I'll tell you, most women who are kidnapped and disappear into the sex trade aren't so lucky. They're never found, and spend the rest of their lives being raped, used, and abused before dying what is most likely an undignified death and being buried in an unmarked grave somewhere."

Allye knew he was right, but it was really hard to look at the positive side of things when she was being towed through the waves in the middle of the ocean.

"Let me put it this way," Gray went on. "On average, there are an estimated ninety thousand missing people in the United States in any given year. Roughly forty thousand of those are female. You were probably an hour or less away from being one of those forty thousand women. I'd say whatever good things you're doing in your life . . . keep doing them. Karma is definitely on your side. She might take a while to show her face, but she's there."

For the first time since she was little, Allye felt tears prick the back of her eyes.

All her life, she'd felt like the unluckiest person alive. But with just a few sentences, a stranger had made her see her entire life differently. No, not a stranger. Gray. And honestly, he was right. Yeah, she'd had shit happen to her, but who hadn't? And the fact that she wasn't chained inside a cage begging her "master" to let her eat was proof that maybe, just maybe, karma hadn't forsaken her, after all.

"Th-Thank you," she said quietly, not sure if Gray could even hear her.

But he had. "You're welcome."

Allye felt his hand come down and squeeze her shoulder before he began stroking toward their destination again.

She had no idea if she would survive the night—heck, survive for another hour—but she was more thankful than she could ever express that she wasn't alone. That Gray was with her. If she'd somehow escaped the boat on her own, there was no way she would've lasted through the night. She knew that without a doubt.

Her fingers tightened on his pocket at the thought, and as if he could read her mind, Gray said, "I've got you, kitten. Just relax. Sleep if you can. I'm not letting you go."

The last thing she thought before falling into a semi-trancelike state was that she wished he meant his words for more than the here and now.

Chapter Five

10:28 p.m.

Gray had been sidestroking for what seemed like forever. His arms were tired, but he refused to let himself even think about being worn out. When he'd gone through BUD/S—basic underwater demolition training for SEALs—he'd felt like this, and learned he could push his body for hours longer than he'd thought he could.

He looked over at the woman beside him. Allye. A unique name for a unique woman. She'd been dozing lightly, and while he enjoyed hearing her talk—and wanted her to stay awake so he could assess her physical condition—the fact of the matter was that he wanted her to sleep through as much of this as possible. She was freaked out, justifiably so, but she'd held up extremely well.

Thinking back to her upbringing, Gray wanted more than anything to have Meat track down her mother simply so he could pay her a visit and let her know in no uncertain terms what a piece of shit she was. He didn't know Allye all that well, but the word *resilient* came to mind.

She'd survived what most people wouldn't have been able to. It was almost laughable that she didn't believe in karma. She was the epitome of karma working its magic. She was healthy, and seemingly thriving, despite what her mother had done to her in her formative years.

Eyeing the lights twinkling in the distance, Gray looked at his watch one more time. The GPS inside the device told him he was nearing the area where he and Black were supposed to rendezvous. And it wasn't a minute too soon. Allye had stopped shivering a while ago, which was a bad sign.

Stroking again in the direction where he was supposed to meet Black, Gray finally saw what he'd been on the lookout for—a boat in the distance, moving slowly over the water in what looked to be a grid pattern.

He wasn't sure it was Black; it could be a random fisherman, or the person who had bought Allye, coming to pick her up, but he doubted it. Men like the scumbags who bought and sold women never did their dirty work themselves. They almost always hired someone else to do it. And while the boat coming toward him could be filled with bad guys, he didn't think so.

He gently shook Allye. "Wake up, kitten. Rescue is here."

As if he'd flicked on an overhead light in a pitch-dark room, she sat upright, almost drowning herself in the process. After she'd gotten her bearings, she asked, "What? Really?"

Gray tamped down the chuckle that threatened to erupt. He had one hand under her elbow, giving her an extra boost of buoyancy as she regained her full senses. "Really. Can you tread water for a sec?"

"Of course," she said, pulling away from him, but still keeping one hand on the pocket she'd been holding as he'd towed her through the waves. It wasn't quite as dark as it had been earlier, the moon shining bright once again, but she was obviously not taking any chances that she'd float away and lose him. As if he'd let that happen.

He waited for a beat to make sure she wasn't going to sink under the waves, and when she seemed okay, he quickly reached into one of the many pockets on his special suit and took out the small beacon he'd stashed there. While he hadn't planned on anything going wrong, he and his teammates were always prepared for the worst-case scenario. And being lost in the middle of the ocean was definitely one of those scenarios.

Black knew the general area to look for him, had the coordinates where they were supposed to meet, but in the dark, he wouldn't have a chance in hell of finding them. Not without the homing beacon. With a flick of his thumb, Gray turned on the small electronic device. It would send a signal straight to the handheld device Black was probably holding. He hadn't turned it on before now because, unfortunately, it had a very short battery life.

Holding the small, flat black box out of the water to improve its accuracy, Gray looked at Allye.

She was eyeing him, and the beacon, with curiosity. He waited, but she didn't ask. He both liked and disliked that about her. He'd prefer she'd flat-out ask him when she had questions, but she'd obviously learned to keep her head down and her questions to herself.

"It's a beacon. I'm fairly certain that's my buddy in that boat over there."

Allye's head whipped around so fast, he would've laughed if he wasn't so tired. She looked back at him. "Really?"

"Really."

"You mean we don't have to swim all the way to the boat?"

"If that really is Black, then, no. If it's a random person out for a joyride, or someone looking for you and the men you were with, then we'll have to keep swimming in general, because they'll go right by without seeing us."

She looked nervous then, the excitement bleeding out of her unusual eyes as if he'd just taken away Christmas, Thanksgiving, and her birthday in one fell swoop. "Should you be holding that thing up, then? Just in case it's not your friend?"

Noting she wasn't stuttering anymore because her body had stopped shivering violently, and kicking himself for killing her excitement, Gray hurried to reassure her. "It's a prototype, and only me and my team have the capability to pick up its signal. It's not transmitting any kind of light or anything. If that's not Black, they'll go right by us. There's no way anyone would find us out here if they weren't extremely lucky, or weren't following the signal from this little box."

"Don't say that," she mumbled. "Karma likes to fuck with me."

He chuckled. "Didn't we already have this conversation? You and karma are just fine, kitten."

"I think I was in a state of shock earlier when we talked about it. I'm not sure I'm ready to believe you just yet."

Pulling her closer, Gray wrapped an arm around her waist again, using his legs to keep them above water. Her body felt cold even through the wet suit, and her lips were no longer ringed with blue as they'd been earlier—now they were almost completely bluish purple. She needed to get out and get warm. Now. But she didn't complain. Just did whatever he asked of her with minimal questions. He liked that.

He liked *Allye*. A lot. He knew nothing could come of his attraction, as he lived in Colorado Springs and she lived in San Francisco. But it had been a long time since a woman had piqued his interest as she had.

Gray eyed the boat and saw the second Black picked up his signal. The vessel took an obvious turn and changed course to head straight for them. He turned to Allye and gave her a smile. "There are one hundred and eighty-seven quintillion gallons of water in the Pacific Ocean. That's sixty-two-point-four million square miles. If karma had it out for you, as you claim, there's no way that boat would be headed straight for us right now. No one would find us out here . . . especially not in the dark. Chin up, kitten. We're about to be rescued."

She turned once again and faced the oncoming boat. "It's a good thing," she quipped. "My fingers and toes are prunes. I'm not sure they'll ever go back to their original state."

Gray couldn't stop the chuckle that escaped. She never ceased to surprise him.

They waited without another word as the light from the boat came closer and closer.

Finally, Gray heard Black call out his name.

"Yo! It's about time!" Gray yelled back.

He heard his friend laugh as he cut the engine and slowed the boat. It floated toward them, and Gray maneuvered himself and Allye so he could grab one of the ropes on the side of the rubber boat when it got close enough.

"Where'd you pick this thing up?" he asked Black. It wasn't the sleek fiberglass boat they'd been on earlier.

"Long story. Jeez, Gray. Only you could pick up a chick in the middle of the ocean, my friend."

"How about you talk less and help me get her inside?" Gray asked dryly. He wasn't going to introduce Allye to his friend while they were bobbing in the ocean.

"Shit, yeah, sorry."

Gray turned to Allye. "You ready to go home?"

"Oh yeah," was her heartfelt response.

"Grab Black's hand. I'll push from here, and he'll pull you up."

Black reached down, not waiting for her to reach up, and grabbed her under the arms instead. He began pulling her on board the large, inflatable Zodiac boat. Gray did as promised, putting a hand on her ass and pushing upward as Black pulled, and within seconds, she'd disappeared over the side.

He heard her "umph" as she hit the bottom of the boat, but when she didn't scream out in pain or otherwise protest, he relaxed a fraction. She'd still need to be looked over by paramedics, but hopefully her little swim hadn't done her any long-lasting harm.

Black's face returned over the side of the boat a second later, and he held out a hand. Without fanfare, as they'd done this exact thing many times, Gray used his friend's help and his own upper-body strength to haul himself over the side of the boat.

He immediately looked for Allye. He could see her more clearly now with the lights from the boat. She was huddled against the side with her knees drawn up. Her face was slightly blue from the cold water, but she gave him a weak smile.

Ignoring his own chilled body, Gray turned to ask Black for a blanket, but his friend was already there, handing him a stack of them. Gray crawled over to where Allye was huddled. He tried not to look at her long legs, but he was only human. She was built, her thighs thick and muscular, appropriate for a dancer, he supposed. He could see her calf muscles clearly, even through the wet suit. He had the thought that she'd look amazing in a pair of high heels.

Holding out a blanket, he said, "As much as it's gonna suck, you need to get out of that wet suit."

"But I'm freezing."

"I know, kitten, but all that thing will do is make you colder. Take it off, and I'll get you wrapped up in these nice, warm blankets."

She rolled her eyes at the cajoling tone of his voice, but did as asked. She struggled with the zipper, but just as Gray was going to offer to help with it, she managed to pull it down. She wriggled and squirmed as she attempted to pull the wet suit off.

Gray handed the blankets back to Black and kneeled next to her. He pulled on the sleeve of the wet suit as she eased her arm out. He helped her with the other arm, then said, "Lie back. I'll pull it off your legs."

She did as he asked without question, but as soon as he began peeling the material down her legs, she quipped, "If I'd known I'd have a cute guy taking off my pants in the middle of the night, I would've made sure to shave."

Black choked back a laugh, and Gray couldn't help the snort that escaped at her words.

"Trust me, kitten, any guy gets to this point, he's not going to give a shit if you've got a little hair on your legs or not."

Without delay, he threw the wet suit off to the side and reached back toward Black. His friend and partner placed the blankets in his hands and Gray spread one out and covered Allye's legs. He swung another around her shoulders as she sat back up, and she immediately gripped it with her right hand, holding it closed.

Gray moved so he was sitting next to Allye. He wanted to put his arm around her and pull her into him, but now that they weren't in the ocean, and the immediate threat of drowning, freezing, or being eaten by a shark had passed, he felt awkward.

"Allye Martin, this is my friend Lowell Lockard. Otherwise known as Black."

She switched her grip on the blanket and held out her right hand. "It's nice to meet you, Lowell," she said.

Black looked at him for a moment with his brows almost reaching his hairline, but took hold of Allye's hand and shook it. "Please, call me Black. I don't even know who Lowell is anymore. And the pleasure's all mine," he said softly. Then he brought her hand up to his mouth and kissed the back of it.

Gray was extremely irritated at the gesture. "Cut it out, Black," he growled.

His friend turned to him. "Hey, she's the one who acted like we were at a formal party. Far be it from me to remind her there's no need to stand on ceremony since we're floating in the middle of the ocean."

Allye giggled, but pulled her hand out of Black's grasp, and it disappeared under the blankets she held tightly around her body.

Gray was about to say something to his friend he'd probably regret when he felt Allye's weight against his shoulder. She'd been holding herself upright when he'd first sat, but now she was leaning against him. It was subtle, and he knew she wasn't giving him all her weight, but even that slight indication that she wanted to be near him, that she was still relying on him, banked his anger toward his friend. It wasn't Black she was leaning on. It was *him*.

And just like that, the caveman inside Gray raced to the forefront. He'd been the one to save her. He'd been the one to keep her alive in the ocean. He'd been the one she clung to as he towed her through the waves. Finders keepers and all that.

Gray forced the thoughts away. Allye wasn't a thing. She was a human being. A woman who had her own life. He couldn't keep her. *Dammit.*

"You talk to Rex?" Gray asked Black, knowing his voice was a bit huskier and irritated than the situation warranted, but not able to control it.

"Told him you missed the rendezvous point and that I was going to head out and look for you," Black said succinctly.

Gray nodded. Then he turned to Allye. "We should get closer to the helm. As you can see, there's no wheelhouse on this thing, but Black will drive slowly back to shore to reduce the amount of wind."

Allye nodded.

Gray stood. His legs shook, but he ignored them. He held out a hand to Allye. He knew he should probably let Black help her up, but he couldn't. She was his to look after, at least until they reached shore and he had to let her go.

She looked up, and even in the dim light he could see her two different-colored eyes. She unfurled an arm from her cocoon of blankets and held it up to him. It was trembling, but she didn't look away from him as he took her hand in his and pulled her upward. She fell against him with a groan, and Gray would've fallen to the floor of the boat if Black hadn't put a hand on his back to steady him.

"You good?" his friend asked.

Gray nodded. "Nothing a nap and some food and water won't fix."

"Can't help with the nap, but I've got water and a couple of protein bars to tide you over."

"You hear that, kitten?" Gray asked Allye. "Black brought us a feast."

She chuckled against his chest, then looked up. "You boys sure do know how to show a girl a good time. Although for future reference, I would recommend chocolate. You can't go wrong with chocolate."

Black laughed again, but sadness hit Gray. This wasn't a date, and he wouldn't get to see Allye all dressed up for a night on the town. But he could imagine it in his head. She'd look beautiful, of that he had no doubt. "Come on," he said, gruffer than he wanted to, disappointment still riding him hard. He'd never felt this way about someone he'd rescued in the past. There was just something about Allye that pulled on every one of his protective instincts.

He leaned over and picked up the blanket that had fallen as she'd stood, then led her closer to the front of the small vessel. He helped her to the bottom of the boat, then sat at her side, one leg settled against hers, the other bent so he could get as close to Allye as possible. He was still wearing the damp dry suit, but she'd still benefit from his body heat. She didn't protest his closeness, and in fact gave him her weight once more as she relaxed against him. Black helped wrap more blankets around the two of them, cocooning them inside.

A small groan escaped Allye's mouth, and Gray had to smile. He felt her body begin to shiver and allowed himself a small sigh of relief. Shivering was good. It meant her body was fighting the cold and working to warm itself.

He reached up and accepted two bottles of water and two protein bars from Black.

He held one of the bottles out to her. "Sip slowly. I know you're thirsty, but if you guzzle it all down, it'll just come up again, and you'll be in worse shape than you are now. Not to mention embarrassed that you barfed in front of us." He squeezed her arm as he said the last, to let her know he was kidding.

As he expected, she rolled her eyes at him even as she held out her hand for the bottle. She sipped the water as he suggested. Satisfied that she wasn't going to do something she'd regret, like chug the entire bottle, he handed her one of the protein bars. "These taste like shit, but if you can get it down, even a few bites, it'll make you feel one hundred percent better. Promise. Your body needs calories and protein to combat the cold and dehydration. Again, small bites."

She nodded and nibbled daintily on a corner of the protein bar, as if she were the kitten he'd nicknamed her after.

"I'm going to start back," Black said. "I'll keep the speed down as much as I can, but it's going to get windy."

Nodding at his friend, Gray turned his attention back to Allye.

She continued to concentrate on the protein bar, holding on to it tightly because her whole body was trembling, even her hands. Gray was impressed. Not once had she bitched about what had happened to her, other than when she was explaining why she thought karma had abandoned her. She didn't complain incessantly about the cold when they were in the water. She didn't bitch about anything he'd said or done since she'd first seen him. Gray figured it was a result of her upbringing, trying to be as unobtrusive as possible, but still. He actually wished she *would* complain about something, simply so he could do everything in his power to make it better for her.

Shaking his head, Gray once again berated himself. She wasn't his to look after, and in about twenty minutes or so, she'd be out of his life once and for all.

"I've got to say it," Black remarked, once he'd gotten the boat turned around and they'd started heading back toward land. They were going at a much slower speed than Black had taken on the way out, that was for sure. "Your eyes are extraordinary, Allye. And I'm guessing that streak of white in your hair didn't come from a bottle."

Allye chuckled. Gray loved the sound. It was low and full of humor.

Humor. She'd been kidnapped and had faced a terrible future, but she was sitting on the floor of the boat wrapped in a blanket, laughing.

"You'd be right," she told Black. "I have what's called heterochromia iridum, which is a rare condition where one eye has less pigment than the other. It has something to do with my genes." She shrugged. "I don't really think about it much."

"And your hair?" Black asked. "Is that related?"

"No clue," Allye told him. "My mom didn't really care much one way or the other. Certainly not enough to bring me to a doctor to make sure nothing was actually wrong with me. As far as I can tell, it's a simple case of me not having any melanin, or color, in the hair follicles in that part of my head. It's probably related to my eyes somehow, but I have no idea."

"It's unique," Gray said before Black could respond.

"Yeah, and being unique pretty much sucks when you're growing up," Allye retorted. "I tried dyeing that streak for a while, but that had disastrous results. I could never get it to be the same color as the rest of my hair, so I would have this dark-brown streak in my hair that looked just as weird. Then, of course, when my hair grew in, I'd have a patch of white roots right at the top of my head. I finally realized it was more hassle than it was worth and gave up."

Gray's hand moved of its own volition. He stroked her damp hair away from her forehead and fingered the long strands of white hair. He traced the streak from the part in her hair all the way down to the ends. "I like it."

"Thanks," she whispered.

They stared into each other's eyes for a long moment, the connection between them seeming to get stronger with every second that passed.

When they went over one particularly large wave, Black swore. He fumbled with a phone that had been sitting on the console in front of him, but it went flying through the air before he could catch it.

It landed right in Allye's lap, and she jumped.

"Easy, kitten," Gray murmured. "It's only a phone."

As soon as the last words were out of his mouth, the cell in her lap began to vibrate with an incoming call.

"Jesus," she breathed, jumping again. "That was so weird."

Gray chuckled and held out his hand. He would've just grabbed it, but as it was sitting at the juncture of her thighs, he didn't feel it was appropriate. "Hand it here?"

Allye picked up the small black phone and looked at the number on the display for a brief second before giving it to him. "Maybe it's the pizza guy calling to let us know the huge pizza Black ordered will be waiting for us when we get to shore."

Gray smiled and shook his head at Allye. He knew it would be Rex. He'd meant to call him as soon as he got Allye settled with her water and protein bar, but got distracted by Black's conversation about her genetics.

"Gray," he said after he clicked on the green icon to answer the phone.

"Are you all right?" Rex asked.

Gray wasn't surprised at his handler's lack of greeting. He immediately told the other man everything that had happened aboard the other boat, and what both the captain and the escort had said—leaving out the specific details of their deaths for now. Then he informed him about Allye. "And the woman was already on the boat."

"She was?" Rex asked, and Gray could hear papers shuffling on the other end of the line. "She wasn't supposed to be."

Looking over at Allye, who was staring as if she could tell what Rex was saying simply by looking at Gray, he replied, "Yeah, I know. But she's safe. She's sitting right here next to me."

"What does she know?"

"Nothing. At least nothing that will lead us to whoever it was who bought her." Gray hated putting it that way, even more so when he saw Allye's nose wrinkle, but it was what it was. "She was nabbed right off the street on her way home. She was drugged and didn't wake up until she was being carried onto the boat. Then she was guarded by an escort."

"Fuck," Rex said. "Selling women is already going too far. Sending escorts who try to kill them when something goes wrong in the transfer is fucking sadistic. I need to chop the head off the snake to stop this shit."

"Nightingale," Gray guessed.

"Exactly. If we kill that motherfucker, it'll at least stop shipments of women for a while. Of course, someone else will pick up where he left off. Dammit. How's the package?"

The way Rex phrased that rubbed Gray the wrong way, but he controlled the retort that wanted to come out and simply said, "Cold, hungry, and thirsty, but otherwise good, considering." He met Allye's gaze, and she gave him a small smile.

"Was she raped?"

"No." Gray wanted to say more. Wanted to tell Rex that the escort was there to prevent her from being abused by any of the men who transported her to her new master, but he didn't want to douse the light he saw in Allye's eyes at the moment.

"We'll talk later," Rex said, obviously understanding. It was one of the reasons their handler was so good at what he did. He had an intuitiveness that went beyond being able to sniff out sex traffickers and abusers.

"We will," Gray confirmed. Then added, "She's likely still in danger." After hearing what the man on the boat had said about the buyer coming for her, how badly he wanted her, Gray knew she wasn't going to be able to return to her normal life as if nothing had happened.

"Make sure she knows, and tell her to go to the cops and tell them her story. She needs a security system, and if she has family out of state, it might be best to go visit them for a while," Rex said.

She *didn't* have family. Out of state or otherwise. Gray knew that. And he had no idea what the cops would do about an alleged kidnapping victim feeling as if she was still in danger, but not knowing from who. It was an impossible situation.

"Gray? You still there?" Rex asked.

"I'm here."

"Drop her off and get your ass back here. The others are back from their mission—successful, by the way—and I'll get to work finding out what I can about Nightingale. I'm going to use all my connections and see if I can't pin him down. It's possible you and the others will be leaving sooner rather than later to take down that fucker once and for all."

"Yes, sir," Gray told Rex, his mind going a million miles an hour, trying to come up with a solution for what to do with Allye.

As usual, Rex didn't say goodbye, just ended the connection. Gray handed the phone back up to Black.

"What'd he say?"

Gray knew he couldn't remain sitting next to Allye when he informed her they'd be dropping her off, and that she was on her own.

It sucked. Maybe it was a product of them having spent a very intense hour and a half in the ocean. Maybe it was simply her. But whatever it was, Gray didn't want to leave Allye. He wanted to take her back to Colorado Springs and personally make sure she was safe. But he couldn't.

He stood slowly. He could feel her eyes on him, but he refused to look down at her. He checked the small instrument panel and looked beyond the front of the boat.

"Gray?" Allye asked from behind him.

Gray turned, braced himself on the front of the boat, and looked down at Allye. Her hair was drying and blowing in the wind. He saw that it was as curly as he remembered it being when he'd first seen her on the fishing boat. The white streak was almost hidden in the curls, but it still peeked out here and there in the breeze. Her brown and blue eyes gazed up at him, full of worry.

He tried to find words that would convey a need to be cautious, but wouldn't scare the shit out of her. "You know that the man who bought you wasn't on the boat."

"Yeah."

"So he's still out there."

Allye nodded. "And if he paid someone to pick me up once, he can do it again," she correctly deduced. For someone who thought she wasn't smart, she sure was proving otherwise.

"Exactly."

"I figured as much. I'd already planned to make sure one of the male dancers escorts me to and from work, and to call the cops when I get home. What else should I be doing?"

Gray sighed in relief. He didn't know what he'd expected her to do when he explained the man who wanted her for his own was still out there. But this calm acceptance was welcome.

A part of him almost wished she would've begged him to take her with him, to keep her safe, but he knew that would never happen. Allye was independent and didn't seem the type to beg anyone for anything.

They talked for a short while about what she should watch out for and what she should say to the cops.

"So, you guys don't want me talking about you, I'm assuming, right?"

"Why would you say that?" Black asked, inserting himself into the conversation for the first time.

"Well, you came to my rescue under the cover of darkness, Gray killed two people, and you haven't really told me exactly what it is you do. It's not hard to figure out you don't want me blabbing to the cops."

"I own a gun range in Colorado Springs," Black told her. "And Gray here is an accountant."

Allye stared at them for a second, then began to giggle. "Unh-uh. That's a lie."

Black held up his hand. "Scout's honor."

"You've never been a Boy Scout," Allye protested, still laughing.

"True, but I'm not lying. Tell her." Black elbowed Gray.

He shrugged. "He's telling the truth. When I'm not rescuing damsels in distress, I'm an accountant and own my own business back in the Springs."

Allye stopped laughing and stared at him. "But . . . accountants are nerdy and wear glasses and definitely aren't as tall and muscular as *you*."

It was Gray's turn to chuckle. "I think you have a pretty narrow view of accountants, kitten. I'm not sure what height or muscular makeup have to do with being able to put numbers together."

"It's just . . . you were going to swim like a million miles back to shore . . . *towing* me. I can't picture you as an accountant. No way."

"You know that I also used to be in the Navy," Gray told her, not sure why he was overexplaining, just that he wanted her to know. "And that I was a SEAL. So was Black, although we never worked together when we were on active duty. I got out, and now I help keep books for a few businesses in Colorado. It's not a big deal."

"Not a big deal?" Allye asked incredulously. "It's a huge deal! And I have to say . . . if there were more boys who looked like you in my high school who were into math, I might've had a new appreciation for algebra. I might even have skipped the class less."

Both Gray and Black chuckled.

"I'm relieved you guys are some sort of supersoldiers, all things considered."

"Sailors," Black corrected.

"What?"

"Sailors, not soldiers," he repeated. "You never call a SEAL a soldier."

"Oh, *so* sorry," she teased. "Super-SEALs . . . is that better?"

"Much," Black said with a grin.

"You need to be really careful when you get home," Gray said, bringing the conversation back around.

"I will," she told him.

"I don't want to hear that you've disappeared again. I'll be awfully disappointed if I have to come rescue you a second time."

She rolled her eyes, and Gray's lips twitched. She was adorable when she did that, although he'd never admit it.

"You won't," she said. "I figure if whoever this is gets his hands on me again, he'll have learned his lesson, and he won't be as lax next time. I'll be one of those ninety thousand missing people you told me about earlier."

She was joking, Gray could tell, but her words didn't sit well with him. Not at all.

He squatted down in front of her, his knees protesting the move, but he ignored his aches and pains as he rested his elbows on his knees and leaned into her. "You feel even the slightest sense that something is wrong, you act on it. Go to a police station, get a friend—preferably a large male friend—to stick by your side. It might even be a good idea to get a dog. A big one with a loud bark. This isn't a joke, Allye. The man who decided he wanted you most likely has money, lots of it, if the fact he hired an escort for you is any indication. And if worse comes to worst, you call me."

Her eyes widened at that last part.

Gray mentally kicked himself. He hadn't meant to say that, but now that he had, he wasn't exactly sorry. He didn't know what he would be able to do from hundreds of miles away, but he'd feel better if he was able to have some contact with her.

"I'm not sure there's anything you can do from Colorado to help me if I'm in trouble," she said, echoing his thoughts exactly.

"I can give you advice. Be a sounding board," he told her, not going so far as to say he'd drop everything to get to her, even though he knew he'd want to.

She gave him a sad smile then. "I'm sure I'll be fine," she told him, brushing off his concern. "I mean, I've been on my own for a long time now, practically since the moment I was born. I can handle this. Besides, I bet he'll back off now that his little plan didn't work."

Gray hoped so, but he wasn't as confident as she was.

"Hold on," Black said from above his head.

Gray stood and looked past the front of the Zodiac. The dark beach they were nearing seemed deserted except for a lone man.

"Wondered where you got this boat from," Gray said.

"Yeah, long story. Nothing went according to plan. I found the other boat, but the captain had no intention of letting me get anywhere near him. Used a semiautomatic to shoot the hell out of the fiberglass boat. Luckily for me, he fucking ran out of bullets. Idiot. I boarded his boat, intending to use it to meet up with you, but the asshole damaged the motor before I could get there. He wasn't forthcoming with his plans or who he was working for, no matter what kind of incentive I tried to give him. When he went for the radio for backup, I shot at his hand, but he actually leaped *toward* my bullet instead of away from it." Black shrugged. "Told you he was an idiot. I managed to get his piece-of-shit boat back to shore, but it wasn't seaworthy enough to come back and meet you at the rendezvous. I contacted Rex, and he sent me here, and this guy"—Black motioned to the man standing on the shore—"had this Zodiac, fully gassed up and ready to go. We switched. He took the fiberglass boat and hid it somewhere, and I took this one back out to find you."

"Rex scares me sometimes," Gray observed.

"Yup."

"Rex isn't really his name, is it?" Allye asked from right next to him.

Gray startled and almost laughed. It'd been a long time since someone had been able to get as close to him as Allye was right now without him noticing. She'd stood right by his side . . . and he hadn't realized until she'd spoken.

"It's what he goes by," Black told her. "And since he's our boss, we call him whatever he wants."

"I'm confused. Gray said Rex hired him, and you say he's your boss, but you also said Gray's an accountant and you own a gun range . . ."

Gray made a mental note that not much got by Allye. "Remember when I talked about getting a call and going to that pool hall for an interview?" When she nodded, he said, "So yeah, Rex is our boss for this kind of stuff." He nodded his head, indicating the boat and their current situation.

"Ahhh," she said, drawing the word out.

Gray was both pleased and irritated that she didn't ask anything else. For the first time . . . ever . . . he wanted to tell someone all about what he did. All about Mountain Mercenaries and some of the things he'd seen and done. But Black was steering the boat up the sandy beach, and the mysterious man who'd been waiting for them was grabbing the rubber side, holding the boat steady.

Gray motioned for Allye to go first, and he did his best to keep his eyes off her ass as she shuffled to the side of the boat. She still had a blanket wrapped tightly around her waist, but it didn't keep him from admiring what a fine backside she had. He'd seen it up close and personal when he was helping her onto the boat.

Black quickly hopped out and held up a hand to help her climb over the side. Gray reluctantly removed his hand from her waist, even though he wanted nothing more than to pull her into him and never let her go.

That thought alone was enough to have him dropping his hands from her body as if she were suddenly electrically charged. What the fuck was he thinking? She was just another mission. That's it. Wasn't she?

Without analyzing his thoughts, Gray jumped out of the boat and stood by Allye's side. Before he could say something stupid—like invite her to come to Colorado—the man who met them on the beach spoke.

"I've got some dry blankets you can use up at the house. Rex called. I understand you're from the city, right?"

Allye nodded.

"I'll take you in when you're ready." His tone made it clear he wouldn't accept any argument with his plans, and Allye obviously understood, because she simply nodded.

When Black stepped off to the side with the man, talking in a low tone, Allye turned to Gray.

"I guess this is where I say thanks and goodbye."

He stared down at her. Their difference in height was more apparent now than when they'd been in the ocean. He towered over her, but for some reason it didn't annoy him as it usually might. Gray typically liked tall women. They seemed less . . . childlike to him. But when he looked down at Allye from his six-five height, all he could think about was pulling her into his arms and keeping her safe. Her height didn't matter. Her tenacity and stubbornness more than made up for any lack of stature.

"Guess so," he told her. "Remember what I said. Don't let your guard down."

"I won't," she vowed.

Gray opened his mouth to say more, he wasn't sure what, but Black was suddenly at his side. "We need to go."

Gray turned and looked at his teammate. "Why? What's up?"

"Our friend's neighbors are gettin' interested in us, and he's not too happy about it. I'm not sure what marker Rex called in, but I'm guessing his guy won't be helping in the future."

Gray's eyes went from Black to the other man. He was scowling at them with his arms crossed over his chest. Impatience practically oozed from every pore.

"I can't leave Allye like this," Gray said.

Before Black could respond, Gray felt her hand on his arm. "I'll be fine. Go. Whatever you've got going with that Rex guy is more important than dealing with me."

"Now *that* was a stupid thing to say," Gray reprimanded her.

As he could've guessed, she rolled her eyes at him. "Whatever. This man isn't going to hurt me. I'm sensing this Rex of yours has a lot of power and connections. If I don't show up back at work, I'm sure somehow Rex will know, and will send fire and brimstone down on this guy."

"Give me a second, Black?" Gray asked.

"One minute," his friend warned. "That's all I'll be able to hold him off."

Without acknowledging his friend, Gray turned back to Allye. He wasn't sure what to say. Suddenly nothing seemed adequate. He'd never felt as frustrated at the end of a mission as he did right that second.

They'd done this before, gotten a woman, or a group of women, to a safe house and left them there so the Mountain Mercenaries could keep their involvement under wraps . . . but it just seemed wrong this time.

Allye put her hand on Gray's chest and stood on tiptoes as she lifted her head.

Instinctively, Gray put his hand on the small of her back to steady her and lowered his head so she could reach him.

She brushed her lips against his cheek, then wrapped her arms around him as best she could and still hold on to the blankets. "Thank you for giving a shit," she said in a low, intense voice. "I know you weren't there specifically to save me, but thank you for not leaving me on that boat."

"Take care of yourself," Gray said gruffly.

"I will. I always do," was her breezy reply.

Gray opened his mouth to say he'd check in on her. That he'd continue to give a shit, but Black interrupted again.

"Time's up. We gotta jet."

Allye gave him a little push and took a step back. "It was nice meeting you, Black. Be careful out there. The world's a nasty place."

"Will do. You too," Black replied as he took a step away from her.

Gray followed his friend, walking backward a few steps before turning. Where he and Black were going, he had no idea, but he trudged along behind him anyway. When he couldn't take it any longer, he turned and looked back at where he'd left Allye.

She and the man were gone. The only evidence they'd been there at all was the black Zodiac still sitting on the sand and footprints leading toward a house on a bluff.

Chapter Six

Allye let herself into her apartment using the hidden key she'd buried at the corner of the building. She'd learned throughout her time in foster care to always make sure she had a way into wherever she was living. Too many times other foster kids had locked her out, thinking it was funny.

She turned and leaned against the door after she'd locked the bolt, the doorknob, and put on the chain, then sighed. It seemed like a lifetime ago that she'd been here, but in reality, it had been only about forty-eight hours. She felt as if she had a million things she should be doing, but all she wanted was to take a long bath and sleep for eight hours straight.

The man who had been on the beach hadn't said much to her after they'd parted ways with Gray and Black. She'd gone inside the house with him and accepted the dry blankets gratefully. She wasn't exactly dressed appropriately, but as it was basically still the middle of the night, she had hoped she'd be able to sneak inside her apartment without anyone seeing her. The man did give her a pair of old flip-flops, which he said he'd found on the beach one evening. They were big, but they worked in a pinch.

The man had asked for her address and driven her home. He'd stopped outside her apartment, and she'd gotten out. Then, without a word, the man had driven away. It had been a bit weird, but considering he was helping her, she didn't bother trying to make small talk.

Allye had memorized the license plate of the two-door white Toyota she'd climbed out of, just in case, but it seemed as though he was just as anxious to get rid of her as she was to get home and back to her normal life.

She needed to call the police and report her attempted kidnapping, but she also needed to wait until she was thinking more clearly. The last thing she wanted to do was let something slip about Gray and his friend Black. She'd make up a story about slipping away from her kidnapper and having no idea where he went after she'd gotten away. She'd say she swam to shore, not the ten miles that it had been, but maybe one mile instead.

Thoughts about the police and her ordeal made her remember, for the first time, the flash drive in her pocket.

Things had been so intense since her escape from that small bedroom on the sinking boat that she'd forgotten all about it. She peeled off her damp shirt and retrieved the small electronic device she'd grabbed from the boat what seemed like a lifetime ago.

She remembered the escort guy on the boat clicking through a spreadsheet on the laptop as he mumbled about all the slaves he had to train, escort, or move. She'd been surprised he was talking about that kind of thing in front of her, but then again, he'd thought she was about to be picked up by whoever had bought her—until something had gone wrong, and then the man had been prepared to kill her.

She'd taken a guess that the spreadsheet was saved on the flash drive. Her plan had been to give it to Gray if he proved himself trustworthy, but she'd simply forgotten.

In fact, they hadn't even exchanged phone numbers. Gray had said she could call him if something happened, but because of the way he'd had to leave so abruptly, they'd both forgotten to get each other's contact information. She could probably find him on Google or something, but their time together already seemed like a dream of sorts. She would feel weird calling him out of the blue, even though he'd said she could.

Walking into her living room, Allye went straight to her computer and pulled up a search engine. She had no idea if the flash drive would even still work after being immersed in the ocean water for as long as it had been.

What she read buoyed her spirits. She went into her bathroom and got out the bottle of isopropyl alcohol in her cabinet. The people on the forums online said that it would help dry out the components of the flash drive. When that was done, she went into the kitchen and opened a box of rice. Thinking it couldn't hurt, she poured a small amount into a bowl, put the flash drive in the middle, then covered it up with more rice.

Knowing she'd done all she could at that moment, Allye's shoulders sagged, her mind back on Gray.

Leave it to her to be attracted to a man she could never have. Not only did he live in a different state but she'd only met him because he was on some supersecret mission to take down a sex trafficker, and he was obviously really far out of her league. She'd barely finished high school, and he was a former Navy SEAL, an accountant, and some sort of real-life badass.

Yeah, even if they lived in the same place, she wouldn't measure up.

She sighed and rubbed her eyes tiredly. Time for that shower and some sleep. Then she'd get on with gettin' on with her life.

The next morning, Allye was ready for things to get back to normal. It seemed unreal that just last night, she'd been in the middle of the ocean, wondering if she'd live to see another day.

She'd called the owner of the dance company the previous evening, before she'd crashed, and let her know she was alive and well and would be in today. Robin McNeely was in her fifties, and still one of the best dancers Allye had ever seen. She didn't dance much anymore, but she came to every rehearsal. When someone was having difficulty with some of the choreography, she'd come up to the stage and demonstrate.

It had been Robin who had called the cops when Allye had gone missing. The police hadn't done much with the information, since she was an adult. Apparently, adults wandered off without telling anyone where they were going all the time—and ultimately showed up after a couple of days or weeks.

Allye had no idea how Gray, or Rex, had gotten involved in her disappearance, but she thanked her lucky stars they had. If not, she knew she'd be wishing she was dead right about now.

Before leaving for the theatre, Allye fished the flash drive out of the bowl of rice she'd put it in. It felt dry, but she didn't know much about electronics. Holding her breath, she put her laptop on the kitchen counter and inserted the device into the appropriate slot.

Amazingly, the icon popped up on the desktop, letting her know there was a new drive detected. Not quite sure what she was going to find, Allye clicked it open.

An Excel spreadsheet opened, but instead of showing her data, like she'd hoped, a password box popped up.

"Fuck," she muttered, staring at it. She didn't know the first thing about hacking into spreadsheets. She was barely able to get her own laptop to work.

For a second there, she'd had visions of turning the flash drive over to the police and seeing on the news that they were able to find hundreds of missing girls as a result of her taking a risk and grabbing it before the boat sank.

"Stupid," she mumbled to herself, pulling the flash drive out of her computer. She held it in her palm for a long moment, wrestling with herself and trying to decide what to do. She should've given it to Gray before he'd left, but she'd forgotten. Just like she'd forgotten to get his phone number. Shaking her head, she opened her junk drawer and threw the small device in with all the other crap she'd accumulated over the years.

She'd think about it later. She had shit to do, and the new girl in the dance company had probably been doing everything in her power to take the lead away from Allye during her brief absence. Jessie had been a pain in the ass ever since she'd been hired, and Allye refused to let her take all the good dance parts. She'd worked too hard to get where she was.

Deciding she'd take a taxi to work today rather than the cable car, as she usually did, Allye called one of the dancers who lived nearby. Since she offered to pay, he was more than happy to get a taxi and come pick her up. Allye scooped up her bag with her dance clothes and left, making sure to double-check that her door was locked before heading out.

"Fuck!" Gray exclaimed late the next morning.

He'd passed out on the private plane he and Black had taken back to Colorado Springs, the long swim getting the better of him. Then he'd spent a couple of hours with the rest of the team, going over the mission and what had happened. He'd listened as the others debriefed their own mission, and ended up not getting back to his house until late.

He'd fallen asleep immediately, and had woken up feeling as good as new. Glad that he was still as fit as he used to be when he was in the Navy, Gray had checked in with Rex.

His sudden expletive—shortly followed by an epiphany—came during their conversation.

"What?" Rex asked.

"I never gave Allye my number," Gray told his handler. "I told her if she thought she was in danger that she could call me."

"Why? It's not like you could do anything about it," Rex said.

Gray was irritated with his elusive friend and boss. "I get that, but at least she'd be able to talk to someone about it. Someone who might be able to do something if she disappeared again."

He heard Rex sigh and knew he wasn't going to like what his handler was about to say.

"The bottom line is that we have no control over what happens to her from here on out. I don't have much of anything on Nightingale. It's like he up and closed shop. None of my usual information channels are picking up any activity on him, or making any connections between him and recently missing women. Whatever happened on this last op seems to have shaken him."

"What are you saying? That you think Allye is safe? That she's no longer in danger?" Gray asked.

"I didn't say that. What I'm saying is that the son of a bitch is in the wind. He's a ghost. Without more information, I can't continue to track him. I thought he was behind another recent kidnapping, but with no eyewitnesses and no information, I can't be one hundred percent sure."

"So, you're saying that if Allye *does* get snatched again, we can use any eyewitness accounts to try to find out information on Nightingale? That you hope she *does* get taken?"

Rex was silent for so long, Gray wasn't sure he was going to reply. When he did, his voice was low and modulated, and obviously extremely pissed off.

"I'm going to pretend you didn't just say that," Rex said evenly. "You know that's not what I meant. I'd never want anyone—man, woman, or child—to be taken by that asshole. He doesn't have one ounce of compassion in his entire body. He'll do what he wants to whoever he wants, and won't let anyone stand in his way. All I'm saying is that if he does decide to finish what he started for whatever rich client who wants her, there's not a whole lot we can do. It's up to Allye to keep herself safe until he screws up and we're able to kill that son of a bitch."

That didn't sit well with Gray at all. "And if she *does* get snatched again?"

"Then we do our best to find her and get her home," Rex replied.

It wasn't exactly what Gray wanted to hear, but it was the best he could expect. Without him staking some sort of claim on her, Allye was ultimately just another woman. And he had no reason to think she would want anything to do with him on a personal level. Oh, he had a feeling she was attracted to him, and wouldn't complain about spending a night or two in his bed, but the only way Rex would extend his protection to her was if she officially belonged to one of his mercenaries.

Their handler had made it very clear when they'd each started working for him that they were free to find a woman and start a relationship, but the only way they were allowed to tell her what they really did for a living was if the relationship was a permanent one. Gray had already told Allye more than he should've, but spending all that time together in the middle of the ocean had uncharacteristically loosened his tongue.

Rex had said more than once that when any of his mercenaries *were* in a permanent relationship, he'd do whatever was necessary to keep their women, and any children they had, safe.

They'd lost one of their operatives to a relationship just recently. He'd quit the group because he'd not only found the love of his life, he'd gained an entire family he hadn't known about until his mother died.

Ryder Sinclair was now living up in Castle Rock, Colorado, and had a woman of his own, three half brothers, two baby nephews, and countless other friends and family members. He worked for Ace Security now, and Gray still spoke with him all the time, but it wasn't the same. He wasn't an official member of Mountain Mercenaries anymore. Gray knew Ryder was happy, but he still missed him.

He had thought Ryder was crazy for giving up the exciting missions of Mountain Mercenaries for a woman, but now he was having second thoughts.

And *that* was his epiphany. There was something about Allye that had snuck under the shields he'd put up, and that he couldn't shake. If there was a woman out there whom he'd give up Mountain Mercenaries for, Gray had a feeling it would be Allye.

The thought should've freaked him out, but instead it simply felt right. The time they'd spent together in the ocean had stripped away the facade that he usually wore for other people, and he suspected the same had happened for her. He'd gotten to know the real Allye . . . and he liked her a hell of a lot.

Gray wanted to ask Rex if he would find her phone number for him, but refrained. He knew Meat could probably get ahold of it easily, as well, but he ultimately decided it was better that he didn't talk to her. Gray had a feeling he'd find out that talking to her, but not being with her, would be more painful than making the break cold turkey.

He remembered the way she'd turned to him when they were still on the fishing boat and said, in a completely serious tone, that it was illegal to not have flotation devices on the boat. And the way she rolled her eyes all the time. She hadn't complained or gotten hysterical, as many women in the same situation might've. But that didn't mean she hadn't been scared. She'd gripped his pocket so tightly, it communicated her uncertainty and fright loud and clear. She'd held on as if her life had depended on not letting go. And it had.

Gray had saved hundreds of lives over the years, but none had affected him like Allye.

The silence on the phone had gone on way too long, but Gray knew Rex didn't care. He'd hang out on the other end of the line forever if he felt it was necessary.

"If you find out any information on her, will you let me know?" Gray asked at last. "Like if she's being targeted again?"

"Yeah, I can do that," Rex told him.

It was as much as Gray was going to get right now, and he knew it. "Thanks. Appreciate it. I gotta go. I have a P&L sheet I need to do for one of my clients. It was due yesterday, but I'll make something up on why it's late."

"You're a good man," Rex said in a low voice. "You did a great job out there. You got as much information as you could, and you saved a life in the process. I'm proud to have you on my team." And with that, Rex hung up.

Gray could only shake his head. Rex was eccentric, that was for sure. As far as he knew, no one on the team had ever met the elusive man. He seemed to always know what they were doing and when, but would never confirm how he got his information.

He and the others had been recruited several years ago. Gray remembered it as if it were yesterday. He was getting out of the Navy and had gotten the call from Rex about a job. He hadn't told him much, just that the interview was at a run-down pool hall in Colorado Springs called The Pit.

When he'd arrived, Meat, Arrow, Ball, Black, Ryder, and Ro had also been there for their supposed interviews. They'd gotten to talking while waiting for Rex to make an appearance, and three hours later—after they'd decided fuck the job and fuck Rex, and had been drunker than hell—they'd each received a phone call telling them they'd gotten the job.

Apparently, it had been a test. A test to see if the seven of them could get along. And they had. Extremely well. Gray knew the other men all had their own reasons for joining the Mountain Mercenaries, but they never talked about it except to say they were glad their unique skills were being used to rid the world of humans not fit to be walking around, and to save women and children from all walks of life.

As Gray pulled up the database needed to work on the profit-and-loss statement for his client, he tried to put the spunky yet vulnerable woman he'd just rescued out of his mind. They just weren't meant to be.

~

A week and a half later, Allye shut her apartment door behind her—hard.

The week had started out pretty well. Everyone at work had been overjoyed to see her, especially after hearing what she'd gone through. At least the bare bones. Allye had left out most of the details. She'd called the police and filed a report about her kidnapping, although again, that report was lacking in a lot of specifics. She told the cops she was concerned that whoever had snatched her would try again, but without any description or any information at all about him, they didn't have much to go on. They'd simply given her the same advice Gray had. Which wasn't exactly comforting.

She'd fallen back into her normal routine fairly quickly over the rest of the week. She woke up early and ate breakfast. Watched the news for any hint of a story about her kidnapping or a sex-slave ring being taken down, to no avail. Then she headed off to the theatre for rehearsals.

Today was the day the photographer was scheduled to take program headshots for the upcoming show. Robin insisted on every dancer having new pictures for each performance. She didn't want the audience to get bored with the programs, especially since the dancers were often the same, just shuffled around from part to part.

One month they might have a modern-dance routine, the next it might be jazz. Robin prided herself on the quality of her shows and her dancers. She spared no expense with the programs, producing them on high-quality, glossy pages that she hoped patrons would save as keepsakes.

The first time the current photographer had come to shoot the cast, she'd been surprised to see Allye's different-colored eyes, and did her best to play them up in the headshot photos. Allye was honestly over it, but had learned not to complain. Between her eyes and the streak of white in her hair, she knew she was an oddity, and photographers loved to highlight both features.

After today's pictures were taken, during which she'd gotten a lot of attention from the photographer once again, the afternoon began to go downhill. Jessie, the teenager who wanted the lead in the show but didn't get it because Allye had reappeared, had been sullen and uncooperative, going so far as to pout when Robin had to intervene and tell her to go home for the rest of the day.

After rehearsal, Allye had stopped to get a replacement cell phone, since hers had disappeared when she'd been snatched off the street. The phone cost way more than she'd been expecting, but not feeling like she had a choice, Allye paid it.

Then, while heading home, she'd started feeling . . . paranoid. Like someone was following her. But every time she'd looked behind her, no one was there.

The feeling persisted all the way home. Allye even detoured from her usual path, and it took an extra twenty minutes to get to her apartment complex.

The hair on the back of her neck was sticking straight up by the time Allye gratefully slammed her door and fastened all the locks, securing herself inside. She dropped her bag right at the front door and made her way to the couch, where she collapsed in a heap.

It had been two extremely weird weeks. Which she never wanted to experience again. She'd gone from normalcy, to extreme terror and being way out of her league, back to normalcy. Now paranoia. It was almost unreal.

How long she sat there, Allye had no idea. All she knew was that even though she was locked up tight inside her apartment, she still didn't feel safe. It couldn't be all that hard for someone to break down her door. And if they did, they could overpower her, just as the thug had when he'd snatched her from the street. Not one person had stepped up to help her, and she knew it would be the same here in her apartment complex. She didn't know her neighbors, and like most people who lived in the city, she tended to ignore the various shouts and odd sounds that came from the apartments around her.

Shivering, Allye hugged herself. What was she supposed to do? She had a job she had to get to every day. A life. But Gray was right: the man who'd originally paid for her was still out there, biding his time until he could pay someone to take her again. Was he out there watching her right now?

Swallowing hard, Allye shook her head. She'd rather die than go through that again. She'd been scared to death and hadn't had any hope anyone was going to come for her.

She thought back to the moment in the boat after Black had picked them up, when Gray's boss, that Rex guy, had called him.

Closing her eyes, Allye concentrated. She leaned over, with her eyes still closed, and grabbed the pad of paper she knew was sitting on the coffee table in front of her. She fumbled for a pen and quickly wrote down the numbers she was seeing in her head.

Blinking, she opened her eyes and stared down at the pad of paper. She nodded. Yeah, it was the number Rex had been calling from.

Standing, Allye began to pace. She shouldn't be considering doing what she was thinking of doing. But she had to. She knew the asshole who wanted her was still out there. Even if she was hallucinating and no one was following her at the moment. Watching her.

And there were still women who hadn't been rescued.

With every day that passed, the flash drive she'd escaped with mocked her more and more. What if she had the information needed to save someone else? To get the entire horrific operation shut down? What if she had the power to stop assholes from abusing women and children . . . and she did nothing? What would that make her? An accomplice of some sort?

Allye hugged herself harder as she paced in agitation. She needed to give the flash drive to someone who could figure out what the password was and help take down the entire operation. Killing the captain of the boat and the man sent to escort her to her new owner was one thing, but the man who'd actually abducted her was still out there as well.

There had to be many more involved, too, lots of people who helped that Nightingale guy abduct and transfer women. But not one of them had helped *her*, and they all had an opportunity. The kidnapper, the captain of the boat, the escort . . . Who knew how many others had knowledge of what was going on? They all needed to be taken down, and it was possible she was holding on to the one piece of evidence that would do just that.

Walking slowly into the kitchen, she opened the drawer, staring at the innocuous black flash drive with hate in her heart. Closing the drawer, she took a deep breath and went back into the other room.

Picking up her brand-new cell phone, Allye dialed the number she'd only seen once, but had managed to memorize.

"Who is this? How'd you get this number?"

The voice sounded like it was being altered somehow, but at the moment, Allye didn't care. The man didn't sound pleased in the least, and Allye wanted to immediately hang up, but she forced herself to say, "My name is Allye Martin. I'm looking for Rex."

"How'd you get this number?"

"Is this Rex?" she pressed. The last thing Allye wanted to do was tell someone who wasn't Rex what she had in her possession.

"Yeah. It's me. Now, *how'd* you get this number?"

"I saw it on the screen when you called Gray last week. I was the woman he rescued from the sex-slaver's boat." There was a long silence on the other end of the line, and Allye finally asked, "Are you still there?"

"I'm here. You saw my number one time, over a week ago, and remembered it?"

"Yeah. I can't remember names or faces that well, but numbers are easy for me."

"Hmmm. Interesting. What's wrong?"

"Well, nothing's wrong, per se, but I've got something I think you need to have."

"What?"

"Um, well . . . when I was on the boat, the man who was escorting me to whoever bought me was sitting in the bedroom with me, after he'd handcuffed me to the bed . . ." Allye paused, remembering the awful things he'd said.

"And?" Rex asked impatiently.

Allye rolled her eyes, but went on. "He was scrolling on a laptop. Every now and then, he'd pause and murmur a woman's name, and then he'd tell me what happened to her. It was like he was searching through something on the screen, finding the most horrifying cases just to torture me."

"So, what . . . you're telling me you got the laptop he was using?"

"Of course not. It's not like I could drag a laptop through the ocean. But I *did* get the external drive he stuck into the computer when he came into the room."

Rex was silent another second before he asked, "Are you shitting me?"

"No. I have it. I was going to give it to Gray, but I forgot. I figured it probably wouldn't work anyway, but when I got home, I looked up on the internet how to dry it out and did everything people suggested. And when I plugged it in, it worked."

"Holy mother of God. What was on it?" Rex asked, sounding even more impatient now.

"That's the thing—I don't know. It's password protected, and I have no idea how to get into the spreadsheet."

"Does anyone else know you have it?"

Allye shrugged, forgetting Rex couldn't see her. "I have no idea. I mean, I don't think so. I don't know how they would. I haven't told anyone. But . . ." Her voice trailed off.

"But what?"

"It's stupid."

"But *what*?" Rex asked again with more force.

"Recently I've felt as if I'm being followed. It's crazy. I mean, it's probably just because I'm paranoid after what happened. But Gray told me to be careful and to be on the lookout. Anyway . . . I just thought that maybe there was something on this thing that might lead to whoever kidnapped me, and maybe could lead to some of the other women who've disappeared. And if I don't give it to someone, and I get grabbed again, those other women will never get a chance to be rescued."

Allye heard tapping on keys in the background and waited for Rex to say something. It took a couple of beats, but finally he said, "I just bought you a ticket to Colorado Springs. You leave in about two and a half hours."

"What? Why?"

"How else are you going to get that flash drive to me?" Rex asked.

"Well, I thought I could mail it."

"Are you *insane*?" he asked, sounding appalled. "What if it got lost? You willing to risk that?"

Allye sighed. Dammit, he made a lot of sense. "Why can't *you* come out here?" she asked. "I have a job. Stuff to do."

"It's Friday. If you decide to, you can be back by Sunday night."

What did he mean, *if* she decided to come back home?

But he didn't give her a chance to ask.

"Go pack. A carry-on only. I'll call someone to pick you up. Don't leave your apartment until I call back and tell you the driver is there. Don't talk to anyone. Don't do anything but go straight to the airport and to your gate. I'd send the private plane, but it's currently out of commission because of a flat fucking tire. You're going to have to fly commercial to Denver, and then you'll be taking the last flight to the Springs. Don't miss it."

Allye rolled her eyes. She wasn't a baby. She knew how to fly. "Anything else?" she asked, tongue in cheek.

"Yes. I'm arranging for someone to pick you up at the Colorado Springs airport. The driver will take you to the Broadmoor. You'll stay there for the night, then the same driver will come back Saturday afternoon after you check out and bring you to meet me. Got it?"

"The Broadmoor? Isn't that, like, a seriously expensive hotel? Why not a Motel 6?"

"Why don't you let me worry about price, Allye? Just don't let anything happen to that flash drive, and get your ass to the airport. If anything seems off or weird, bail, and call me as soon as you can. I'll get you here one way or another."

Allye sighed. She supposed she should feel grateful Rex was worried about her, but she knew he wasn't exactly worried about *her*. He wanted the flash drive.

"Got it?" he barked.

"Yes, sir," Allye said instinctively. "I got it."

"Stay safe," Rex ordered. "And I know you're thinking it, so I have to say—*you're* more important than whatever is on that drive you're holding. I don't like you being vulnerable out there without someone at your back, especially now that you're feeling like you're being watched. Keep your eyes open. Talk to you soon."

And with that, he hung up.

A warm feeling moved up Allye's chest as she clicked off the phone. She didn't know this Rex guy, but if Gray trusted him, so would she.

Rex hadn't said anything about Gray, but the thought that she was going to the same city he lived in wouldn't leave her brain. Maybe she could ask Rex if he would call Gray and let her at least say hello.

She stood in the middle of her living room for a heartbeat, trying to imagine how a reunion with Gray would go, before shaking herself and looking at her watch. She needed to get moving. She had a plane to catch.

Gage Nightingale hung up the phone, satisfied that his special future pet was home safe and sound for the night. He absently scratched his scruffy black hair as he pushed his chair away from the desk and leaned back. Placing his hands on his protruding belly, he thought over what could have happened with the transfer of his property last week. Obviously, something had gone terribly wrong. He couldn't get ahold of the man he'd paid handsomely to escort his new acquisition, to find out how he'd screwed up.

She'd somehow escaped.

But it didn't matter. She'd be his eventually.

Allyson Mystic. He still remembered the first time he saw her. He'd gone out one night to a new theatre, one he'd never been to before. As soon as he saw the program, he was intrigued. The photograph of her caught his attention and wouldn't let go. He'd never become so enamored from a simple photo.

Her eyes called to him. One blue and one brown. That, along with the streak of white in her hair, made him want to come back. To see more of her.

Then he'd seen her *outside* the theatre. He'd recognized her immediately. She'd been with another dancer, but the other woman hadn't interested him in the least. Only Allyson. He'd watched her that night. Saw how she'd rebuffed all other men, as if she were saving herself just for him. He was intrigued and fascinated.

By the end of the night, he'd already begun to plan how to make her his own.

He was a collector of the unusual. In the specially designed compound on his hundred-acre property outside San Francisco, he had endangered animals, dinosaur fossils, relics from the Middle East . . . and a few very special acquisitions.

He had a woman who, when he'd acquired her, had tattoos covering seventy-five percent of her body. He was working on making that one hundred percent.

He also had a little person, a pair of identical twins, and, just last month, he'd found and acquired an albino woman. Every hair on her body was the most beautiful white color.

Nightingale kept his treasures in special rooms behind a secret door so they wouldn't be accidentally discovered by any of the many staff and visitors he had on his property. He visited them when he wanted to be amused. Oh, he made sure they knew he was their master in every way, shape and form, but sex wasn't all he wanted from them. He found great amusement in the way they begged for food and water whenever he came around, pounding against the soundproof glass.

And of course he kept them naked, as wild animals should be.

But Mystic would be solely for personal use. She was his good-luck charm. Ever since the night he'd seen her dance, he'd had nothing but good luck. His stocks had made him more money since that night than in the entire previous year. He'd been able to purchase the pair of rare and endangered birds he'd had his eye on.

And, most important, his libido was back.

For a while, he'd been afraid he wouldn't be able to get it up again, but with one look at his Mystic's eyes in the program, he'd gotten hard. Right there in his seat in the theatre. His cock had lengthened and had stayed hard throughout her entire performance.

Yes, Mystic would be his pet. His very special pet. She would be given the gift of his sperm, and she would pass her genetically beautiful eyes and hair on to his offspring. She'd obey his every command and would learn, in time, all his likes and dislikes. Not only that, but she'd dance for him. *Only* for him. He was building a special stage, one that would punish his Mystic for daring to escape from his grasp the first time, and where he could watch her perform anytime he wanted.

Yes, he'd have good luck for the rest of his life with her in a cage at his bedside.

But first he had to catch her. She was as wily as any wild animal, well worth his time and effort to capture.

The man he'd hired to keep his eye on her had reported that her schedule had resumed since she'd returned home. His pet really should learn to alter her routes to and from work a little more. But if she did, he wouldn't have as many chances to snare her.

"Soon, my precious pet," Nightingale murmured, rubbing his hand over his crotch. "Soon."

Chapter Seven

Allye stood in front of the run-down building and stared at it in disbelief. *This* was where she was supposed to meet the elusive Rex? She turned to ask the driver if he was sure he'd gotten the address right, but all she saw were taillights turning onto the street before they disappeared altogether.

She sighed and turned back to face the building.

She'd made it to the airport with no time to spare. The flight to Denver had been uneventful and, luckily, on time, as she had twenty minutes to run to catch her plane to Colorado Springs. It had been late when she'd arrived, and the small airport was nearly deserted when she'd landed.

A man had been waiting for her with her name on a sign, and he'd whisked her to the Broadmoor hotel. It was as beautiful as she'd heard, but because she'd been exhausted, she hadn't really had much time to appreciate it. She'd slept in and had been awakened by the phone ringing on the nightstand next to her.

It was the concierge, letting her know lunch would be brought up momentarily and that her driver would be waiting for her around three o'clock.

And now, here she was. Standing in front of a dilapidated bar called The Pit.

Sighing, Allye hitched her backpack farther up her shoulder and reached for the handle of the door. She blinked a couple of times once she was inside, trying to give her eyes time to adjust. The interior was surprisingly . . . nice. Especially compared to the exterior. A large wooden bar was to her right, taking up almost the entire wall. There were tables and chairs sprinkled around the rest of the room, with a small wooden dance floor and a jukebox off to the left side.

A large doorway atop a couple of steps sat at the back of the room, and Allye could see pool tables in a room beyond the open entrance. It was early, so there weren't many people around, but there were a few.

She wandered over to the bar, not sure if any of the people were Rex or not, but she figured he'd come to her. She put her backpack on the floor at her feet and hopped up onto a tall bar stool.

She rested her elbows on the wooden counter in front of her and waited.

Within moments, a tall, fairly scary-looking man began to emerge from a back room behind the bar. He was wiping his hands on a dishcloth, and his gaze pierced hers as soon as he came through the door.

He was at least half a foot taller than Allye, and his dark hair was cropped close to his head. A rather scraggly beard covered most of his face, gray hair liberally sprinkled through the strands. She could see a scar snaking down his neck and disappearing into the neckline of the blue T-shirt he wore. His complexion was dark, and he had black tattoos covering both arms. Allye knew if she had encountered this man on the streets of San Francisco, she would've gone out of her way to avoid him.

"Hey," he said, his voice deep, his southern accent easy to hear even in that one word.

"Hi," Allye replied.

"Can I get you somethin'?"

"Just a water, please."

The bartender eyed her for a long moment, then he put down the cloth he'd been using and held out a huge hand. "Dave. I'm the bartender around here."

Allye hesitantly reached out and placed her hand in his. "Allye. Like the space between buildings, but the *y* comes before the *e*."

He chuckled and shook her hand, not squeezing overly hard, and dropped it after an appropriate amount of time. "Haven't seen you around here before. You new or just passin' through?"

"I'm supposed to meet someone here," she told the bartender, relaxing into his polite conversation. He wasn't putting out any scary vibes, and the slight smile on his face made her let down her guard even more.

Dave reached below the counter and pulled out a bottle of water. He held it up and asked, "Would you like me to open it for you?"

Allye's brows drew down. "Bottled?" she asked. "Tap water is fine. I don't have a lot of cash on me."

"In my bar, a lady doesn't ever get a glass of water unless she specifically requests it. It's harder to mess with a capped bottle than an open glass. And water in my bar is always free."

"Oh, that makes sense," Allye said. "Thank you."

"So . . . you want me to open this for you, or do you want to do the honors?"

"You can do it."

Dave cracked the seal on the water, placed it on top of a napkin, and slid it in front of her. "You want anything else, just yell. I'll be around."

"Thanks."

"You're welcome."

Allye took a sip of the water and watched as Dave turned and began to clean the top of the bar farther down from her. She spun and took in the rest of the place. There was a man and a woman sitting at a table in the back corner, and the sounds of pool balls hitting against each other came from the back room.

After about twenty minutes, she began to get antsy. No one had come up to her, asking if she was Allye, and the flash drive in her pocket seemed to get heavier and heavier the longer she waited. What if someone had figured out she had the information and was going to give it to Rex? What if he'd gotten hurt on his way to the bar?

Knowing she couldn't just sit there anymore, Allye turned back to the bartender. "Hey, Dave?"

"Yeah, darlin'?" he asked as he wandered over in front of her.

"Can I leave my backpack here while I walk around?"

"Of course. The person you're meeting with hasn't shown up yet?"

She shook her head.

"You call him or her?"

"Him, and yeah, I tried ten minutes ago, and he didn't answer."

"Bummer."

"Yeah."

Dave held out a hand. "Give me your bag. I'll put it behind the bar so no one will mess with it. Although no one would dare in *my* bar."

She chuckled and rolled her eyes. Now *that* she believed. "You're not going to spill anything on it, are you?" she teased.

Dave's eyes narrowed. "I realize you don't know me, woman, but I'm the best bartender in the city. I don't spill. Ever."

Allye laughed. He sounded so put out that she couldn't help it. She held up her hands in capitulation. "Sorry! I didn't know."

Dave smiled at her. "Now you do. Hand it over," he ordered, wiggling his fingers.

Allye picked up her backpack and handed it over the bar to Dave. He took it and placed it somewhere behind the bar. "You go on, explore. And you should know, you're safe in The Pit. I know it looks rough, but I'd vouch for any man or woman in here. They're good people."

"Thanks," Allye told him, feeling relieved even though she hadn't realized she'd been tense in the first place. She hopped off the bar stool and turned to head toward the back room.

"Allye?" Dave called.

She turned around. "Yeah?"

"Cool eyes."

She smiled. She'd had people gush about her eyes to the point where it embarrassed her. They'd asked questions about the streak in her hair and wanted to know if she was wearing contacts. Sometimes they went on and on, and it got extremely awkward. Dave's simple compliment was friendly and not intrusive in the least.

"Thanks."

Dave gave her a chin lift, and she smiled again, then turned and wandered around the room. Maybe she'd spent too much time in San Francisco, but the alpha-male chin lift did something for her. She hadn't really noticed it before, but from the moment she saw Gray giving his buddy Black the same chin lift, she'd decided she liked it. A lot.

Allye meandered over to the jukebox and perused the song selection. It was an eclectic mix of pop, country, and rock and roll. The couple in the corner didn't even look up as she went by them. She headed toward the back room, curious as to what a pool hall might look like. She stopped in the doorway and looked around.

It was a huge room, with about a dozen pool tables strategically set up so none of the players would have to worry about hitting anyone as they were playing. Two of the tables were in use, and by the looks on the players' faces, the games were intense.

There were a few small circular tables randomly strewn around the room. Some short, so people could sit and drink and chat, and others were bar height, so pool players could rest their drinks on them as they were playing. There were lights hanging over each pool table, which gave the room a dim glow, but there weren't any overhead lights on.

Allye turned to her right and glanced at the group of men sitting at the only square table in the room—and froze.

Her breathing increased, and her fight-or-flight instinct kicked in. The men weren't paying any attention to her and hadn't seen her yet.

Allye took one step backward toward the doorway she'd just walked through. But she was too late.

"What the fuck?"

The exclamation had come from Black. The man she'd met just over a week ago on a mission she knew wasn't exactly public knowledge.

Five more heads swiveled to look in her direction, and Allye could do nothing but stare. It was as if she could actually feel the amount of testosterone in the room increase.

All six men at the table were big. And good-looking. And staring at her as if they'd never seen a woman before.

But it was Grayson Rogers's eyes that she couldn't look away from.

Without a word, he stood, a fluid movement that was as graceful as those of any dancer in her troupe, and walked toward her.

"Kitten, what the hell are you doing here? How'd you find me?"

She loved the sound of her nickname on his lips, but his second question sounded more like an accusation than an actual "Boy, am I glad to see you again" statement.

"I . . . I didn't know you'd be here," she stammered. "I wasn't looking for you."

He looked confused.

"I called Rex, and he arranged to meet me here. But he hasn't shown up yet. I was sitting out there"—she pointed at the doorway—"talking to the bartender, Dave, and got bored waiting. I didn't know you'd be here," she repeated.

"Fucking Rex," Gray said under his breath, then held out his hand. "Whatever the reason, I'm glad to see you again. Are you okay?"

Allye liked this gentler Gray. She nodded and put her hand in his outstretched one. The second she touched his palm, his fingers closed around hers. The warmth from his body seemed to seep into her. She hadn't even known she was chilled until she felt how warm his skin was. "I'm okay," she said softly.

"No one's been following you?" Gray asked.

Allye shrugged. "I don't think so. I've felt uneasy recently, but it's probably just a result of what happened to me before."

Gray frowned and tightened his fingers. "Maybe, maybe not. Come on, I want you to meet my friends."

He turned, and would've tugged her across the room to the table full of over-the-top-masculine men, but she stopped him.

"I'm not sure that's a good idea."

His eyebrows went up. "Why not?"

"Because . . . well . . . after what happened, you weren't supposed to be there . . . I'm kind of a real-life, in-your-face reminder that what 'didn't happen' . . . happened."

He stared at her for a heartbeat, then grinned and shook his head. "Come on, kitten. Come meet my friends and teammates."

She allowed him to lead her over to the table. If he wasn't concerned about her meeting his friends, then she supposed she shouldn't be either.

He stopped at the table and wrapped an arm around her waist. Their hips were smashed together, and she felt every finger as he gripped her opposite hipbone.

"Guys, I'd like you to meet Allye Martin. Allye, these are the guys. Meat, Arrow, Ball, Ro, and you know Black."

"Hi," she said awkwardly. "It's nice to meet all of you."

Her greeting was returned by all the men, and she couldn't help but squirm under their scrutiny. The man Gray called Meat got up, snagged a chair from a nearby table, and placed it next to the empty one. She sat when Gray gestured to it. She didn't lean back in the chair but instead sat fully upright, wondering what in the world was going on.

"So . . . you're the woman Gray rescued the other week, huh?" Arrow asked.

Allye swallowed, then gave him a small nod.

"What I'm about to tell you, kitten, isn't common knowledge. But after what you've been through, and given the fact that you're supposed to be meeting Rex here, so he obviously trusts you, I'm comfortable telling you. These men and I are all part of a group called Mountain Mercenaries," Gray said quietly. "Rex is our leader, so to speak. He contacts us when he has rescue jobs for us to do, mostly involving women and children who are being abused or were abducted. And before you ask, we're highly qualified. All of us are former military, all different branches, for the most part, and we've been through extensive training."

Allye stared at him for a second, then her eyes went to the rest of the men around the table. She was surprised that he'd explained as much as he had, but she had no trouble believing that these men had the skills and strength to operate rescue missions.

Then something Gray said sank in.

"Mercenaries?"

He nodded.

Allye was confused. "You have a name? Can I look you up online? Hire you?"

"No."

"Then why have a name?"

Allye thought it was Ball who answered. "Because Rex decided, rightly so, that we would become more well known if we were associated with a name. He wanted the bad guys to fear hearing the Mountain Mercenaries were coming for them. And it's worked. There was a situation not too long ago where a bad guy in Chicago was desperate to keep Rex and his Mountain Mercenaries out of his business. Desperate enough to kill his own son when he couldn't control him anymore."

Allye wasn't sure she wanted to know the details about that. But she was still a little confused. "But mercenaries are guns for hire. Like, they go where the money is and don't care about right or wrong, good or bad. They're *all* about the money. Aren't you more like vigilantes or something? Working around the law to do what's right and good?"

Gray stared at her, but the other men around the table chuckled.

Finally, Gray grinned. "Knew you were too smart for your own good," he said. "You're right, but when Rex formed our little group, he thought Mountain Mercenaries sounded tougher than vigilantes."

Allye rolled her eyes. "Yeah, I guess *Vengeful Veterans* doesn't exactly have the same ring, does it?"

And with that, the other men burst out laughing.

Allye couldn't decide if they were laughing *at* her or *with* her, until Gray controlled himself enough to say, "I can't wait to pass that on to Rex. Vengeful Veterans. Classic." Then he sobered himself. "What we do is technically against the law. Most police departments would frown on us going into any kind of situation and taking the law into our own hands like we do. But in most cases, time is of the essence. We can't exactly wait for the police to get the facts, decide if they think the threat is viable, and then make a move."

Allye nodded. "If you'd done that in my case, I would've been long gone."

"Exactly," Gray told her, covering her hand with his own.

"And it's not like we're out saving the world every minute of every day," Ro chimed in. "We all have regular jobs. Well . . . sorta regular. We make our own hours so we can leave at a moment's notice if we need to."

"What do you all do?" Allye asked, eyeing the men critically. "Other than save people like me. That is, if I'm allowed to ask? Gray told me he's an accountant, which is still really hard for me to believe."

"I make furniture," Meat said.

"From scratch?" Allye asked.

"Yup."

"And he's got a waiting list a mile long from people wanting him to make dining room tables and outdoor furniture," Arrow added. "I'm an electrician. I generally get hired by people who are flipping houses, to rework the wiring in their properties."

"I'm a web page designer," Ball added.

"And I'm a mechanic," Ro said, his British accent sounding sexy even with only four words spoken.

"And you know I own my own gun range," Black added. "You ever shoot a gun, Allye?"

She shook her head. "No. And before you offer, I'm okay with that."

The other man eyed her for a long moment before shrugging. "If you change your mind, all you gotta do is ask."

She nodded, then bit her lip and turned her eyes back to Gray. "Um . . . so . . . is Rex going to join you guys? Is that why he sent me here?"

"We've never met Rex," Gray told her.

"What? How is that possible?"

He shrugged. "It just is. He runs the missions from the background. Gets the intel and sends us where we need to go."

"But . . . he told me he was going to meet me here. I've got the . . ." Her voice trailed off.

"You have what?" Gray asked when she didn't continue. His eyes narrowed as he looked at her.

Allye considered what to tell him for a long moment. It wasn't as if she didn't trust him. She was going to give him the flash drive before he left California anyway, but Rex seemed really interested in it, and she didn't want to make the man mad. Not after all the money he'd spent getting her to Colorado Springs.

"Kitten, what? You never did say why you were here, other than to see Rex. How'd you find The Pit? And while we're at it . . . how'd you get in touch with Rex in the first place?" Gray asked.

"Can we talk in private?" she asked, well aware of the other men listening intently to their conversation.

"No," was his flat response. "I trust these guys with my life. More importantly, I trust them with *your* life. If I wasn't here, I'd expect them to do whatever it took to make sure you were safe, just as I'd do for them in the same situation. Now spill."

Allye wanted to reject his words. Tell him that she didn't trust him enough to tell him all her secrets, but that would be a lie. She'd told him about her upbringing. About how horrible her mother had been. He'd literally saved her life many times over. She had no reason not to trust him. And if he trusted the other men, then she had to as well.

"Remember after you unlocked the handcuff and we were leaving the bedroom on that boat, and I ran back?"

"Of course. Thought it was stupid then, and I think it's stupid now."

"You never asked *why* I went back."

Gray's gaze stayed locked with hers. "What was so important that you risked your life to go back and get it?" he asked quietly.

Allye reached into the pocket of her jeans and pulled out the flash drive. She placed it on the table in front of her. "That."

Gray's eyes flicked to the small device, then came back up to her face. "What's on it?"

She shrugged. "I don't know. I was going to give it to you before you left, but I forgot. Then I wasn't sure the data on it even survived being submerged for as long as it was. But I did what I could, and when I plugged it into my laptop, it worked. But there's only one file on it. And it's password protected."

"Leave it, Meat," Gray ordered, not taking his eyes from hers.

Allye blinked and turned her head to see Meat's hand inches from the flash drive. He looked like a little kid caught with his hand in a cookie jar.

"Come on, Gray. You know I'm the man for the job," Meat whined. "Rex probably sent her here so I could get my hands on the drive."

Gray rolled his eyes, and Allye wanted to laugh. "Let's get all the info before you head off into your geek cave to hack into it," Gray told him. Then he turned back to Allye. "He might make furniture for a living, but Meat is our resident computer genius. He can hack just about anything. Has a knack for everything electronic. Now let's get back to Rex. How'd *he* get involved with this? He call you?"

Allye shook her head. "No. I called him."

"How'd you get his number?"

She looked down at her fingers in her lap. "I remembered his number, from when we were on the boat after Black picked us up. I handed you the phone, and his number was on the screen."

"And you remembered it after seeing it once?" Black asked.

"Yeah. I have a good memory for numbers."

"So you called and got Rex," Gray murmured. "I'm sure he was surprised."

"He wasn't exactly thrilled at first," Allye told him. "But when I told him why I was contacting him, he got interested real fast."

"I bet he did," Ro said from the other side of the table.

"It might be nothing," Allye said. "But on the boat, that guy, he was clicking on something on the laptop and talking about other women, telling me details about what had happened to them, as if he was reading about them on the screen. He wanted to scare me, and he did, but when we were leaving, I just thought that maybe whatever was on the flash drive could help find them. Save them."

"If you don't want her, I do," Arrow drawled.

"Fuck off," Gray told his friend as he glared at him before turning back to Allye. "So, you told Rex you had it, and he brought you to the Springs so you could give it to him?"

She nodded.

"And he told you to come here?"

"Not exactly. He sent a guy to my hotel, and this is where I was dropped off."

"You honestly didn't know anything about The Pit before you got here?" Gray asked.

"No. It's weird that you guys just happened to be here at the same time as me, right?" Allye asked.

"Nope," Ro chimed in. "We meet here every week. Same time, same place. Rex knows that just as well as the locals around here do."

"Rex wasn't ever going to meet me, was he?" Allye asked.

"No, kitten. He sent you to us," Gray told her softly. "Remember when I told you he brought me and my friends here for an interview, and never showed up?"

Recollections of the conversation he'd had with her in the ocean shot through her. "Oh. Okay. Well . . . I guess I need to figure out how to get back to California now. I thought I'd give the info to Rex, and then he'd give me info about my flight home."

"Stay. For a little while," Gray said.

"I can't."

"At least until Meat gets into the flash drive and sees what we're dealing with."

Allye bit her lip and looked away from Gray. She wanted to stay. She really did. "But I have work next week. We're starting a new production number, and I need to be there for rehearsals."

"Rehearsals?" Ball asked.

"I'm a dancer," she told him.

"I bet you're like, really flexible, aren't you?" Arrow asked.

She frowned at him wryly. "Yeah, I am."

"You always get the good ones," Arrow told Gray, leaning back in his chair and crossing his arms over his chest in a good imitation of a pout.

Gray glared at his friend once more before turning his gaze to Allye. "Stay," he said again. "At least for tonight. We'll see what Meat has found out, and, if necessary, I'll make arrangements for you to go back Sunday night."

Allye thought about that. It wasn't as if she had anything to do this weekend. And as long as she got back before rehearsal on Monday, no one would even know she was gone. "Where would I stay?"

"With me," Gray said immediately.

Allye wasn't stupid. She was well aware of the feelings she had toward Gray but wasn't sure what he thought about *her*. Would he ask her to stay at his place if he didn't like her at least a little bit? What if he just felt responsible for her? Like, since he'd saved her life once, he wanted to make sure she was safe now? It wasn't as if she had a lot of options. She could stay at a hotel, but she didn't have a ton of disposable income. Living in San Francisco was expensive. Most of her salary went toward rent and food.

Gray didn't press her. Didn't plead his case, simply waited for her to make a decision. Which actually made it harder. If he'd pushed, she could've given in gracefully.

Throwing caution to the wind, Allye made her decision. "Okay. But just until tomorrow. I really do have to get home."

With that, Meat's hand darted out, and he snatched the flash drive off the table like an experienced pickpocket. He was up and moving toward the door before Allye could think about protesting or even moving.

"I'll be in touch," Meat called out as he disappeared through the door to the other part of the bar.

Allye looked at Gray with a hint of concern.

"He'll take good care of it," he soothed. "He'll get the information to Rex, and Rex will do his thing too. You made the right decision in bringing this to us."

"I didn't bring it to you," Allye grumbled. "I *thought* I was bringing it to Rex."

"Rex is us, and we are Rex," Ball said philosophically.

Allye rolled her eyes. When she was done, Gray was looking at her and smiling.

"What?"

"I can't believe I'm saying this, but I think I missed those eye rolls," he told her, then stood, not giving her a chance to respond.

"You'll let us know what's up, right?" Black asked, also standing.

"Of course," Gray said.

"Should we plan to meet back here tomorrow?" Ro asked.

"Let's play it by ear. Rex might contact us with different plans after getting whatever information is on that drive," Gray told him.

"See you both soon," Ro said. "I'll close out the tab with Dave on my way out."

"'Preciate it," Gray said.

The others left, and then Allye and Gray were the only two at the table.

"You hungry?" Gray asked her.

"A little," Allye admitted.

"Come on. I'll stop at the store and get us some steaks on the way home."

"I don't eat meat," she told him as they headed for the doorway.

Gray stopped in his tracks. "You don't?"

"Nope. But I wouldn't be opposed to some grilled veggies or something."

It was Gray's turn to roll his eyes, but he took her hand in his and continued toward the door. "Whatever."

Allye giggled. They stopped by the bar to say bye to Dave and to grab her backpack, then they were headed out of The Pit to Gray's two-door black car.

"What kind of car is this?" Allye asked as he held open the passenger-side door.

"Audi S5," he told her.

He walked around the vehicle and lowered himself into the driver's seat. He looked even bigger sitting next to her in the small space. "I've never heard of it, but it's nice."

He smiled over at her. "Yeah. And more importantly, she's got some power under her hood."

Allye rolled her eyes at him as he started the engine and pulled out of the parking lot, presumably heading toward the store.

"What do you mean, she's not there?" Nightingale huffed into the phone. "It was your job to watch her and know where she was at all times."

"I'm sorry, sir. After we talked last night, and I thought she was in for the night, I went and got something to eat. When I came back, the lights were still on in her apartment, and I figured she was still there. When she didn't leave her apartment to go to the store, like she does every Saturday morning, I pretended to be someone who was looking for a friend so I could check on her. She's not there."

Nightingale ground his teeth together. "Find her, you idiot! I want to know where she is and who she's with. Got it?"

"Yes, sir. I'll be in touch."

Nightingale clicked off the phone and paced. Allyson Mystic was *his*. She had no right to go *anywhere* without his knowledge. The sooner he had her under lock and key, the better.

He tried to calm himself by thinking about the things he was going to do to her, and how she'd look in his collar and under his control, but it didn't help much.

"How *dare* she," he mumbled.

As the hours went by and his man had no updates on her whereabouts, Nightingale got more and more enraged. Until finally, he realized he had only one option.

"You drove me to this, Mystic. This is *your* fault!" he ranted. "If you'd behaved, I wouldn't have had to resort to this."

Nightingale picked up the phone and called one of his best men. "I have a job for you. I need a girl."

"Any girl?" the man asked.

"No, not this time. A specific one. Her name is Jessie Callahan. She's a dancer with the Dance Theatre of San Francisco. Bring her to me. Alive."

"Yes, sir," the man said, then disconnected.

Nightingale nodded to himself. Yeah, Mystic would come running back home when she found out. She had to. He was counting on it. And when she did, Nightingale would have her brought to him.

Ignoring the fact he was throwing caution to the wind, and that the collections he held near and dear to his heart could be at risk, Nightingale smiled. He needed Mystic and her beautiful mismatched eyes. She would be his, come hell or high water.

Chapter Eight

Allye sat in Gray's living room. She'd obviously been surprised by his house, if her wide eyes and "Holy cow" comment were any indication. It was huge. Four bedrooms and two vast open spaces, one on the first floor and one in the basement. He also had a gourmet kitchen with all the bells and whistles. Gray had a feeling she'd expected an apartment or a bachelor pad. Not this huge family-style home.

His house sat up on a hill, and there were two enormous windows on the main floor that faced Pikes Peak. The view was breathtaking, and Allye couldn't take her eyes from it.

"It's why I bought this house," Gray said, loving how intently she'd taken in his home. "I know it's way too big for me, but the second I saw that view, I knew I had to have it."

"It's extraordinary," she said, still in awe. "I can see why you wanted it."

"After getting out of the Navy and joining Rex's team, I was restless. Unsettled. I didn't like to be around people and wanted my space. This house satisfied that need inside me. It calms me to look up at the mountain and think about all the people who came before me who have stared up at that exact same pile of rocks."

"I never thought about it like that before," Allye said softly. "I mean, I've looked at the Golden Gate Bridge and Alcatraz, but never really thought too much about the people who built them or were around when the prison was actually in use."

They were quiet for a while, lost in their own thoughts.

"How are you really doing?" Gray asked after some time, keeping his eyes on Allye. She was sitting directly across from him, her legs drawn up. Her arms were curled around her knees, and she looked a little lost.

"I'm good."

Gray snorted. "Don't give me the party line, kitten. Tell me how you *really* are. Are you scared? Have you seen anyone suspicious around? Are you sleeping at night? How's your appetite? Talk to me."

She sighed and rested her chin on her knees, looking at him from across the coffee table. "I'm okay. As crazy as it seems, I think my past has helped me put what happened in perspective."

"How so?"

"Well, it's not the first time shit has happened to me. Of course, I didn't end up in the middle of the ocean or anything in the past, but being left at the mall wasn't exactly fun and games. Then finding out my mom had literally abandoned me sucked pretty hard. I've had so much practice with bad stuff happening, I guess I'm almost used to it."

"Do *not* get used to this," Gray said with more heat than the conversation probably warranted. "Just because some asshole decided he wants you for himself doesn't mean that bad shit will continue to happen to you."

Allye rolled her eyes at his words, which made Gray want to smile, but he was too irritated to do so at the moment.

"It's just . . . I'm fine. Which makes me almost feel even worse. I mean, I *should* be having nightmares. I *should* be having trouble sleeping and eating. But I'm not. It's as if those two days didn't actually happen."

"Can I be blunt?" Gray asked.

Allye smiled. "Because you haven't been so far?"

He didn't return her smile. "It's gonna hit you. When you least expect it. You'll be going about your day, and boom, you'll see something that reminds you, and you'll have a reaction. Or you'll wake up in the middle of the night and remember. And it's okay. If I've learned nothing else in my life, I've learned that it's okay to freak out or have a bad reaction to something that happened to you."

"What happened to *you*?" Allye asked, so insightfully it was almost scary.

Gray sighed. He had a decision to make. Open up and let Allye all the way in, or continue to keep himself closed off.

The problem was, if he opened up and told her about the skeletons in his closet, he'd want to keep her forever.

He knew himself—he already wanted her. If she heard his story, and accepted it, it would be almost impossible to let her go again. But if he made up some bullshit, he was admitting to himself that he didn't think she was the woman for him.

He'd obviously taken too long to make his decision, because Allye turned her head and rested her cheek on her knees once more, breaking eye contact. "Sorry, that was rude. Forget I asked."

His body moved, making the decision for him. Gray stood and walked over to the other couch. He sat next to Allye and boldly took her into his arms. She went without protest, settling herself against his side and shifting until she was comfortable. He had his arm around her shoulders, and her knees were now resting against his thigh. Her head was lying against his pectoral muscle, and her hand fiddled with the buttons on his shirt.

It was an intimate embrace for two people who hadn't ever really touched much before now. But it felt right.

"I was a damn good SEAL once upon a time. I went where I was sent and never questioned orders. I thought I was making a difference in the world." He paused, realizing telling her this story was going to be harder than he thought it'd be.

Allye's hand patted his stomach, as if she was reassuring him. He forced himself to continue. If she didn't take this well, it was better to know now rather than after he fell in love with her.

Halting thoughts of love before they could take root in his brain, Gray kept speaking. "We were in Kandahar, Afghanistan. My team was told there were insurgents gathering in a specific building on a side of town known to be a hotbed of activity for terrorists. We went in and all hell broke loose. It was a trap, and two of my friends were immediately killed, shot in the head. Two others were mortally wounded, and when we tried to get them out, they died in our arms.

"The other three teammates and I hunkered down and tried to fight our way out of the situation, but it was no use. They captured all of us. Jones and Blue they killed outright, because they were African American. The assholes who took us captive were racist as hell. Then they tortured me and Hick. When that didn't get them any information, even though what they were asking wasn't exactly top-secret shit, they . . ."

Gray's voice trailed off. He didn't like *remembering* what had happened next, never mind talking about it.

"It's okay," Allye whispered. "You don't have to tell me."

And that right there was why he wanted to. She didn't demand answers. Didn't insist he tell her everything that was on his mind. He remembered thinking when they were floating in the ocean that she was peaceful to be around. He actually liked the sound of her voice. It was soothing. Even if what she was saying wasn't peaceful, her tone was.

"They decided to stop torturing us . . . and start up on innocent civilians. They first brought in a woman old enough to be my grandmother. As they were beating her, she spat at us as if *we* were the ones breaking her fingers one by one, and not her own countrymen. When we still refused to tell them numbers of bombs and ammunitions the United States had stored in their country—numbers that didn't even matter to them because they changed daily—they brought in younger and younger women to try to convince us to talk.

"I finally broke when they dragged in the tenth woman, and started hitting and . . . assaulting her. And laughing. I told them what they wanted to know. But they abused that woman anyway. And laughed while she and I both screamed."

Allye shifted then. She threw one leg over both of his and straddled his lap.

Surprised, Gray just sat there and let her adjust herself on top of him. She tucked her head into the space between his neck and shoulder and wrapped her arms around him. She didn't say a word, and the moment wasn't sexual in the least.

Gray immediately felt comforted. And less alone. He slowly wrapped his arms around her, and she shifted until she was closer. They ended up chest to chest, her legs hugging his thighs. He could feel her warm breath against his neck, but she didn't urge him to continue speaking. Simply held on, offering her support the only way she could.

"My friend Hick actually got out of the ropes that had secured him to a pole in the middle of the room. He rushed the man on top of the woman. He was shot in the back of the head. I watched the whole thing. Unable to help my buddy or those women. When it was over, the men simply smirked at me and left, dragging the bleeding woman along with them but leaving Hick dead on the floor. I spent the next three days there. With Hick staring at me with his sightless eyes. I wished *I* had been the one to get free so I wouldn't have had to be there at that moment."

"How'd you get free?" Allye asked, not lifting her head.

"A second team of SEALs found me after the third day. The insurgents had cleared out of the area and left me there to die. It turns out, the brass who sent my team in knew the area was unstable, and knew there was an increased threat for any US personnel. They told me they would've sent a team to liberate us earlier, but the Air Force was running an operation on the other side of the city, and they couldn't risk jeopardizing that mission, so they didn't send the other SEALs to come get us until after it was completed."

Allye's head lifted then. "I'm sorry, Gray. That sucks."

"Yeah. It sucks," Gray agreed. "I went a little crazy after that. I killed a lot of people. I can't even say they were all terrorists either. But I didn't care. As far as I was concerned, they were all the enemy."

"Is that when you got out?"

"Yeah. The Navy shipped me back to the States for extensive psychological care. But I didn't want their fucking shrinks messing with my head. The government had messed with me enough at that point. So, I put in my papers to be discharged, and they gladly signed them."

"And then Rex got in touch with you," Allye said.

"Yeah. I didn't trust him for the longest time either," Gray told her, looking through the window at the beautiful mountain peak in the distance. "But I did trust the rest of the guys. They've all been through hell, just as I have. The bond we have is deep. They're my brothers in every sense of the word, except for blood."

"I'm glad you have them," Allye said softly.

"Me too." He turned his gaze back to the woman in his lap. "My point is . . . I thought I had dealt with what happened. I'd been on dozens of missions for Rex. Killed people. Scum who didn't deserve to live. But one day I was in the middle of helping a busload of kids escape a Mexican drug lord who had kidnapped them, when one of his assholes grabbed a little girl. She had dark-brown hair and huge brown eyes, and she stared at me just like that last woman back in Afghanistan had. Begging me without words to help her. And just like that"—he snapped his fingers—"I was back there."

"What happened?" Allye whispered.

"Ro. He walked up behind the bastard and shot him in the head before he could get his own round off. Probably scarred that little girl for life, but at least she's still alive and wasn't hurt. It took me three days to completely come out of the stupor that flashback put me in. I'm just saying, shit that happens to you can come back to haunt you out of the blue."

"Okay, Gray. I'll be on the lookout."

"Don't be ashamed if it happens."

"Are you ashamed?" she asked.

Gray thought about her question for a beat, then said, "*Ashamed* isn't really the word. Sad. Frustrated, maybe. And helpless."

Allye nodded.

"You need help processing, let me know. I'll be there for you."

"Okay," she whispered.

He stared into her unusual eyes for a long moment before blurting out, "Does knowing I've killed, and will kill again, bother you?"

"No."

Her answer was immediate and heartfelt, and Gray had to swallow hard at the feelings that one word evoked within him. He wasn't sure he believed her, though. Her acceptance couldn't be that easy. "I'm an accountant, but if Rex calls with a mission, I'm gone."

"Good."

He wanted to shake her. Make sure she understood. "I could be sent to India to help fight against the people who force children to marry men four times their age, or halfway across the world to help rescue a boatload of refugees."

"Or maybe even to the coast of San Francisco to help a lone woman, who was kidnapped and about to become a sex slave, escape and return to her life."

"Exactly."

Allye sat up then and put her hands on either side of his face. Her palms were warm against his cheeks. "The world needs more men like you and your friends. I wish there were more people willing to stand up for what's right and good than assholes like the two who you killed on that boat. I don't feel bad for them, because they made their own choices, and died as a result of them."

Her eyes darted to his lips before coming back up to his eyes—and that was all the encouragement Gray needed. His hands gripped her hips hard enough that he knew he was probably leaving bruises on her delicate flesh, but he didn't loosen his hold. Moving slowly, giving her a chance to pull away, Gray lowered his head.

But she didn't pull away. In what he was beginning to learn was typical of Allye, she went after what she wanted, lifting her chin and meeting him more than halfway.

Their lips touched, and Gray jolted as if he'd just been electrocuted. Then he slanted his head and took control. Or tried to. Allye wouldn't let him. She gave as good as she got. The slight noises coming from deep in her throat egged him on, encouraged him to take more, to give more of himself to her.

Their tongues dueled and danced together as if they'd kissed a thousand times before. Gray could taste the mint she'd eaten an hour earlier. For the first time, her position on his lap turned sexual. The heat between her thighs burned him with its intensity. His cock was hard, lengthening quickly, ready to push inside her. For a second, he contemplated the best way to rip off her shorts so he could take her right now, just like this.

But when she pulled back, breathing hard, and Gray saw a blush make its way up her chest into her cheeks, he reined himself in. He wasn't going to fuck her like that. At least not this time. She deserved more, and for the first time in his life, he cared about what the woman he was with deserved.

In the past—the very distant past, as it had been more than a year since he'd last been with a woman—he hadn't cared much beyond getting off . . . and chose women who felt the same way.

But Allye was different. He knew it deep down inside. When she licked her lips and then bit one uncertainly, Gray rushed to reassure her.

"Thank you."

She looked confused. "For what?"

"For listening. For not judging me. For accepting me the way I am."

"Of course," was her reply. And Gray realized that for her, listening and not being judgmental was a way of life. It was simply who she was. With the way she'd been brought up, with a mother who didn't give a shit about her, and then being shuttled from foster home to foster home, her ability to be empathetic and down-to-earth was simply a fucking miracle.

And suddenly the thought of anyone getting their hands on her and abusing her, and changing who she was as a person, was absolutely abhorrent to Gray.

He opened his mouth to tell her that he was going to make sure she was safe to live her life, where and how she wanted, when his cell phone rang.

Allye smiled shyly at him, and started to move off his lap.

Gray's hands tightened, not wanting to lose her.

"You need to get that. It might be Meat calling to tell us what he found out."

Gray knew she was right, but it didn't mean he had to like it.

He leaned close and kissed her forehead before helping her climb off him. With his dick still semihard, Gray stood and stalked over to the other couch where he'd left his phone.

"Gray here."

"Turn on channel eight."

Gray immediately looked to find the remote to the TV and do as Rex ordered. He didn't ask why, simply turned on the television and changed it to the correct channel.

The tail end of a story about another woman who had been kidnapped in San Francisco that afternoon was playing. Apparently, she'd been taken off the streets kicking and screaming, and there were several witnesses and even a blurry cell-phone video of the incident. When the weatherman came on and began to talk about the week's upcoming weather, Gray asked cautiously, "Why did I need to see that?"

"Ask Allye."

Gray wasn't surprised Rex knew she was there. He seemed to know everything. His stomach churning, he turned to Allye. As he feared, she was sitting at the edge of the couch, one hand over her mouth in shock, her eyes wide with horror.

"Kitten," he said soothingly.

"That's Jessie," she said, her words mumbled from behind her hand.

"Who?"

"Jessie Callahan," Rex answered from the speaker at his ear. "Nineteen. Five-ten, one hundred and twenty pounds. She's a dancer at the same place your Allye works."

"Fuck," Gray swore, then clicked off the TV and strode over to where Allye was sitting, still in shock. "Nightingale?" he asked Rex.

"I don't have all the details yet, but I'm assuming so, yes."

"What's the plan?"

"No plan," Rex said immediately.

It didn't sit well with Gray. "Allye knows her." He told Rex something the man obviously already knew. "We can't just do nothing."

"If this is Nightingale, he did it on purpose. It's as much proof as we're gonna get that he was the one behind Allye's kidnapping. He wasn't taking her for someone else. He wanted her for *himself*. And now he's pissed that she's disappeared. He took this new woman to send a message. He's reacting, not thinking. That can be good for us."

Gray ground his teeth together. He knew exactly how Allye was going to react to the fact that he and his team weren't going to do anything to find the other woman. Hell, he'd just talked about the exact same thing happening to *him*, and how *he'd* reacted when the terrorists had tortured people to get a reaction from him.

"Has Meat figured out what's on the flash drive yet?" he asked his handler.

"No, but he says he's close."

"Call me when he's got information," Gray ordered.

"You know I will. Take care of Allye," Rex said before hanging up.

Gray sighed and clicked off his phone. He sat next to Allye and put his hand on her knee. "What do you know about her?"

She was still staring at the television even though the screen was black. "Jessie's a lot younger than me. She joined the troupe about four months ago. She's a really good dancer, but jealous. She wants to be a star, and doesn't like the fact that she has to work her way to the top."

"Are you friends?" Gray asked.

Allye shook her head. "Not really. I mean, we're courteous to each other, but that's about it." She turned those big expressive eyes his way. "Is it the same guy who took me?"

Gray wanted to lie. Wanted oh so fucking badly to lie, but he couldn't. Not to her. "Probably."

"It's because I left, isn't it?"

Gray nodded. He let her think about the situation for a minute, then asked, "You okay?"

Allye looked down at her lap before answering. "If I say yes, I'm a horrible person for being glad it's her and not me. If I say no, then I'm being hypocritical, because I don't really even like Jessie all that much."

Gray brought his hands up and physically turned her to face him. He put his palms on her cheeks, much as she'd done to him earlier. "This isn't your fault," he told her fiercely.

She shook her head. "Technically, it is."

"*No,* it's the fault of the man who kidnapped her. Period."

"What do you think is happening to her?"

"Don't think about it," he said.

"How can I not?" she returned in anguish.

Her eyes filled with tears, but she brushed his hands away from her face and pressed her thumb and index finger to her closed eyelids in an effort to hold them back.

Gray leaned into her and said urgently, "Don't give him that power over you. The terrorists who held me and Billy did the same thing, and I fell into their trap. What he's doing is on *him*, not you. Even if you flew back to California right this second and gave yourself up to that asshole Nightingale, it wouldn't change whatever he has planned for her. Remember that."

He saw Allye take a deep breath, then she opened her eyes and looked up at him. "What can I do, then? How do I make this stop? Will I ever be safe? Or is he going to slowly kidnap and torture everyone I know? What do I *do*, Gray?"

The last question was so agonized, it almost tore Gray's heart out.

He moved slowly so he wouldn't startle her, and wrapped his arms around her shoulders.

Not sure what her reaction would be to his attempt at comfort, he was astounded when she melted into him as if they'd been a couple for years.

"Trust me," he said. "That's what you do. Trust me, Rex, and the rest of the guys to fix this for you."

She didn't respond verbally, but the small nod he felt against his chest was enough. In fact, it was everything.

Allye Martin might have been a stranger a week and a half ago, but now, he had a feeling she'd just become the most important person in his life. More so than his team. More so than his mother and brother.

It was an odd feeling, knowing that he'd do whatever it took to protect someone. It was more than the feeling he had on missions, where he did his best to bring justice to the countless women and children he'd been sent to rescue. This was a bone-deep feeling of rightness that he couldn't shake. That he didn't *want* to shake.

Chapter Nine

Allye lay in the double bed in Gray's guest bedroom that night, unable to sleep. For the first time in a really long while, she was struggling to figure out what her next steps should be.

Right after high school, when she'd aged out of the foster-care system, she'd drifted, not able to figure out what it was she wanted to do for a living. College was out. She didn't have the grades, the desire, or the money to attend. But she also couldn't get any decent jobs with only her high school diploma, so she'd used what little money she had and fled west. She'd ended up in San Francisco, and luckily had befriended some nice people who let her live with them in a small house, and from there, she'd eventually found the dance theatre.

She'd always loved dancing, and Robin had taken pity on her, giving her a job while Allye continued taking dance classes. She'd cleaned the theatre for a year before Robin finally let her join the troupe on a month-to-month basis. Allye had worked her ass off, proving to Robin, and herself, that she was serious about becoming a dancer. It wasn't until two years ago that she'd finally earned the lead spot in a few performances. It had taken almost eight years, but she'd done it.

She'd never be a millionaire, but it was enough for her to live on.

But now . . . Allye didn't know what to do. Going back to California would surely mean whoever was out there would continue to try to grab her. But what would she do if she *didn't* go back? Where would she go? Where would she live? How would she support herself?

She finally managed to fall into a restless sleep an hour later . . . only to wake up screaming not too long after that.

Her door flew open, and Allye screamed again when she saw the shape of a very large man looming over her.

"Jesus, it's me, kitten."

Allye recognized Gray's voice immediately and opened her arms.

Gray gathered her up, and it wasn't until her face was pressed against his neck that she realized she was panting.

"Shhh. You're okay. I know I said it was fine to remember and have bad reactions, but you didn't have to be an overachiever and do it your first night here."

Allye snorted against him, but didn't pull away. His gentle caress on her back was soothing rather than stifling or patronizing. He didn't say anything else, just rocked a little with her in his arms.

When she felt she had herself somewhat under control, she pulled back and roughly scrubbed a hand over her face.

"You want to talk about it?"

She sighed, but didn't hesitate. There was just something about Gray that made it impossible for her to hold back from him. "There was a guy. He had Jessie, and he was hurting her. Telling me that if I went with him, he'd let her go. You were there, too, but you couldn't get to me. You were behind a piece of glass or something. You were pounding on it, yelling something at me, shaking your head, but I couldn't hear you. When I looked back at this faceless guy—literally, he had no face—he took a knife and slit Jessie's throat from ear to ear. That's when I woke up."

"Jesus, kitten. That's one hell of a dream."

"Uh-huh." Now that Allye wasn't scared out of her mind and her heart had slowed down to its regular rhythm, she was exhausted.

"You tired?" Gray asked.

"Yeah," she mumbled.

"You gonna be able to go back to sleep?"

She stared at him for a second before blurting out, "Can I sleep in your room?"

Gray didn't answer, just stared at her with an unreadable look on his face.

"Never mind," Allye backtracked, pulling out of his arms. "Stupid question. I'm fine. I'm sure I'll fall right to sleep now and—"

"Look at me, kitten," Gray ordered.

She raised her eyes and waited for him to tell her she was being silly. That she was a grown woman, and if she just relaxed, she'd sleep fine.

"I want you in my bed. But I need you to answer a question for me first." He paused as if waiting for her to answer.

"Okay."

"Do you want to be there only because you're scared and worried about Jessie? Or is there another reason?"

Allye swallowed. Was she brave enough to admit that she liked Gray? That being with him made her feel not quite so alone in the world? She thought about her response for a long moment. He was quiet, letting her think and answer in her own time.

"I'm twenty-nine years old," she said softly. "Mature enough to be blunt about what I want. I've never been afraid to come right out and tell a man that I'm attracted to him or that I'm interested. But with you, I'm scared to death because I'm afraid you only see me as someone you rescued. That you'll look at me with pity if I admit how I really feel. And most of all, that you won't feel the same."

"Tell me," Gray both ordered and begged at the same time.

Feeling as if she were standing at the edge of a fifty-foot drop-off, Allye looked Gray in the eyes and said, "I'm attracted to you. I don't know if it can go anywhere because it seems like we have a million factors working against us. All I know is that when I'm with you, I feel safe. As if nothing and no one could ever hurt me. But I also feel energized. Excited. My stomach feels funny, and when I think about leaving tomorrow and never seeing you again, it makes me want to cry. And I already told you, I never cry. I want to sleep in your bed because I'm scared, yes. And you make me feel safe. But it's more than that. A lot more."

Gray had an intense look on his face that Allye couldn't decipher. He stood, and she was afraid for a second that she'd said all the wrong things and he was leaving. But when he leaned over and picked her up as if she weighed no more than a child, she relaxed, curling her arms around his neck and laying her head on his shoulder.

He walked across the hall to the master bedroom and carried her over to his bed. He placed her down and followed her onto the mattress. Allye quickly slid over, giving him some room. She turned onto her side to face him and sighed in contentment when he gathered her to his naked chest and pulled the comforter up and over them.

Just when she didn't think he was going to say anything, he spoke. His words rumbled through his chest, making their way into her own.

"Leaving you alone in that guest room earlier almost killed me. But I didn't want to move too fast. I haven't been able to stop thinking about you since I left San Francisco. I've never thought about any of the women I've rescued before, after they were safe. But I couldn't get you out of my mind. Every time my phone rang, I thought it would be Rex calling to tell me that you'd disappeared again. And that scared the shit out of me."

Allye raised her head and blinked at him. "Really?"

"Really. And I'll tell you something else."

"What?"

"Nothing would've kept me from coming after you again."

The pressure behind her eyes built, and Allye ducked her head against his chest to keep the tears at bay. What was happening to her? She *never* cried, and yet here she was, holding back tears because of something he'd said . . . again.

She felt his lips against the top of her head. "And for the record, I want you too. But not tonight. Sleep now, kitten. You're safe here. No need to dream bad things."

She smiled against him. "I don't think I can control that."

"Sure you can. Just know that you're here with me, and it'll keep those nightmares at bay."

It was an arrogant thing to say, but Allye had a feeling he was right. After a moment, she whispered, "Do you want to . . ." She told him she'd never had a problem asking for what she wanted before, but for some reason, she couldn't just come right out and ask if Gray wanted to have sex with her.

But he seemed to know what she was asking without her having to say it. "Yeah, kitten, I do. But not right now. I'm tired and feeling mellow. I just want to hold you."

"Okay. But later?"

He chuckled. "Yeah, Allye. Later for sure."

Smiling, and feeling happier and more content than she'd felt in a long time, Allye fell asleep in Gray's arms. And didn't remember one dream.

Gray didn't remember falling asleep. One minute he was enjoying having Allye in his arms, and the next . . . nothing.

But he woke up suddenly when he felt someone moving next to him. For a split second he was confused, because it had been a really long time since anyone had been in his bed other than him, but then he remembered. Allye.

He was lying on his back, and she was against his side. Her hand was slowly caressing his chest. He wore just a pair of sweatpants, and she had aroused him even in his sleep. The cotton was pulled taut over his groin. She'd pushed the comforter down, and he saw her lazy caresses getting closer and closer to his growing cock.

"What are you doing?" he asked sleepily, a languorousness he hadn't felt in a long time moving over him.

"What does it feel like I'm doing?" she retorted, her hand pushing his sweats down a little more with each pass.

He caught her wrist when he felt her fingers brush against his cock. She gazed up at him with a look both innocent and carnal. Her mismatched eyes twinkled, and her hair was a tangled mess. The white streak looked even more adorable, mussed the way it was. But it was the mischievous smile on her face that made his wayward dick jerk. He liked that look on her. A hell of a lot.

"It looks like you're about to get yourself into trouble."

She raised her eyebrows as if to say, "Who, me?" Her fingers played with his nipple, and he felt it harden in the chilly predawn air.

"You want something, all you gotta do is ask," Gray told her seriously.

Without pause, she whispered, "I want you."

Before the last word had even left her lips, Gray was kissing her. He wasn't thinking about what time it was, or worrying if he should take a shower before being with her. All he could think about was making Allye his.

She opened for him immediately, and his tongue plunged inside her mouth eagerly. Even as he kissed her long and hard, his hand was roaming her body. She was wearing an oversize T-shirt and a pair of sleep shorts, but she might as well have been naked. The amount of pleasure he got by being able to freely touch her where and how he wanted was immense.

His hand slid under her shirt, and he felt her suck in her belly as his fingers trailed up her body, but he didn't stop. He homed in on her breast, his large hand easily covering it. Her hard nipple stabbed into his palm as he squeezed and fondled. He felt her hips shift, and Gray turned so that she was on her back next to him.

Lifting his head, Gray licked his lips, relishing her taste on them. "Now's your chance to change your mind," he said in a husky tone.

"I'm not going to change my mind," Allye replied, arching her back into his touch.

"I'm a big man," Gray told her seriously. "And I'm not sure I know how to be gentle." He wanted to warn her, but not scare the shit out of her. He liked what he liked in the bedroom. And what he liked was to be in charge. To take what he wanted. He made sure his partner was satisfied, but nothing got him off faster than hard, rough sex.

"I can take it. I can take *you*."

"I sure as fuck hope so," he murmured. "If I go too fast, or you don't like something I do, tell me. The last thing I want is to hurt you, or coerce you into doing something you don't want to do." Gray kept his gaze on her as he squeezed her breast once more, a little harder. Instead of seeing doubt or pain in her eyes, they sparked with excitement.

She rolled, surprising Gray, and ended up on top of him. She straddled his hips and ground her pussy against his rock-hard dick. "I want you, Grayson Rogers. Any way you want to take me."

Without a word, Gray pushed her shirt up and over her head, leaving her in nothing but her sleep shorts. Her small breasts were topped with large pink, areolas and long, hard nipples, which were begging for his touch.

He sat up and latched on to one of those nipples without another word. He sucked. Hard. Allye's back arched, and he felt her fingernails digging into the back of his head, urging him on, not tugging him away from her body.

Unleashing the lust she'd purposely brought forth with her not-so-innocent caresses, Gray let himself go. His mouth ate at her. He licked, bit, and sucked on her tits. She was squirming nonstop on him, and his cock felt as if it was going to burst any second. She felt tiny on top of him. *Was* tiny compared to him. He had almost a foot in height on her, and it only made him feel more in control. And that, in turn, fueled his need.

He flipped her without effort, and she landed on her back next to him once again, but he never took his mouth off her breast. Gray shoved her shorts down, and she cooperated by lifting her hips and using a hand to push them to her knees and off. He palmed her pussy, gratified to feel her excitement coating her outer lips and his palm.

He stared down into her eyes as one finger delved into her hot heat. She was snug, his finger pushing past her inner muscles with difficulty as he plunged it in and out of her. "You're so fucking tight," he said. "You're gonna strangle my dick when it gets inside you."

He'd always loved dirty talk, and it seemed as if she did too.

Allye dropped her knees open, giving him more room, and her hips raised just a fraction as he played with her. "It's been a while," she told him, her eyes closed into slits as she licked her lips.

"How long?" he asked. He eased another finger into her, and she moaned. When she didn't answer him, he held his fingers still and asked again. "How long, kitten? How long has it been since you've had a cock inside this luscious body?"

"Three years or so," she gasped. "Please, Gray. More."

Three years. Fuck. Deciding to tease her longer, simply because it was fun, he asked, "Why?"

"Why what?" she panted.

Gray put his other hand on her lower belly to hold her down as he slowly stretched her with his fingers. She was feisty, wriggling and squirming under him. Her body demanded he give her what she wanted. But he was having fun making her wait. "Why so long?" he asked.

"Because I've been busy at the theatre. Didn't have time. And didn't want anyone."

Her words were disjointed and staccato.

"But you want me."

She rolled her eyes, and that only made Gray harder. Fuck, he loved when she did that. It was insane, but that little act of defiance made him want her all the more.

"Yes, Gray. I want you. I think it's more than obvious. *Please.*"

And with that, Gray was done waiting. She was soaked. His fingers were covered with her essence. Even though he was big and she was tight, he knew he'd slide right inside her as if he was meant to be there.

Without a word, he quickly stood and pushed his sweats down, his cock catching on the elastic before bobbing upward once it was released. He could see a bead of precome on the almost-purple tip. He reached into the drawer next to his bed and fumbled with the box of condoms there. He'd bought them last week. He'd been restless after leaving Allye in California. Needing something. Wanting something. He thought maybe he'd try his hand at dating again and had bought the condoms just in case.

But what he'd needed was Allye. Not some random hookup—*her*.

Gray rolled the condom onto his cock without fanfare and got back on the bed. Allye had been watching him, the fingers of her right hand lightly rubbing her clit, and the fingers of her left pinching a nipple.

Without a word, Gray grabbed her and turned her onto her belly. He then lifted her hips, and she bent her knees, getting them under her. Putting one hand on her upper back, Gray smiled when she immediately lowered until she was resting on her elbows.

Her ass was up in the air, and he'd never seen anything so delicious and beautiful in all his life. His plan had been to take her immediately, but the second he saw her pussy lips glistening, he knew he needed to taste her first.

Sitting back on his heels, Gray lowered his mouth and licked from her clit to her asshole.

She groaned, arched her back, and slid her knees farther apart, giving him more room to work.

Without warning, he began to eat her as if she were his last meal. She squealed when his scratchy day-old beard chafed her inner thighs, and moaned when he licked over her clit hard and fast. If he wasn't as strong as he was, he wouldn't have been able to hold her still as she bucked and rolled under his mouth.

Wanting to see her come apart, Gray put his hands on her inner thighs and picked her up, lifting her to his lips and allowing himself better access to her clit. She was suspended in the air, holding herself up on her elbows, and he knew he wouldn't have been able to put her in this position if she weren't a dancer. She was flexible and in shape, and he'd never been more turned on.

Without mercy, Gray lashed at her small nubbin until every muscle in her lower body tensed and she began to come.

God, she tasted good. Gray could've stayed there all night, drinking down her excitement as he forced her to come again and again, but he needed more. His cock was so hard it hurt, and he couldn't remember a time he'd been so fucking needy for a woman.

He put Allye down, still in the midst of her orgasm, and pushed her legs apart. He eased inside her with one long thrust. She squealed once more and momentarily tried to pull away from him, but he grabbed hold of her hips and pulled her closer to him instead.

The feeling of her inner muscles around his dick, still contracting with her orgasm, was heaven. Gray held himself still, experiencing her orgasm wane with her. When she finally stilled under him, he leaned over her back.

His bulk cocooned her body, making him feel more masculine and powerful than he'd ever felt. He moved his hips away a fraction of an inch, then shoved back inside her. Her upper body was pressed to the mattress, her ass up in the air, taking everything he gave her.

Even though he took what he wanted when it came to sex, he'd never try to hurt her. "You all right?" he murmured in her ear, before taking the lobe between his teeth and biting down not so gently.

"Yeah. Oh yeah."

"I'm going to take you now, kitten. You ready?"

She nodded her head frantically.

"You sure?"

Once more, her head bobbed up and down where it rested on the bed.

Gray leaned up, and, bracing himself with both hands on the mattress by her shoulders, he began to move. He knew he wouldn't last long, he was too close to the edge. Seeing her pleasure, having her under him, was too exciting. Too good.

He moved his hips until only the head of his dick was inside her, then slammed all the way back in. He did it again and again. He pounded his cock into her body as if this would be the last time he'd ever make love. Each time he bottomed out within her, Gray grunted with exertion.

God, she felt amazing. Like nothing he'd ever experienced before.

Then Allye moved under him. She braced herself on her elbows, and he felt her pushing back against him with every thrust. She wasn't just taking what he gave her, she was a willing and enthusiastic participant.

Her breasts were swinging with every thrust, and the carnality of their lovemaking only made Gray harder. He reached under her and found her clit, roughly manipulating it as he continued to push in and out. The sounds their bodies were making were loud and sensuous, and only increased his pleasure.

"Gray, fuck . . . oh my God, Gray!"

He smiled at her words, knowing she was as lost to the pleasure as he was.

His orgasm snuck up on him. One minute he was enjoying the sensations of having her under him, and the next he was coming without warning. He pushed inside her as far as he could go, and felt the come shoot up from his balls and out the tip of his cock. Warmth filled the condom, and he groaned; it felt as if he would never stop coming.

When he was done, he realized that Allye was still squirming beneath him. She hadn't come again and was obviously on the verge. Without a word, and without pulling out of her, Gray renewed his assault on her clit. Mercilessly rubbing it as fast and as hard as he could.

"Too much," Allye groaned, trying to squirm away from his touch.

But he wouldn't let her. Pinning her in place, with his cock still inside her and his fingers working their magic, he leaned down and bit her earlobe once more. "Come for me again, kitten. Come all over my cock. Squeeze me, show me how much you like my touch."

And with that, she came. Once again, the feeling of her inner muscles spasming around his semihard dick was indescribable. She trembled all over, every muscle tightening and relaxing as she experienced her bliss.

The moment she began to relax, Gray eased out of her, smiling at the moan of protest that escaped her lips when he slipped free. She straightened her legs and lay flat on the mattress. Gray knew he needed to go and take care of the condom, but he couldn't take his gaze from her.

She was red and swollen, and he could see the evidence of her satisfaction between her legs. It was sexy as hell—and she was all his. No way was he giving her up now. Not when she'd just given him everything he wanted in a partner and more.

Gray knew it wasn't going to be easy. She'd have to leave behind everything she'd built in San Francisco, as he couldn't be a part of Mountain Mercenaries from California, but he'd do everything in his power to make sure she never regretted moving to Colorado Springs to be with him.

He reached out and ran a thumb between her swollen pussy lips, collecting some of her juices. He brought his hand up and sucked his thumb into his mouth. Her taste exploded on his tongue.

His gaze went to her face. Expecting to see her eyes closed in postcoital bliss, he was surprised to find her watching him.

"Good?" she asked.

Grinning, Gray could only nod.

Allye reached out and grabbed his hand, wrapping her tongue around his digit and treating it much as he imagined she would his cock when it was in her mouth.

She nipped the pad of his thumb, then gazed up at him with a saucy smile.

"Jesus," Gray groaned. "I need to go clean up. Don't move."

Allye lay back down and put her hands under her cheek. Her legs were splayed slightly, and she kept her eyes on him.

Gray turned from the bed and headed to the bathroom. He threw away the condom and used a washcloth to clean himself. Then he rinsed it and walked naked back into his bedroom.

He saw the pleasure in Allye's eyes as she looked at him. He'd never been modest, but there was something about having *her* look at him—as if he were an ice-cream cone and she was starving—that made him want to be nude around her all the time.

He sat on the edge of the mattress and pressed the warm washcloth between her legs. She smiled and moaned a little, opening her legs more, giving him room.

"Did I hurt you?" he asked. "I was a little rough."

"I loved it. And no, you didn't hurt me the way you mean. It was a good hurt, if that makes sense."

It did. More proof that she was made for him. Wiping away the remnants of their lovemaking, Gray threw the washcloth toward the bathroom, not caring that it landed a few feet short of the tile. He gathered Allye into his arms and pulled the comforter, which had been pushed all the way to the end of the bed, up and over them both.

"What time is it?" Allye asked, after throwing an arm around his chest and hitching a leg over his thighs.

"Around three thirty. Not time to get up yet."

"Good." She fell asleep almost immediately, her body going lax next to his.

Gray lay awake for a long time, memorizing the way she fit against him. Loving the way she seemed to claim him in her sleep, hugging him to her. It was hard to believe that two weeks ago, he hadn't even known her. Because already he couldn't imagine living without her.

Chapter Ten

The next week went by in a blur for Allye. Gray convinced her not to go back to San Francisco with Jessie still missing. After her dream, and really thinking about it, she decided that her safety was more important than any job.

She'd called Robin and explained what was happening, and, luckily, the owner of the dance theatre agreed that it was best she stay away for now. They'd talked at length about the performance, and Allye reassured her boss and friend that she'd practice the routines even if she wasn't in California. She also promised to call if she needed anything.

She'd hung up feeling pretty good about her friendship with the older woman and about the security of her job. Allye didn't know what would happen in the future, but for now, she was taking things one day at a time.

Living with Gray was amazing. He hadn't lied, he wasn't gentle when it came to sex, but since she enjoyed everything he did to her, and he made sure she was always satisfied—often making sure she came more than once—it wasn't exactly a hardship. She loved when he physically lifted and moved her where he wanted her.

One afternoon after he'd arrived home from a meeting with the rest of the team and saw her in the kitchen making dinner, without a word, he'd pulled her over to the kitchen table, pushed her down, shoved her pants to her ankles, and fucked her until she was a puddle of goo. Then he'd picked her up, carried her to the couch, covered her with a blanket, kissed her on top of her head, and told her to nap while he finished dinner.

Then there was the time she was in the shower, and, without asking, he'd joined her. He'd proceeded to push her to her knees and hold her head while he'd fucked her mouth. It should've been debasing, but throughout it all, he'd never forced her to take more of him than she could comfortably take. He'd caressed her hair the entire time she was sucking him off, and afterward, held her in his arms as she masturbated herself to orgasm while he watched, then washed and conditioned her hair.

He was a dichotomy of rough and gentle, and the more time Allye spent with him, the more she got to understand him. He didn't put up with a lot of bullshit and said whatever was on his mind. But he never tried to manipulate her into making a decision that *he* thought she should make, which she appreciated. He was also very aware of her being smaller and weaker than he was, and never crossed the line between rough and hurtful when they made love.

But she had no idea if whatever they had was going to last. Yeah, Gray liked having her live with him. What guy wouldn't? He had access to uninhibited sex all the time, and she'd pretty much taken over in the kitchen just to keep herself occupied. She loved making vegetarian dishes for him. Meals that he'd never make for himself but obviously loved.

Deep down, however, Allye wanted to believe she meant more to him than just a convenient sex partner. And whenever she asked if he had more information about Jessie or if she'd been found, he'd frown and ask her to try not to worry about it.

But she couldn't continue living in limbo. Her job and her life were back in California. She couldn't hide out with him forever, as much as the thought appealed to her.

She was making lunch when she heard the door to Gray's house open. She turned with a smile to greet him, but her smile died when she saw the look on his face.

"What happened?" she asked immediately.

Gray walked over to her and took the knife out of her hand. He put it on the counter, then led her into the other room, to the couch. He sat her down and pulled the coffee table over until it was in front of her. He sat on it, encasing her legs between his own, and scooted closer, holding both her hands in his.

Allye took a deep breath. This was bad. Very bad.

"Jessie was found."

Allye breathed out a sigh of relief. "Oh, thank God. Is she okay?"

Gray slowly shook his head. "No, kitten. She's dead."

Allye blinked. She couldn't have heard him right. "What?"

"She's dead," he repeated. "A tourist found her body in Golden Gate Park. She'd been tortured."

Allye tugged at her hands, needing to pace. Something. But Gray wouldn't let go.

He continued. "She had ligature marks on her wrists and ankles, and it looks like she'd been starved. He probably didn't give her anything to eat the entire time he had her."

"Oh my God. Poor Jessie! I mean, we weren't exactly friends, but that's awful!"

Gray stared at her, his gaze unwavering.

"What? Is there more?"

"There's more," he confirmed. "Her hair had been dyed brown with a white streak, and she was wearing a pair of contacts when she was found."

"One blue and one brown," Allye whispered.

Gray nodded and tightened his grip on her hands. "There was a message carved into her body as well."

Allye closed her eyes. She couldn't bear to hear any more. But Gray kept on talking.

"He used a knife and cut the words *come back* into her belly. Investigators think it was done while she was still alive."

"No!" Allye yelled, yanking her hands out of Gray's grasp and pushing past him after she stood up. "No, that's a lie! You're just saying that to scare me!"

She ran for the front door, not knowing where she was going or what she was doing, but Gray caught her. He wrapped both arms around her and pulled her into his body.

Allye fought him. Fought to escape her reality. Fought to get away from words she didn't want to hear.

Her struggles didn't even seem to faze Gray. He picked her up so her feet weren't touching the ground and carried her, squirming and flailing, back to the couch. He sat her down, then pushed her sideways until she was lying on her back and he was crouched over her.

Allye ineffectively beat her fists on his chest, trying to get him off her. "God, Gray—please tell me he didn't really do that to her!"

"Calm down, kitten," he said, grabbing hold of her hands and pushing them to the cushion above her head.

All the fight left her in a rush. Allye went limp and gazed up at him sadly. "He tortured her because he wants *me*."

Gray didn't respond, but he didn't have to. His eyes and facial expression said it all.

"Was she raped?"

Gray hesitated, then admitted, "With the amount of damage to her lower body, it can't be determined."

Allye closed her eyes, not wanting to know what kind of torture Jessie had gone through that was so bad that the coroner couldn't tell if she had been violated sexually. "What now?"

"You stay here so we can keep you safe. Rex is investigating."

Her eyes opened. "For how long?"

"He'll keep on it until he finds Nightingale's location."

"No, I meant, how long am I going to have to stay here?"

His expression changed then. Allye couldn't read it.

"As long as it takes."

That wasn't exactly the answer she was looking for. She'd begun to think she'd *love* to stay here with Gray. Forever. But not because he had to protect her—because he wanted her here. With him.

She nodded. "I'm okay now. You can let me up."

Gray cautiously eased his hold on her hands and sat up. She brushed her hair out of her face and let him pull her upright.

"Have Rex and Meat figured out what the spreadsheet means yet?" They'd cracked the password the night she'd given the flash drive to Meat, but the entire spreadsheet was in code, and they'd been having a hard time figuring it out. Apparently, the man sent to escort her wasn't exactly stupid.

"Some of it. There have been a few locations and names, but they're vague enough that there's nothing concrete Rex can use to send us to check out."

Allye blew out a breath in frustration. "So, it's not helpful. Me risking both our lives to grab it was for naught."

"I didn't say that," Gray said, leaning over and kissing her forehead. "Rex has gotten confirmation about several men who he'd believed were involved in sex trafficking, but he hadn't been able to prove it. Their names were on the spreadsheet. He also . . ."

Gray continued to talk, but Allye tuned him out. All she could think about was Jessie. The woman hadn't been nice, and frankly, was a pain in Allye's butt, but she never would've wished her dead. Especially not the way it had apparently happened.

"Are you listening?"

Allye jerked when Gray put a hand on her leg. She looked up at him and sheepishly shook her head.

"I said, I have a surprise for you today."

"You do?"

"Yeah. I know you've been stressed, and today's news, while maybe not entirely unexpected, wasn't good. I also know you've been cooped up here. Colorado Springs doesn't exactly have the public transportation system you're used to, and you said you weren't comfortable driving my car. So, I made you an appointment today."

Allye mentally cringed. She'd never been the type of woman who liked going to the spa. It just seemed like such a waste of money. Especially when she never had any extra. She couldn't think of any other kind of appointment Gray would've made for her.

"Great," she said, trying to drum up some enthusiasm. She wasn't sure she wanted to do *anything* after hearing about Jessie and the damn message that had been left on her body. But Gray was going out of his way to be sweet to her, so she'd suck it up and pretend to want to be pampered and coddled for an afternoon.

They both knew the message on Jessie's body was for her. Knew the man who'd had her kidnapped wanted her back in the city so he could grab her again.

"I know when I work out, it really helps me refocus and get rid of stress. I figured the same would work for you. Come on," he said, standing and holding out his hand.

Allye sighed and put her hand in his. So, he wasn't taking her to a spa. At least that was something. She wasn't in the mood to work out either, but she needed to. She'd been trying to practice the steps of the dances she'd be performing back in California, whenever she got back there, but it was hard to do while on her own and not in a dance studio with the rest of the dancers. And being lazy wasn't the way to keep her lead role at the theatre. She needed to start practicing again. Big-time. Gray had also bought her some clothes, but she missed her own workout things, her own T-shirts and fat pants. Frankly, she missed a lot of things about California and her life there.

Gray led her to the garage door, then turned. "Stay here a sec, okay?"

"Why?"

"Because," he retorted.

Allye rolled her eyes.

He smiled and kissed her hard on the lips, then jogged back into the house.

Allye bit her thumbnail as she waited for Gray to return. She worried about what was happening with the dance theatre. Wondered what Robin was really thinking about her future with the troupe. Did the other dancers know that Jessie had been taken and tortured because of her? She also worried about what her kidnapper was going to do next. It was all just too much, and Allye was as close to crying as she'd been in years.

Just when she'd decided to go looking for Gray to find out what was taking him so long, he returned. He had one of his gym bags in his hand, and he was smiling. When he looked at her, though, the smile faded.

"Fuck, kitten, don't."

"Don't what?"

"Don't look so damn sad. We're going to get through this."

Allye leaned toward him and put her forehead against his chest. She gripped the shirt at his sides and asked, "You think so?"

"I know so. There's no way I've found you, only to have you taken away from me."

It was a sweet thing to say, but all it did was stress Allye out. Their whole relationship was impossible. Him saying such sweet things only made her yearn to stay even more, though she knew the possibility of that working out was slim. What if she moved here and they broke up? She'd have given up everything, and he'd be able to continue on with his life as if she'd never sacrificed anything for him.

"Stop thinking so hard," he said softly. "You're killin' me."

"I can't help it," she mumbled against his chest.

"Come on, kitten. I think what I planned is just what you need."

As usual, he opened the passenger door of his Audi and waited until she was seated and comfortable before shutting her in. He went around to his side and put the bag he was carrying in the back seat. Then he got in, started the car, and they were off.

They made small talk as he drove them toward downtown Colorado Springs. Allye really liked the small city. It was big enough to have most of what she needed, but way smaller than San Francisco. It had a homey feel to it.

She blinked when Gray stopped the car. He got out, grabbed the gym bag, then came around to her side. When she stood, she couldn't help but stare at the building in front of them in shock.

"Gray?"

"Yeah?"

"Is this . . ."

He chuckled. "Yeah, kitten. It's a dance studio. I know you must miss it, and I'm guessing dance is a good stress reliever for you."

Allye sighed in ecstasy. Gray got her. He really did.

"I did some research and made an appointment with the owner, Barbara Ellis. She said you were welcome to practice here as much as you want. There are classes most afternoons, but the mornings are pretty much open. Though she said there was an empty studio this afternoon because one of the classes is away at a competition."

Allye could only stare up at Gray. She'd thought he was going to bring her to an aerobics class. She should've known better. This was so much more enjoyable.

He handed over the bag. "I packed some of your things. I wasn't sure what you usually practiced in, so I threw in a bunch of stuff, just in case."

Would he ever cease to surprise her? Allye threw her arms around him and gloried in the fact that he immediately returned the hug.

He gently ran a hand over her head, caressing the white shock of hair as he spoke. "I'm worried about you. I know you have a lot of stuff going on up here"—he tapped her temple—"and I'm doing the best I can to make it so you can feel safe and free."

She noticed he didn't say *so that you can go home.*

"Is two hours enough? If it's too much, just let me know," he said.

"It's perfect."

"I'm going to go and meet with the guys while you're dancing. If you need me, just call. We'll be at The Pit, which isn't too far away. Okay?"

"Okay. Thanks, Gray. This is amazing."

Then he blew her mind even more. "I researched as much as I could about dance studios here in Colorado Springs. Unfortunately, they seem to merely hold classes. But I talked to Cleo Parker Robinson. She has a professional dance troupe up in Denver that gives performances year-round. I told her your name, and she hadn't heard of you, but when I told her you danced at the Dance Theatre of San Francisco, I heard her clicking on a keyboard, obviously looking you up. She informed me that your stage name is Allyson Mystic." He grinned. "She was impressed with what she saw online, and told me she'd welcome you with open arms. She liked the fact that you're able to do a broad range of dance genres."

"She said that?" Allye asked, her eyes wide.

"Yeah, kitten. I know it's unfair of me to expect you to make all the sacrifices. But I would do anything to make this relationship work out. I need to stay here in Colorado Springs, which isn't exactly fair to you. But if you staying here means I have to call every dance studio in a hundred-mile radius and brag about you and your talent in order to get you a job you love, I will. It's not ideal to have the troupe up there in Denver, but Cleo said you could practice down here most days, and you'd only have to travel up to Denver once or twice a week."

Allye smiled up at the huge man in front of her. She never in a million years would've guessed he could be so sensitive. He looked unbending and downright frightening at times. But she'd seen the vulnerable and tender side. "You're amazing," she said softly. Then, looking around to make sure they were alone, she stood on tiptoe and nipped his chin before saying, "You're *so* getting some tonight."

He grinned and moved his hands to her ass, pulling her into him. She could feel his hard cock against her belly. "You might be sore after dancing for two hours."

"You can run me a bath," she told him suggestively. "Then join me in it."

"We've fucked just about everywhere in my house but there," Gray mused with a glint of lust in his eyes.

"Thank you," Allye said with all the gratitude she could muster in her tone. "Not just for being amazing, but for this"—she motioned to the dance studio with her head—"and for making me feel safe. And for just being you."

"Go, dance," Gray ordered. "Try not to worry. I'll be back in two hours."

He bent his head and kissed her. A long, heartfelt, lustful kiss that was inappropriate for a public sidewalk. But Allye didn't care. When someone whistled out a car window as they drove past and yelled "Get a room!" Gray finally pulled back. Allye rolled her eyes.

"Have fun," he said as he backed away toward his car.

"I will. You'll let me know what you guys talked about later?"

"Of course. Go."

Allye smiled at him and turned to enter the dance studio. She should've been thinking about Jessie, San Francisco, and what the madman who wanted her for a sex slave was going to do next. But all she could think about was losing herself in music. It had always been her safe and happy place.

"So it's a list of women, the men who bought them, and how much they paid?" Gray asked Meat.

All six of the Mountain Mercenaries were sitting around their usual table at The Pit. Meat had had a breakthrough with the code and had finally cracked it.

"Yeah. It lists the requirements of the buyers, like one wanted a blonde-haired, blue-eyed virgin; another wanted a woman under five-three; and still another requested a voluptuous African American woman. Then the women's names are filled in after they're tagged for acquisition."

Arrow scanned the list and whistled. "These women didn't come cheap."

"Nope," Meat agreed. "The cheapest was seventy-five thousand. The set of twins? Two hundred K."

"Buyers are listed with only initials, which isn't helpful at all," Black added.

"Bloody hell," Ro swore, slamming his hand down on the table. The crack of sound echoed through the pool hall. "This is like the Cadillac of sex-slave trading."

"Exactly why we need to shut this shit down," Ball growled. "Is Nightingale the mastermind?"

Meat shrugged. "There's no indication on the spreadsheet. The escort Gray sent to the bottom of the Pacific didn't make note of Nightingale; the dumbass just seems to have put his orders in the document. Probably yanked off to it late at night."

"It's Nightingale. It has to be," Gray said in a low, deadly tone.

"Rex thinks so too," Meat agreed. "But there's no proof. Not on this spreadsheet, anyway."

Gray stared at the line that had Allye's information on it.

Allyson Mystic, Dancer, 5'7", white streak in hair, 100K, San Fran., T.B.

"Who's T.B.?" he asked. All signs pointed to Nightingale being her buyer. If he had a known pseudonym, maybe they could nail him.

"No clue. Rex has his ear to the ground, but there's no one he knows in the trade with those initials. It could be anyone rich enough to drop a hundred grand on a woman. Some businessman who decided he wanted a piece on the side. A Mob boss who wants in on the sex-trade game. There's no telling."

Gray clenched his teeth together so hard, he was in danger of cracking a molar. "How do we find out? This asshole paid someone big bucks to kidnap Allye. He's not going to just let that go."

"Obviously," Meat said, still looking down at the spreadsheet.

Gray couldn't hold back his frustration any longer. He got up so fast, his chair hit the floor behind him with a loud thump, and he reached across the table for Meat. He grabbed his shirt and twisted his hand, forcing Meat to stand or be choked. "This is not some random woman we're talking about. It's *my* woman. He's killing people she knows in order to get inside her head and force her back to California so he can grab her again. Stop treating this so flippantly!"

Meat's eyes narrowed, and he glared at Gray. He didn't struggle in his grasp, merely waited for his friend to calm down.

"Put him down," Arrow ordered. "Beating Meat to a pulp won't solve anything."

Gray hesitated for a split second, then let go of Meat's shirt abruptly. He paced back and forth next to the table. "He has to have seen her before. She only goes by the name Allyson Mystic when she dances. Maybe he went to one of her performances. Can we check everyone who paid for a ticket via credit card?"

"Well, sure, but it's going to be a huge number of people," Meat said, obviously not holding Gray's outburst against him. "I'd be surprised if the kidnapper was stupid enough to buy a ticket using a credit card in his own name, but I'll look into it and let you know if I find anything."

"Whoever it is seems to be obsessed with your Allye," Ro commented. "By forcing that Jessie girl to wear those contacts and by dyeing her hair brown and white, he recreated the object of his fantasy."

"Or he just wanted to mentally torture Allye," Black threw in.

"We could try to see who's gone to several of her performances to help narrow it down," Ro finished.

"Sit down, Gray," Ball said. "You're making me dizzy."

Gray huffed out a breath and sat.

"Speaking of, where's Allye?" Black asked.

"I dropped her at a dance studio downtown to blow off some steam," Gray told his friends.

"You're really serious about her, aren't you?" Ro asked.

"Yeah. I am. She's . . . I can't really describe it."

"Tough, compassionate, funny, pretty, and fun to be around," Black said.

Gray narrowed his eyes at his friend.

Black held up his hands in capitulation. "Easy, friend. I was around her just a little bit, and I can see the appeal. She's different from a lot of women. Hell, most chicks I know would've been freaking out if they'd found themselves in the middle of the ocean. But not her. From what I saw, and what you've said, she just rolled with the punches. Don't see that very often."

Gray nodded. "True. Even when I told her it was quite a ways to shore, she didn't panic. Just lay back and trusted me to get her to safety." He looked around at his friends. "I want her to stay, but I want her to *want* to stay. Not because she has no other choice. Help me figure this out."

"We're tryin', Gray," Meat said.

"This guy is going to do it again," Arrow observed. "When his first message doesn't work, he'll escalate until he gets what he wants. Namely, Allye."

"Not going to happen," Gray said, his fingers clenching into fists.

"Your job is to stick close to Allye," Black said. "We'll do what we can to investigate. I'll see if Rex will approve a couple of us going to San Francisco and poking around. We'll talk to the other dancers at Allye's work and see if they saw anything, or know anything about Jessie's disappearance. He's pissed that she escaped, and he's getting desperate. We'll track him down, Gray. I know it."

"I hope so," Gray said quietly. "I really hope so."

He shook hands with each of his friends and left The Pit, giving Dave a chin lift as he went. It had only been an hour and a half since he'd left Allye, but after all the talk about missing women and what might be happening to them, Gray needed to see her. Make sure she was all right. Even though the chances of Nightingale figuring out where she was were slim, he should've put a guard on the dance studio. Or watched over her himself.

He drove back to the small dance studio faster than he should've and parked. He went in, a bell tinkling over his head announcing his arrival. A group of young girls turned and stared as he entered. An older woman, probably in her sixties, greeted him. It wasn't Barbara, as he'd met the owner. He assumed it was another instructor.

"Let me guess, you're here for Allyson Mystic?"

Gray blinked. How had she known Allye's stage name? He supposed word got around quickly. "Yeah, I guess I am."

"She's been quite the hit here today. She might not be nationally known, but when Barbara is impressed, we're *all* impressed. Word got around to the students, and they've been thrilled, taking turns watching a professional dancer. If you want to take a peek, you can use the observation window down the hall and to your left."

Gray nodded his thanks and headed in the direction she'd indicated.

He knew exactly which window she was talking about, as there were four girls gathered around it, their eyes wide, watching Allye dance.

Gray stopped a few feet behind them and stood without saying a word, his eyes glued to the woman dancing on the other side of the glass.

She was amazing.

He'd never seen her practicing when she was at his house. She'd said that she felt self-conscious with him watching her, so he'd left her to it when she went downstairs to practice. Intellectually, Gray knew she must be good to have a full-time job as a dancer, but whatever he thought he knew about dancers went out the window as he watched Allye.

She'd pulled her hair up into a ponytail on the top of her head, the slash of white peeking out as she moved. He couldn't hear the music from his vantage point, but he didn't need to. She was graceful as she bent and swayed. Her arms seemed to be attached to her body by strings, with the way they waved and undulated to the beat. The muscles in her legs flexed with every bend and arch. She was wearing a pair of skintight pants, her feet bare except for a band of tape wrapped around the ball of each, giving her traction. She had on a tank top that clung to her curves.

The music must've sped up, because her movements became faster, more energetic. She began a series of spins, her arms outstretched, one knee bent, her weight all on one foot. Her head marked her place as she spun in circles, never slowing down, never misstepping. It was beautiful and awe inspiring all at the same time.

The young dancers watching must have thought so, too, because they were murmuring to each other about how amazing "Miss Mystic" was, and how they hoped to one day be as good.

Allye suddenly stopped turning and fell to the floor. But she hadn't really fallen, she'd collapsed as part of the choreography of the dance. Her palms on the floor, one foot flat on the wooden planks below her, the other stretched behind, toes pointed.

Gray could see her chest moving up and down with her labored breaths, but it was the serenity on her face that struck him the hardest. This was her happy place.

He hadn't realized it, but she'd been extremely stressed over the last week, and had very effectively hidden it from him. She did a very good job of hiding *all* her emotions from him, from everyone.

He remembered that she said she never cried. She needed this. Needed to dance as much as he needed fresh air every day. Needed it to feel complete.

It was at that moment, watching Allye in her element, that Gray realized he loved her.

He would do anything possible to make sure she always had dancing in her life. If it meant moving to Denver so she could be closer to the Cleo Parker Robinson Dance Theatre, that's what he'd do. He wanted to always see the sense of peacefulness on her face she had at that moment.

She stood and smiled at someone on the other side of the room. Wiping his hands on his pants, Gray made his way to the door. He opened it slowly, and was gratified when Allye turned to him and gave *him* a big smile.

"Has it been two hours already?"

"Just about. If you want to stay longer, it's not a problem."

If anything, her smile got bigger. "No, I'm good. Like you said, I'm going to be sore as it is. I think you promised me a bath, though."

Gray almost blurted it out right there. Not caring about the woman who had been manning the stereo. Almost told Allye that he loved her. But he managed to hold it back. Barely. "That I did, kitten."

He stood by the door, not trusting himself as she collected her belongings. She threw a T-shirt on over her tank top, and Gray was both upset that he couldn't stare at her tits anymore and glad that she'd covered herself so no one *else* could stare at her tits.

She picked up her bag, and Gray took it from her as soon as she got near him. She linked her elbow with his and stayed by his side as they walked out of the room toward the front door. They were stopped half a dozen times by little girls who wanted to say hello to Miss Mystic, and then again by the owner of the dance school.

"It was wonderful to have you, Allyson," she said. "You're always welcome here."

"Thank you, Mrs. Ellis. And please, call me Allye." She looked up at Gray. "Would it be okay if you brought me here in the mornings? Barbara said that the first class doesn't start until ten, and she's willing to let me in around eight to do my workouts."

"Of course," Gray said immediately. "Whatever works for you."

She beamed up at him before turning back to the owner. "I appreciate it very much. And I'm happy to spend time with some of the classes in return for using your space."

The other woman looked like she was going to explode with happiness. "That'd be wonderful! Simply wonderful," she gushed. "I'll make sure everyone knows you'll be rotating in and out of the various classes. They'll all just be tickled pink to know you're here."

Allye smiled and gave a few more goodbyes before they were finally out of the small dance studio and on their way home.

"They seem to know who you are," Gray observed after they were in the car. He'd grabbed her hand after he'd pulled onto the road, and she'd intertwined her fingers with his.

"Yeah, well, the dance community is actually smaller than you'd think. And I've been dancing professionally for a while now. I guess word gets around." She shrugged. "How did your talk go?"

The last thing he wanted to do was talk about Nightingale, the missing women, or the spreadsheet she'd pilfered from the sinking ship. "Can we talk about it later?" he asked.

"That bad, huh?" she said, the smile slipping from her face.

Gray moved his hand up to her face and brushed the back of his fingers against her still-flushed cheek. "I just can't bear for you to lose this content, relaxed look just yet," he told her honestly.

"Okay," she said, tilting her head and rubbing her cheek against his hand.

"I'll run you a bath when we get home. Then I'll make us something to eat afterward. Okay?"

"Sounds heavenly," Allye said. "I don't think anyone has ever started a bath for me before. Not even when I was a kid. I started showering when I was four because Mom said that baths wasted too much water."

Gray clenched his teeth together. It seemed like he was doing that a lot lately. But instead of saying something derogatory about her mother and upbringing, he merely said, "Then I'm glad I get to be the first."

An hour later, Allye lay completely boneless on top of Gray. He'd done just what he said he was going to. He'd run her a bath. But after he'd helped her in, she'd held on to his hand and tugged, saying, "Will you join me?"

She'd never seen him strip so fast. He was in the tub with her in five seconds flat. Things had almost gotten out of control, and he'd actually slipped all the way inside her before swearing and pulling out. He'd leaped out of the tub and run into the bedroom. Allye couldn't stop giggling at his urgency, and the fact that he was walking around soaking wet, dripping water all over the floor and not seeming to care.

But when he'd returned, he'd had a condom rolled over his cock, and he'd climbed right back into the tub and thrust inside her so forcefully, she could do nothing but moan in delight.

Now, she was sitting astride him, her face tucked into the space between his shoulder and his neck, loving the way he was stroking her back in long, languid movements. He'd removed the condom, and she could feel his semihard dick tucked between their bodies, but for now at least, they were both sated.

"Thank you for letting me dance today," she said softly.

"I watched for a while there at the end," he told her. "You're amazing."

She shrugged. "I'm okay. There are a lot of people better than me."

"Don't do that," he scolded. "You're good. Really good. I doubt Robin would've made you lead if you weren't. Not to mention all those little girls today had stars in their eyes when you actually talked to them. Praised their outfits."

"It felt good," she told him. "I'd forgotten how much I enjoyed being around kids."

"You taught before?"

She nodded against him. Steam still rose from the tub, and she could feel the beads of sweat on her brow from both the temperature of the water and their earlier exertion. "Yeah. Part-time when I first signed on to the dance theatre. I wasn't getting paid as much as I am now, and it helped supplement my income. There's just something so freeing about teaching little kids. For the most part, they haven't learned to be critical of their bodies or each other. So even the kids who are overweight don't seem to notice or care. And there was this one class where a little girl with Down syndrome was enrolled. She always started the class with big hugs for everyone, and that little act of joyfulness carried through the entire session. Everyone seemed happier and just plain had more fun than any of my other classes. No one cared that little Rory was different from them. They didn't care that she wasn't very verbal. Her enthusiasm and joy in jumping around and dancing was contagious. There was more laughter in that hour of class than any other. I'd love to teach again. Maybe have a class that integrated special-needs kids with regular kids. I think it would do everyone a lot of good."

"I think so too," Gray said, kissing her on the forehead.

They stayed like that, bodies mashed together, enjoying the intimacy of the moment.

"Will you tell me about your meeting?" Allye finally asked.

She felt Gray tense under her, but he didn't prevaricate. He told her about the spreadsheet and what Meat had learned. He told her how much the mysterious T.B. had paid for her to be brought to him. He even told her that some of the team would be traveling to San Francisco to talk to her friends and coworkers at the dance theatre.

When he was done, Allye said softly, "I'm not going to be safe until you guys figure out who this T.B. guy is and stop him, am I?"

"I'm going to keep you safe," Gray swore even as he leaned over, grabbed a washcloth, lathered it up, and began to tenderly wash her back.

Allye sighed. It wasn't exactly an answer. Deciding she couldn't deal with any more at the moment, she sat up. She shivered, the air much cooler than the water and Gray's body. "Promise me you'll keep me informed. Don't keep anything about this from me. Please?"

She could tell he wasn't happy, but her trust in him grew when he nodded and said, "I promise."

"Thank you."

"How about we finish cleaning up, get out, and I get some food in you? You worked off quite a few calories today, I'm guessing. I bought a steak for me last night, and I'll make you some veggie kabobs, if you'd like."

She smiled. "That sounds great. And since you'll be taking me to dance every morning for a while, I'll need to make sure I go to bed extra early then too, huh?"

He grinned back. "I'll make sure to tuck you in nice and tight."

She rolled her eyes. "I'm counting on it."

She smiled at him, and they quickly finished soaping up and getting clean. When they were done, Gray put a hand at her nape and pulled her to him. He kissed her as if he'd never get to kiss her again.

Then again, *every* time they kissed, it was as intense as if it were their last. She loved that about him.

Allye froze. *Loved.* Had she completely fallen head over heels for Gray?

When she scooted back, giving him room to stand, she stared up at his chiseled body and nodded to herself. Yeah, she loved this man. He used his strength to fight evil in the world. He could be absolutely lethal, yet he'd been nothing but protective and gentle with her. Well, *gentle* wasn't the word she'd use when they were making love. *Intense* was more like it.

He held out a towel and wrapped his arms around her as he wrapped the towel around her body, trapping her arms at her side. He kissed the side of her neck, his beard rough and scratchy against her heat-flushed, sensitive skin.

"You smell good," he said, inhaling deeply.

"You do too," she told him, bending her neck and inhaling his scent at his upper arm.

"Since we were in the same tub, I'd say we smell like each other."

She turned in his arms and smiled up at him. "I like that."

"Me too," he agreed. Then he stood back, turned her, and smacked her ass. "Now go get dressed, woman. And stop distracting me."

Laughing, Allye did as he ordered and skipped into the bedroom to grab some clothes.

Gage Nightingale, otherwise known as "the Boss" to those who worked for him, frowned, standing in a hallway in front of a huge window, behind which were two of his women.

A secret door led to the long passage. Similar windows were spaced all along the hall, allowing him to look into the rooms where his pets lived.

He gripped his hands behind his back as he stared at the twins lying listlessly on the floor of their cage, not even looking at him when he rang the bell that hung inside their enclosure. When they heard the bell, they were supposed to get up and face front, letting him get a good look at them. Sometimes he went inside and took them, other times he forced them to have sex with each other, but today they refused to budge.

Making a mental note to discipline them later, Nightingale moved to the next window.

The little woman he'd acquired was doing as she had been taught, kneeling with her legs apart, staring at the floor. She hadn't been fed yet, he could see her water and food bowls were empty, and he'd have to reprimand the zookeeper for making her wait when she was being so good. Holding back food was only for the bad pets, not those who were doing what they were told.

The tattooed woman was not in her cage, but Nightingale knew that was because she'd gotten more ink done today. She'd had to be sedated because they were working on her face now. The last time she'd been brought in for tattooing, she'd been combative and weepy. There was nothing Nightingale liked less than a slobbering, crying woman.

But once her face was tattooed, she'd be ninety-five percent complete. He just needed to have the bottoms of her feet and her palms inked, and she'd be the first woman to be one hundred percent covered by tattoos. Even the insides of her labia and lips had been marked. And *he* owned her. It was a heady feeling. He'd submit pictures for the *Guinness Book of World Records* as soon as she was ready.

His albino was in the next cage. Nightingale flipped a switch outside her enclosure, which turned on the spotlight over the area where she was chained, and smiled. She'd proved to be a wild one. Refusing his attempts at training her. Until he'd brought in the head box.

One of the trainers had inadvertently found her weakness after she'd freaked out when a moth had entered her room one night and flitted around the light bulb on the ceiling.

So, the next time she'd refused to do what he wanted—namely, not fight him when he entered her cage—he'd had her chained down and the box slipped over her head. It was filled with moths. The way she'd trembled and screamed as the creatures flitted around her face, brushing against her cheeks, getting stuck in her hair and even crawling into her ears, made him laugh hysterically.

He kept the box of completely innocuous creatures inside her cage, as a deterrent to more inappropriate manners. So far, it was working. Nightingale much preferred her subdued and docile, if not terrified, to her out-of-control behavior. It made strapping her to the bed so he could have his way with her much easier. He hadn't been with an albino before. Her skin pinked up so nicely when he smacked her, and the bruises he left on her skin were vivid, so much easier to see than on regular women . . . He liked that.

Nightingale smiled. He loved owning unique things.

That led him to think about his Mystic once more. He'd been so sure, after she'd learned about the warning he'd left for her, that she would return to the city—yes, he was convinced now that she'd fled San Francisco, maybe even the state—to prevent any more of her friends from being killed. Then he'd finally be able to add her to his collection. He had a cage by his bed for her when she wasn't in the empty room at the end of the long hallway. Everything was all ready, including her special stage.

He couldn't wait to wake up in the mornings and see her beautiful eyes staring at him, full of fear. There was nothing like terror to help him start his morning right. He'd tried to make the other woman—he didn't even remember her name now, not that it mattered—look like his Mystic, but it hadn't worked. She was too tall. Too skinny. And all she'd done was cry.

Even after he'd dyed her hair and put in the beautiful swath of white, it wasn't the same. The contacts had helped, but he shuddered remembering how she'd screamed and carried on when she was strapped down and her eyelids were removed so she wouldn't be able to hide her brown and blue eyes from him.

Nightingale scowled and stomped to the end of the row of cages. He pounded on the zookeeper's door and waited impatiently for him to open it. The albino and the little woman needed food, and the twins needed to be separated. He'd agreed to keep them together, but only if they behaved. And they were not behaving right now.

He knew his anger was all out of proportion. He was usually much more patient with his pets. It was all Mystic's fault. If she would just come home, he'd be able to concentrate again. Train his pets better. It was time to send her another message. She'd eventually get the hint. If she didn't, he'd just keep on communicating. *His* way.

The man who took care of his special pets finally opened the door, and Nightingale lit into him. By the time he left for the night, he was confident all would be well with his pets when next he returned.

Chapter Eleven

The longer Gray spent with Allye living in his house, sharing his space, the more anxious he got. It wasn't her, per se; it was the feeling of impending doom. Something was going to get screwed up. He'd either do something, or she'd decide she had to go back to her life, or the mysterious T.B. would find out where Allye had gone and come after her here.

It was as if the more perfect things were between them, the stronger his feeling of dread.

She'd been in Colorado Springs for three weeks now. Three of the best weeks he'd ever had. She just seemed to fit seamlessly into his life and routines. They'd get up in the mornings and shower, sometimes together, other times apart. He'd make them breakfast, then he'd take her downtown to the dance studio. She'd begun spending more and more time there, sometimes not texting him to pick her up until well after lunchtime. The kids and the owner loved having her. Barbara had even begun to pay her for helping out with the children's dance classes.

They'd gone shopping to buy her more clothes and other odds and ends that she needed to feel comfortable. Gray had wanted to pay for everything, but she'd flatly refused, saying that she had plenty of money at the moment to clothe herself.

While she was at the studio, Gray would meet with the guys or stay home and do research, trying to find something that would lead to the elusive Nightingale, then go and pick up Allye when she let him know she was done. They'd have lunch together, sometimes eating out, other times going back to his house and eating something there. Then he'd do some accounting work in his home office, creating spreadsheets and doing other financial work for his clients.

In the evenings, they spent time together. Making dinner, watching TV, or making love.

He'd learned that she could be stubborn—not just about not letting him pay for new clothes—and didn't give in gracefully when she wanted to do something and he disagreed. But she was also fairly easygoing about most things. She didn't care if his furniture was a mishmash of expensive masculine and college student, didn't seem to get wigged out if the floors weren't immaculate or if he hadn't dusted. In fact, she was somewhat messy; he was always picking up her clothes from the middle of the master bedroom.

Then again, she'd begun to complain about the small beard hairs he left in the sink after he shaved in the mornings. Or the way he never rinsed out his dishes, just left them in the sink to deal with later. She claimed they were harder to get clean that way because the food was dried to the dishes by the time they went into the dishwasher.

But none of that ultimately seemed to matter to either of them. They spent every night wrapped in each other's arms. The first week they'd lived together, they'd made love every day, at least once, sometimes twice. Gray hadn't been able to get enough, and Allye seemed to gladly take whatever he gave her. She never complained when he was in the mood to take his time and be gentle or when he needed to take her roughly.

But he'd already begun appreciating the nights he simply got to hold her. They were intimate, if not passionate. He'd memorized the way she nuzzled into the space between his neck and shoulder, warming her nose. And the way she ran her fingers over his chest, lightly playing with his nipples. Not to arouse him, but just . . . exploring.

With every day that went by, however, it seemed as if whatever danger lurked above their heads was getting closer and closer. And Gray had a feeling when push came to shove, he was going to lose Allye. Somehow. Someway. She'd slip through his fingers. And that was making him dread waking up each morning, wondering if today was the day he'd lose her.

Last night they'd been making out on the couch, not watching whatever movie Allye had insisted they watch, when his phone rang.

He'd seen it was his mother and immediately answered. Allye hadn't been all that receptive to him inviting his mother to Colorado so she could meet her, and wouldn't talk about why. He'd decided that moment was as good a time as any to make introductions, even if they were over the phone.

"Hey, Mom."

"Hello, son. How are you?"

"I'm good. Can I put you on speaker?"

"Sure."

Gray clicked the phone on speaker and hugged Allye to him. She'd tried to sit up—to leave the room, he knew—but he wouldn't let her. "Mom, I'd like to introduce you to someone. Allye, this is my mom. Mom, meet Allye Martin."

"Oh, hello, Allye. How are you?"

Allye had looked up at him, her eyes wide and stricken, and had mumbled hello. Then she'd crawled out of his arms and went upstairs to the master bedroom. He'd let her go, because the look in her eyes wasn't irritation—it was unadulterated terror. She was scared to death to talk to his mom, and he hated it. He'd told her how great his mother was, and he'd tried to reassure Allye that his mom would love her, but he obviously hadn't gotten through.

He'd talked to his mom for a while, avoided telling her all the details about how he'd met Allye, admitted that she was *the one*, talked her out of immediately planning his wedding, and told her to tell his brother hello for him next time she talked to him. Then he'd hung up and gone to find Allye.

"Allye?" he said as he opened the door.

She was in bed, the covers pulled all the way up her body, her back to him. They'd gone to bed at this time before, but when they did, it was because they both wanted to make love, not sleep.

Gray sat on the side of the bed. He ran his hand over her head. "Are you okay, kitten?"

She nodded.

"What's wrong?"

She turned her head to look at him, and he almost flinched at how sad she looked.

"What? Talk to me, Allye."

"I'm not good with moms," she said quietly. "They never like me."

And with that, Gray's heart just about broke. He stripped off his shirt, took off his jeans, and climbed under the covers with her. He wrapped his arms around her, pulling her back to his chest, and simply held her as tightly as he could. "I don't believe it."

"It's true. The first boy I dated in high school . . . he and I were getting along fine. I went over to his house one night, and when his mom found out I was a foster kid, she turned cold. The boy never asked me out again."

"His loss," Gray murmured.

"Then there was the mother of a guy I dated when I first started working at the dance theatre in San Francisco. He thought it would be fun if we went out to dinner with his parents. She took one look at the cheap dress I was wearing and turned up her nose at me. I think I had two more dates with *that* guy before he ended it."

"My mom isn't like that," Gray told her.

"I think I have some defective mom gene," Allye said softly. "My own mom didn't like or want me, so no one else's does either."

Gray turned her onto her back, forcing her to look at him. "After you left, my mom interrogated me about you. She even looked you up on her computer as we were talking. She gushed about how pretty you are, and then even had the nerve to ask what you were doing with a reprobate like me." He smiled to let her know he was teasing. "I had to talk her down from calling all her friends and telling them I was getting married." He ran his hand over her head again in a gentle caress. "I'm not saying you'll be best friends, but she's going to love you."

Allye had just shaken her head and sighed. Then she'd inched her way down his body and begun to make love to him. He knew what she was doing, distracting him so she didn't have to talk about his mom anymore, and he let her. But he knew his family. They would embrace Allye as if she were one of their own . . . if she'd allow it.

There were a lot of things he didn't know about the woman he loved. Things he couldn't wait to learn. But in return, there were things she didn't know about *him*. He'd told her about his time as a SEAL, and what had happened to make him leave, but she didn't know that sometimes it still affected him. He didn't have nightmares too often anymore, but certain situations sometimes threw him right back there. Where he'd been helpless to do anything but watch as his captors hurt those women right in front of him. When it happened, he tended to shut down. To block out any kind of emotion so he didn't have to feel.

Would she understand? Would she take it personally? He had no idea and no desire to find out.

His phone ringing snapped him out of his reverie. Allye was at the dance studio, and he was alone in the house. He was supposed to be working on taxes for a client, but he couldn't concentrate. The feeling of impending doom was too thick to let him effectively think about tax laws or do any kind of math.

"Gray."

"It's Rex."

Gray's stomach dropped. "What happened?"

"He got another one."

Gray knew exactly what his handler was talking about. "Who?"

"A woman named Melany Brewer. She actually took Allye's place as lead since she's been here in Colorado Springs."

"Fuck," Gray swore. "Fuck, fuck, *fuck*. She's not going to take this well."

"Then, don't tell her."

"I'm not keeping this shit from her. I promised I wouldn't, and she has a right to know. Are we any closer to tracking down T.B. or Nightingale?"

"Yes and no," Rex said reluctantly.

Gray's stomach clenched again. He had a feeling he wasn't going to like what his handler said next. "What?"

"T.B. *is* Nightingale."

"How is that possible? His name is Gage. T.B. doesn't match."

"You know that Arrow and Black are in California. They've done some digging. Talked to a lot of shady folks. Word on the street is that there's a man, known only as 'the Boss,' who takes orders for specific kinds of women."

Gray stood up abruptly and began to pace. "Shit. So that's it. Proof that the head of the most notorious and elusive sex-trafficking ring *does* want to get his hands on my woman."

"Looks that way," Rex said, his voice seemingly unruffled.

"You don't sound too fucking worried," Gray barked. "In fact, you make it sound like this is just another day for the Mountain fucking Mercenaries. Well, it's fucking not. This is *my* woman's life on the line, Rex. And I'm telling you right now, there's no way Nightingale is getting his hands on her. I'll take her and disappear so he can't ever find us. Hear me?"

"Calm down, Gray," Rex said evenly.

Gray sighed and ran a hand through his hair, absently noting that he probably needed to get it cut. "Does anything *ever* ruffle your feathers?" he asked. "Seriously, you're always so fucking calm. Never show any emotion. Do you give a shit about *anything*? Because from where I'm sitting, it doesn't seem like it."

"Yeah, Gray. I give a shit about a lot of things. Women disappearing and never being heard from again. Their loved ones never knowing what happened to them, if they're dead or alive. That's what I give a shit about. That, and taking down people like Nightingale so it doesn't happen to someone else's family."

Gray blinked in surprise. He'd never heard his handler say anything as personal as what he'd just revealed. They'd all guessed the man had some experience with a loved one going missing or somehow being involved in the sex-slave industry, but they'd never had confirmation—until now.

Someone else's family.

Before he could say anything, like apologize for being insensitive, Rex spoke again.

"Talk to Allye. Tell her about Melany. Arrow and Black are doing what they can from California to track her down. We're also trying to figure out what the deal with the boats was all about. I mean, if he kidnapped both Jessica and Melany and simply had them brought to him, why didn't he do the same with Allye? Why bother with the damn boats in the first place? Was it just an elaborate ruse to throw people off? Or was there a deeper reason behind it? Maybe we'll know more when we find Melany . . . or when her body shows up. In the meantime, call if you need me." And with that, Rex ended the call.

Looking at his watch, Gray saw that it was only ten, but he needed to see Allye now. He had the same questions about the boats, but they could wait. Talking to Allye couldn't.

Pocketing his phone, he headed for the garage.

Thirty minutes later, he was ushering Allye into his Audi, her apologies to Barbara and the little girls echoing in his head. She'd been in the middle of a dance lesson when he'd barged in and said he needed to talk to her.

Without complaint, she'd said her goodbyes and gone with him.

As soon as they were in the car, she put her hand on his thigh. "What's wrong?"

"When we get home," Gray told her.

Allye bit her lip but nodded. She kept her hand on his thigh, but Gray couldn't make himself touch her. He wanted to, wanted to comfort her, but he was too on edge. Too worried that she was going to lose it when she heard.

The rest of the trip was done without either of them speaking. Gray tried to go over in his head how he was going to break the news to Allye. She had to know Melany. Had to have been friends with her. Hearing about Jessie had hurt, but hearing about Melany might break her.

They got home and entered the house. As soon as the garage door closed behind them, Allye turned and said, "Tell me."

"Go and sit," Gray said. "Do you want something to drink?"

"No," she said a little testily. "I want to know what happened."

Gray sighed. He put his hand on the small of her back, feeling the dampness from her workout earlier. She was wearing a pair of yoga pants and had on her normal tank top under a T-shirt. For once, he wasn't thinking about how sexy she was, but how vulnerable and small she seemed next to his six and a half feet.

Gray encouraged her to head into the living room and sit.

She did, but he could tell her patience was about over.

As soon as they sat, he told her the bad news. "Do you know someone named Melany Brewer?"

Allye's eyes widened, and she nodded.

"She's disappeared."

Allye leaned forward and covered her face. She stayed hunched over as she asked through her fingers, "Was it my kidnapper?"

"Probably."

She sat up. "What's being done to find her? To rescue her?"

"Arrow and Black are in San Francisco now. They're questioning her neighbors and the other dancers to see what they know. Rex is using his contacts too. The same ones that had the lead on your transfer."

Her eyes dulled, and the truth registered on her face. "She's going to show up dead, too, isn't she?"

Gray tried to soothe her. "We don't know that."

"She is. We both know it." Allye pushed to her feet and paced in front of him in agitation. "Why is he doing this?" she asked in a shrill voice. "Why is he so obsessed with me? It doesn't make sense! He can't *have* me. I'm not something he can purchase and lock away and do whatever he wants with. I'm a *person*. A human being! He doesn't have the right to steal my friends and kill them. He doesn't have the right to play God! You have to stop him, Gray! You *have* to. Make him stop—please, God, make him stop!" And with that, she crumpled to the ground, shaking uncontrollably.

Gray hated seeing her like this. He bent and scooped her up as if she were a child rather than a full-grown adult. He carried her up the stairs and into their room. He put her on the bed and curled himself around her, doing everything he could to make her feel safe.

She shook for quite a while, but never cried, her emotions coming out through her trembling body rather than in the form of tears. Then she spent the next twenty minutes telling Gray everything she could about Melany. Her favorite kind of dance, what she liked to snack on during rehearsals, everything she knew about her family. She talked about her quirks, how she had to wear pink underwear when she performed. How she would knock on a piece of wood along the stage of the theatre every time before she went onstage. How she lived alone, but always asked one of the male dancers to accompany her home.

Gray let her talk. Let her get it all out, always alert to anything that he might pass on to Rex that could assist in finding her.

Finally, her words trailed off, and she sighed. "He's not going to stop."

"He will when we find him and kill him." In the past, with other girlfriends, Gray would've never been so blunt, but he'd found over the weeks that Allye honestly didn't seem to mind what he did for a living. Maybe it was the way they'd met, and the fact that he'd killed two men rescuing her from a fate worse than death. Maybe it was her background. Whatever it was, Gray knew he could always be who he truly was with her.

"He wants me," she said softly.

"And he's not going to get you," Gray retorted immediately.

"But what if it's the only way he'll stop?" she asked.

Gray used his greater strength and turned her in his arms. He put a finger under her chin and forced her to look up at him. "No, kitten. Absolutely not."

"No, what?" she asked, trying to sound innocent, but he knew her well enough by now to know there was nothing naive about her question.

"You will *not* put yourself in harm's way. I won't allow it."

"But if you're there with me, you'll keep me safe."

"No," Gray repeated, tucking her head into his chest, not able to look into her beautiful eyes anymore. "Just no."

She didn't say anything else, and eventually he felt her grow lax in his arms. It didn't matter that it wasn't even noon yet. She'd fallen asleep, probably to try to block out some of the pain she was feeling over what was happening to her friends.

Gray slipped out of her arms and replaced himself with a pillow, waiting until Allye had settled before easing out of the room and heading back to his office. He needed to get online and do whatever he had to do to find Nightingale and end this. Before Allye insisted on being involved.

~

Nightingale grinned as the escort he'd paid ten thousand dollars entered the room, dragging a struggling woman on her back. He always paid his people above and beyond what they'd get for doing the same jobs for someone else. He found that by shelling out good money to those who snatched the women—and to the men who collected payments from others and escorted his own special pets—the more careful and loyal his employees were.

The service he provided wasn't cheap. There were a lot of risks in the human-trafficking business, and the more difficult the woman was to obtain, the higher the fee. But he had no problem shelling out money to good escorts and kidnappers.

The woman being dragged into the room really didn't look anything like his Mystic, but Nightingale knew he could work on that. He indicated to the zookeeper to take off the blindfold around her head. She blinked once it was removed and squinted as if the light hurt her eyes. She was about the same height as Mystic, but her hair was black. Her dark eyes would be tough to lighten, but he'd already considered that.

"Welcome, Melany," he said congenially.

The woman had a piece of duct tape over her mouth, so her response wasn't clear, but what *was* clear was that it seemed full of venom and not at all pleasant.

Knowing he had to start training her now, even if she wouldn't be around all that long, Nightingale walked over to where she was lying on her back on the hard floor and grabbed the hair at the top of her head. She was breathing hard, and her eyes were dilated with fear. He wrenched her up slightly, then tilted her head back until she was struggling to pull in air through her nose.

"Is that any way to greet your new master?" he asked. "Why don't you try again, and be nice, or I'll have to show you what that defiance gets you. Welcome to your new home, Melany."

She glared at him through her dark, boring eyes, and mumbled something through the tape.

Without remorse and without delay, Nightingale shoved her head back down, not caring that it met the concrete floor with a loud thud, and grabbed one of her kicking feet. She wasn't wearing shoes, as per his instructions, and he reached into his back pocket and pulled out a small nutcracker. He positioned her big toe in the middle of it and squeezed.

The sound of the bone breaking was loud in the room, but her scream, even muffled as it was by the tape, was louder.

Nightingale dropped her foot, satisfied he'd made his point. After all, dancers protected their feet at all costs. He crouched by her head once more.

"Welcome to your new home, Melany," he repeated.

He grinned when his new pet meekly said a garbled "Thank you." Nightingale was disgusted by the tears leaking from her eyes and the snot dripping from her nose, but at least her attitude had improved. His Mystic would never debase herself like this whore was doing. He stood, nodded to the escort, and gestured for the man to follow him.

The zookeeper stepped forward to take control of the new pet. He had his orders as to how to groom the new addition. He had some bleach for her right eye, and some blue dye, and her hair had to change color as well. The bleach would also work for the streak in her hair, but would need to be followed up with some plain ol' matte-white paint for it to look as Nightingale wished.

The zookeeper took hold of the new pet's foot, the one with the broken toe, and began to drag her toward her new living quarters as Nightingale and the escort left the room without a backward glance.

Chapter Twelve

The next two days were tense. There hadn't been any word from Arrow or Black about Melany's whereabouts, and Rex hadn't called with information about Nightingale either.

So Allye had spent two horribly long days worrying about what was happening to her friend and what she was going through. And she knew in the pit of her stomach that it was bad. It had to be. After hearing about some of what had happened to Jessie, Allye knew Melany was probably suffering the same fate.

The more she thought about it, the sicker she felt. This was her fault. No matter what Gray tried to tell her, it *was*. The man wanted *her*, and since he couldn't get to her, he was systematically attacking her friends. And she knew without a doubt he'd keep doing it. Who would be next? Molly? The sweet young dancer who'd just started? Bethany? The girl who wasn't that good, but had so much enthusiasm Robin couldn't help but let her have bit parts in some of the smaller productions? Would he go after some of the kids she used to teach before she began dancing full-time?

It had to stop, and Allye knew deep down, she was the only one who could stop it. If Rex hadn't been able to find this Nightingale guy yet, it was unlikely he would without some help.

The problem was Gray. He was adamant that she stay right where she was. With him. In Colorado Springs. He'd said time and time again that there was nothing she could do that he and his team weren't already doing.

But it sure didn't feel that way to her.

It was later in the afternoon, two days after Melany had been taken, when the doorbell rang. Allye couldn't make herself move from her spot on the couch. The television was on, but she wasn't watching it. Gray had gone into his home office, like he did most afternoons, but she had no idea what he was doing in there.

Things had been tense between them, and she hated it. They still slept in each other's arms every night, but they hadn't made love since they'd found out about the second abduction.

She watched as Gray walked toward the front door and answered it. When she saw Ro, Ball, and Meat enter, she stiffened even more.

"Oh shit," she whispered as the four men came toward her solemnly.

She knew without them having to say a word that they'd found Melany. And it wasn't good.

"Just say it," she begged softly as the men settled around her.

Gray sat next to her and took her hand in his.

"They found her in the same place Jessie was found. Golden Gate Park."

"Was she tortured?"

Gray nodded.

Allye pressed her lips together.

"Contacts? Her hair?"

"No contacts this time. It looks like he tried to use bleach to lighten her right eye. It didn't work. It just blinded her. Her hair was dyed brown, though. And the streak was added."

"Was there a message like on Jessie?"

Gray hesitated for the first time, and Allye braced for the worst.

"It said, *How many more? Come back.*"

Allye felt cold inside. This was worse than Jessie.

"There was a witness to the dumping of her body this time," Ball told her, as if that would make her feel better.

"And?" she asked. Allye knew her voice was flat and emotionless, but she couldn't make herself feel right now. If she did, she'd lose it.

"And Black and Arrow are working the lead."

Which meant they had nothing. If she could cry, now would be the time, but no tears came. She was uncomfortably numb. "So what now?"

"We continue to do what we can to find him. And you continue to stay here and be safe."

Allye wanted to refute Gray's words. Wanted to yell that it just wasn't right that others were being tortured and dying because of her. But she didn't. She stayed sitting. "Thank you for all that you're doing to try to help," she told the other three men. "It means a lot."

She looked down at her hands, not wanting to see their reactions to her words.

"We're going to find the arsehole," Ro said, emotion making his accent thicker than usual.

Allye nodded.

"He's going to pay for what he's done," Meat added.

"Good."

"We've got this," Ball said, when she didn't say anything else.

"What are you thinking, kitten?" Gray asked, lifting her chin with his finger and turning her head to his.

"I'm kinda hungry. Are you guys hungry? I can make something." She wasn't hungry in the least, but she needed to *do* something. Anything other than sit around and worry about who would be next to fall into the hands of the madman who wanted her.

"Yeah, that'd be great. Maybe some sandwiches?" Gray asked.

Allye nodded and stood. She walked around Gray, feeling his hand trailing on her hip as she went past.

~

"Bloody hell," Ro said when Allye had left the room. "What the fuck was that?"

Gray ran his hand through his hair tiredly. "That was Allye not dealing well with hearing another one of her friends is dead at the hands of this asshole. What did Black get from the witness?"

"Not much. Just that he saw a four-door sedan parked along one of the side roads near the park, and it caught his eye because there were literally no other cars around, and it's not the safest place to be at two in the morning," Ball shared.

"What was the witness doing there?" Gray asked.

Ball shrugged. "Don't know. Frankly, don't care. But he said he saw a man between five-ten and six feet, carrying a large bag. Then later, when the man was getting back into the car before he left, he didn't have the bag anymore."

"Could've been the body," Ro observed.

"Did he get a plate number?" Gray asked.

Ball shook his head. "Not that I know of."

"So, he's completely useless," Gray huffed. "Fuck, why can't we get a break?"

"Maybe, maybe not," Ball said. "Rex told me he did add that there was some sort of hangtag on the mirror of the car. He only noticed it because it was reflecting off the streetlight nearby."

"What was it?" Gray asked.

"He couldn't tell for sure, but he thought there was some sort of paw print on it," Ball told the group of men.

"A paw print? What does that mean?" Ro asked.

"A zoo? Does the San Francisco or Oakland Zoo have passes like that?" Gray asked.

"I don't know, but I'm going to find out," Meat said decisively.

"Maybe it's some kind of private animal reserve or something," Ro added.

Meat nodded and stood. "Let me know if you guys think of something else, or if you hear from Rex, Ball. I'm headed back home to see what I can dig up."

"Will do," Ball told him. "And with that, I'm going to go too."

"You want to stay for lunch?" Gray asked Ro.

The other man shook his head. "Naw, I'm thinking you and Allye need some time alone."

Gray nodded. He wasn't glad, exactly, that his friends were leaving. Things had been awkward with him and Allye lately. But he did want to do what he could to comfort her.

He walked his friends out and shut the door. When he turned, Allye was standing there.

"They left?"

"Yeah, kitten."

"They didn't want lunch?"

"No. They wanted to see what else they could find."

"Oh."

The word was low and sounded uncertain.

"Come here," Gray said, and held out his hand. She came to him immediately, ignoring his hand and cuddling right up to him.

Gray sighed in relief. Holding her felt so right. He didn't know what he'd do without this. Without *her*. He shuffled them back into the living room and sat them down on the couch.

They sat glued together for several minutes without speaking. Then Allye pulled back and looked him in the eye. "Make me forget?" she asked softly.

Gray's cock immediately hardened, but he shook his head. "I don't think—"

"Please, Gray. You're the only thing that makes me feel safe. I feel like the world has gone crazy, but when you're inside me, it all fades away, and the only thing I can think about, or feel, is you."

She was killing him. But he felt exactly the same way when he was balls deep inside of her. He stood and took hold of her hand. He led her to the bedroom and slowly began to strip her. He treated her as if she were as fragile as a piece of glass. He removed her blouse and bra. Then unzipped her jeans and slid them down her legs. He carefully eased his hands under the elastic of her panties until she stood in front of him completely bare.

Then she returned the favor, pushing his shirt up until he took if off the rest of the way. She unbuttoned his jeans and kneeled as she slowly eased them over his hips. His cock was hard against his briefs, and when she tugged the elastic down, the head popped out, nearly smacking her in the face. But instead of pulling his briefs all the way off, she left them there, with nothing but his dick sticking out, his balls still encased in the cotton.

She put her hand around him and, without any warning, sucked him into her mouth as far as she could.

Allye didn't want tenderness. She didn't want Gray to treat her like she was going to break. She wanted *her* Gray. The rough, take-what-he-wanted-and-damn-the-consequences Gray. But she knew she wouldn't get him if she didn't make the first move. If she didn't force him to forget the last hour and what they'd learned.

She knew she'd surprised him when she engulfed his cock in her mouth. His hips jerked, and she gagged when he pushed past what she could take, but she didn't let him ease up. Using her hand to jack him off at the same time, she licked and sucked him. She knew the exact moment when he broke.

He picked her up with his hands under her armpits and practically threw her onto the bed. He jerked off his underwear and reached for the drawer in his nightstand. Allye licked her lips as she played with herself while he rolled the condom down his length.

"You want this?" he asked huskily.

"Yeah, Gray. I want that," she replied.

"You're gonna take it how I want to give it to you," he warned.

She nodded. Because how he wanted to give it to her was exactly how *she* wanted to take it.

He crawled up between her spread legs, pushing her thighs farther apart. He pushed her hand away from her clit and took over manipulating it.

"You like sucking my cock, kitten?"

Allye could only nod as his knees pushed her legs open even farther. She could feel the burn in her inner thighs, but welcomed it. The physical pain pushed away the emotional anguish she could still feel.

She felt his fingers press into her body, making sure she was ready for him. He might like rough sex, but he always made sure she was wet and willing before he took her. He apparently was satisfied with what he found, because before she knew it, she felt the head of his cock pressing against her pussy.

With one hard thrust, he was suddenly inside her. Groaning, Allye threw her head back and closed her eyes. The slight burn made her forget everything but him.

"No. Look at me, kitten," Gray ordered.

Allye was helpless to do anything but respond to the order in his tone. She picked her head up and looked into his eyes.

"That's it, kitten. Let me see those beautiful eyes. Fuck, you're gorgeous, you know that?"

She couldn't answer, as he was thrusting powerfully in and out of her. Making her take all of him. Chasing away the demons that were trying to suck her under.

He reached out and grabbed a pillow, shoving it under her head, making it easier for her to keep her eyes on his. He put one hand next to her shoulder and leaned down, his gaze piercing into hers.

Each thrust moved her body up and down the bed, but she felt grounded by the intense look in Gray's eyes. His other hand moved between them, and he caught her clit between his thumb and forefinger. Every time he pushed inside her, he squeezed his fingers together, and when he pulled back, he relaxed his grip on her extremely sensitive bundle of nerves.

Between his unrelenting pounding into her body and his assault on her clit, she was on the edge of orgasm within seconds.

"You gonna come for me, kitten?"

"Mmm-hmmm," she managed, words beyond her.

"Don't close your eyes," he ordered. "Look at me as I push you over the edge."

And with that, he pinched his fingers together tight enough that it would've hurt if she wasn't so turned on, and he shoved himself so far inside her, Allye swore she could feel him at the entrance to her cervix . . . and she came.

Her eyes closed into slits, but she never shut them all the way, keeping her gaze on the man who owned her heart.

As soon as her breathing slowed, Gray pulled back and sat on his heels. He reached for her and turned her onto her stomach. Then he grabbed her hips and forced her backward.

"Reach down and put me back inside, kitten."

Allye immediately did as he ordered, getting in one long caress before he warned, "Allye," in a deep cautionary tone. She notched his cock head at her opening, and he immediately pressed back inside her. He pulled her onto his lap, her legs spread on either side of his thighs.

She couldn't move, and neither could he with the way she was sitting on him. She squirmed, wanting more. Needing more.

One arm wrapped around her waist, and the other went to where they were joined. She could feel how wet she was. Her excitement was smeared on her thighs, and now his too.

He held her to him for a while, petting her clit, pinching her nipples, and generally working her back up to an excited, frustrated frenzy. His cock pulsed deep inside her, and she moaned.

Finally, either reaching the end of his own control, or maybe he was just taking pity on her, Gray lay back. She was facing his feet, and started to turn around to ride him, but his hands stopped her. "Like this, kitten. Take me exactly like this."

It wasn't a position they'd done before, and she was unsure at first. Gray pushed on her back until she leaned forward, bracing herself on his shins. He slapped her ass once, then did it again when she froze.

"Ride me, Allye. Take me hard. Make me come."

So she did. He didn't allow her to be on top very often, and once she started lifting herself up and down on his shaft, she realized that he touched her differently inside this way. Whether it was the way she was bent over, or how his cock was rubbing a different spot than it usually did, it felt amazing.

Before long, she was frantically humping him, trying to go faster while at the same time trying to get him deeper. She was getting frustrated because she knew she was on the verge of coming, but needed to rub her clit in order to do so. But she couldn't touch herself and stay balanced at the same time.

Seeming to understand her predicament, Gray said, "Kneel over me. Touch yourself, and I'll do the rest of the work."

Trusting him, Allye did as he suggested. She sat up straight, and slid her knees out a little more. The position gave him a little room to thrust, and more important, allowed her easy access to the small bundle of nerves at the apex of her thighs.

Gray took hold of her hips with his hands and began to pound into her, much as he did when he took her from behind. Her breasts bobbed up and down with each thrust, and she frantically rubbed herself. Within seconds, she was shouting out her release, and would've collapsed if Gray hadn't been holding her above him. He pounded into her without mercy for another dozen or so thrusts before pulling her down on him and groaning. He held her locked to him for a heartbeat before pulling her upper body backward.

Allye gave him her weight, knowing he'd catch her. She lifted her hips as she shifted, not wanting to break his dick in half, and moaned when his heat left her. As soon as she was on her side and they were facing each other, Gray reached down and put himself back inside her. He was only semihard, but it was enough for her to sigh in contentment.

Her entire crotch felt soaked, but she was so relaxed and sated, she didn't care.

"Fuck, I love you," Gray breathed, more to himself than her.

But she heard it.

And upon hearing his words, she knew everything would be all right. With Gray's love, they could get through anything. They were a team. No sex-slaver/kidnapper/killer could come between them. No way. No how.

Chapter Thirteen

"You are not going to San Francisco," Gray said a week later, his arms crossed over his chest. "No way. No how. Not as long as I'm breathing."

"Gray," Allye said, trying to placate him, but he wasn't to be swayed.

"I said *no*, Allye. I'm not going to let you go back there only to be kidnapped and killed like your friends were!"

"But he got to Robin," Allye said softly. "She's my mentor. My boss. My friend. I know if you're with me, I'll be safe."

"No," Gray said for the thousandth time.

"I know you're worried about me, but if we talk to the guys, they'll think of something that will help keep me safe."

"Do you remember when I told you about what happened to me, what ultimately made me quit the SEALs?" Gray asked in a harsh tone. Allye didn't even recognize this Gray, and he was scaring her.

"Yes, Gray, but—"

"How I had to sit there and watch those bastards hurt a woman right in front of me?"

"Yes," Allye tried again. "But this isn't—"

"They wanted me to do something I didn't want to do. Tell them something I didn't want to tell them. And they were hurting others in order to achieve that. *That's* what's happening here, Allye. Nightingale is doing the exact same thing to you. He's trying to use *them* to get to *you*. But you know what? Back then, when I was in that fucking joke of a house, I knew all along that if I broke, and I told those assholes what they wanted to hear, they were going to beat and rape those women and kill me anyway. They just wanted me to suffer. That's it. It's the same thing Nightingale is doing. He's *not* going to let Robin go if you return to San Francisco. He's going to use her to make you suffer. Probably torture her in front of you. So there's no point in you going back. If you do, you're signing your death warrant."

"And if I don't, I'm signing Robin's," Allye protested.

First thing that morning, they'd gotten word that Robin had been reported missing an hour earlier. Her boss. The woman who had been nothing but supportive and understanding and sympathetic to Allye. She'd agreed it was a good idea to stay in Colorado Springs for the time being. And now she was gone.

Rex had called and suggested that maybe it would be best if Allye went back to San Francisco. Maybe then, Nightingale would hold off on killing Robin.

Allye had been arguing with Gray ever since.

It was nearing midmorning . . . and he'd gotten colder and colder with every minute their discussion continued.

"She's going to die either way," he said between clenched teeth.

His voice was so unfeeling, and Allye hated it. Hated the harsh words coming out of his mouth.

"I thought we had something good going here," Gray told her, his eyes narrowed.

"We *do*," Allye insisted.

"And you're willing to just throw it all away. Give yourself over to someone who will abuse you, treat you like shit, and eventually kill you."

Goose bumps broke out on Allye's arms at Gray's words.

"No."

"If you leave, that's what you're doing. You're saying that our relationship is worth less than this asshole. That you'd rather die than trust me to keep you safe."

"Gray!" Allye said sharply. "You're twisting things around. That's *not* what I'm saying. Just because I want to keep my friends from dying doesn't mean that I don't love you!" The words just spilled out. She hadn't really meant to say them now, in the middle of this huge fight, but now that they were out there, she was glad.

He snorted. "Love? Love isn't walking into a firefight without a gun. Love isn't being stupid by walking into the clutches of a man who wants to enslave and possibly kill you. Love isn't saying 'I love you' one second, and turning your back on that love the next." He clutched her shoulders. "If you loved me, you would stay *here*. With me. Safe."

Allye swallowed hard. She hadn't thought Gray was a selfish man. After everything he'd done for her. The danger he'd been in when he'd climbed aboard that boat. After hearing about the other missions he'd been on. She hadn't once thought he was selfish. But hearing him so easily dismiss the lives of others . . . of Robin, her other friends . . . her heart hurt. She knew he'd been through something awful, but it wasn't the same as what Nightingale was doing. The difference was that Gray hadn't *known* the women who had been tortured in front of him.

"He'll just continue to kidnap, torture, and kill other people if I don't go," she implored. "I'm asking—no, I'm *begging* you, Gray. If you have any feelings for me at all, come with me. Help keep me safe while we figure out how to trap this guy. I'm not all that thrilled at being bait, but I'll do it if it'll stop the killing. If you're with me, I know I can get through it without being scared out of my skull."

"I can't," Gray said in defeat, dropping his hands.

He took a step away from her, and Allye's heart broke in two.

"I can't be put in the same situation I was in when I was a SEAL. How do you think I'd feel if I was helpless to do anything, and *you* were the one being tortured in front of me? Did you think about that? I can't go through that again. I won't. Not even for you. Not for anyone."

"But it won't be just you and me. The other guys will be there too. We can work together to stop him," Allye pleaded. She couldn't let this go. Couldn't let this be the end of them.

"You can't guarantee that," Gray said softly.

"And you can't guarantee that I won't be hit by a car tomorrow or that I won't have a sudden heart attack. *Life* isn't guaranteed, Gray. We have to live the life we're given to the fullest. If I did nothing, stayed here and let more and more people die, what kind of life would I have?"

"At least you'd be alive to live it," he responded.

Allye stared at the man whom she loved with all her heart. He wasn't going to change his mind.

She was terrified to go back to California, but she would've been stronger with him by her side. Protecting her. Guiding her. Giving her advice on what she should and shouldn't do. He was the expert, not her. But he was disappointing her right now. When things got tough, he wanted her to hide out and think only of herself. She couldn't do it.

He didn't know her. Not if he thought she'd be okay with staying here while others suffered.

Knowing the answer she was going to get, she still tried once more. "Please come with me, Gray. Be by my side, like you've been almost since this started. Help me swim the last ten miles to shore. I can do it if you're with me. Without you, I'll end up being eaten by sharks."

"No," he said wearily. "I won't have anything to do with you offering yourself up on a silver platter to that asshole. If you go, you're on your own. I honestly thought you were the woman I was going to spend the rest of my life with. You know why I have this huge house? Because I want kids. Lots of them. And for the first time, I thought I'd found the woman I wanted to give me those children. But if you're willing to give up our future, our kids, you aren't the woman I thought you were."

They stared at each other for a long moment.

Allye felt the tears well up from somewhere hidden. From a place she'd buried so deeply, she hadn't thought it would ever come to light again.

Water filled her eyes and spilled over. She didn't take her gaze from Gray's. The tears flowed as if a faucet had been turned on inside her. They dripped from her cheeks onto the floor, and still neither of them moved.

She didn't bother asking him again. Begging him. He'd broken her heart, and it would never be the same. Talking about children was a low blow. He knew how she felt about them. They'd talked about it one night. How she was scared to have kids because she'd never had a good role model for a mother.

He'd reassured her that she'd make a wonderful mother. That she was amazing with the children at the dance studio. They all loved her. He'd even said that her experiences growing up would serve as a reminder of what *not* to do with her own children and would make her a better mother.

Now the dream of ever having kids had withered and died with his words.

He stared at her, his face impassive, before he turned and headed for the garage.

Allye heard his car start up and the garage door close as he left. And still the tears came. Twenty years' worth of pent-up emotions flowed out of her eyes. Even as she turned and grabbed her cell phone, the tears fell.

She texted the one person she knew would help her end the killings once and for all. Rex.

Gray might not help her, but she knew Rex would. He wanted to find and kill Nightingale even more than the rest of the team did.

Yeah, Rex and the other guys would help her. It would suck doing it without Gray's support, but she was damned if she did and damned if she didn't.

She couldn't stay, knowing she was signing countless death warrants. Couldn't have that on her conscience. But she also knew Gray would hate her if she left. Knew he wouldn't easily forgive her. Even if she did live through whatever was waiting for her in San Francisco, she and Gray wouldn't get back together. He'd turned his back on her, and she was defying him. They were done.

Gray drove around aimlessly for quite a while before deciding to take the winding road up to Pikes Peak. He hadn't been up there for years, and today seemed like a good day for it. As the road twisted and curved upward, he thought about Allye.

Maybe he'd moved too fast with her. He'd certainly been attracted to her from the very beginning, but lust didn't make a good relationship foundation, obviously.

Hadn't she heard him when he'd told her what had happened that day so long ago over in Afghanistan? How he'd felt? Hadn't she understood what it had done to him to be helpless, to watch women be tortured and abused in front of him?

By refusing to allow her to go back to California, he was saving her from feeling the same anguish. She might be upset now, but she'd see reason. She had to.

He parked the car and got out, amazed anew at how thin the air seemed at fourteen thousand feet. He bypassed the small gift shop and restaurant and headed for the boulders off to the side. He sat about ten feet below the only building on the mountain and gazed down at the city of Colorado Springs.

It was a beautiful day. There were big, white, fluffy clouds lazily floating by, and the sky was a bright blue. It was the kind of day that made you happy to be alive. Gray almost wished it was cloudy and rainy; it would fit his mood better.

He glanced at his watch. He'd been gone for a couple of hours. He knew he probably should get back, but he couldn't make himself move yet. He didn't want to fight with Allye. He just wanted to keep her safe. And going back to California was definitely *not* safe.

Gray was so lost in his head, he didn't hear or see the little boy approaching until he was sitting right beside him.

"Hi," he said.

"Hey," Gray replied.

"Whatcha doin'?"

"Just thinking."

"Hmmm. Isn't this cool?" the little boy asked, using his arm to indicate the view in front of him.

"It sure is."

"My house is over there," he said, pointing off to the south. "We moved here two years ago. Before we lived here, we were in Georgia and Washington and California. It didn't snow much there, but here it does. I really liked skiing when we lived in Washington, but we had to drive really far to do it, and it rained a lot. I mean a *lot.* Is this your first time up here? It's weird how it's kinda hard to breathe, huh? My mom says it's because we're *way* up in the air. Did you get sick on your way up here? The road was so curvy, I almost puked, but Mom let me roll down the window and get some fresh air, and I felt better. Do you get carsick? My brother does all the time. It's why he's not here today. He totally would've barfed if he was in the car. Gross!"

Gray smiled at the boy's prattling and nodded distractedly. He continued on, talking about his teacher, his school, how he thought it was unfair that his older brother got the bigger room, and how, after they left the top of Pikes Peak, his mom was going to take him to get an ice cream.

"So . . . where are your parents?" Gray asked when the kid took a breath. He had no doubt the youngster could babble on forever, but he really wasn't in the mood, and he figured he'd been polite long enough.

"My mom's shopping. She loves to shop. No matter where we go, my dad says she could find someplace to spend money. My dad's in the Army. He's currently overseas being brave."

"He is, huh?"

"Yup. He didn't want to go. I heard him and my mom arguing the night before he left. She didn't want him to go neither. She said she was scared he was going to die and leave us alone."

"What did he say in reply?" Gray asked, interested now in spite of himself.

"He said that he was kinda scared too. But that serving his country was more important in the big picture. That he never wanted to leave us, but if something happened, he knew we'd be okay. Mom asked him how did he know, and he said because he married the most amazing woman on the planet, and if the shit hit the fan, he trusted her to do the right thing."

Gray froze and stared at the little boy, who was still looking out at the view. He kept talking.

"Mom cried, and Dad hugged her and told her not to cry, that she rarely cried and she shouldn't waste her tears on him. Then they started kissing, which was gross, so I went back to my room. When I grow up, I want to be in the Army too. I want to serve my country just like my dad." He looked up at Gray then. "Were you in the Army?"

Gray shook his head. "Navy," he croaked.

"Oh. My dad says sailors aren't as brave as soldiers because they stay out on their boats while the *real* fighting is on land."

Gray could've set the boy straight, but he was still thinking about his earlier words.

A woman called the boy's name, and he stood. "It was nice meeting you, mister."

"Same," Gray said absently, and didn't look back as the boy climbed up the rocks to his mom.

He thought back to his argument with Allye earlier that morning. It hadn't penetrated through his anger then, but now it did.

She'd been crying. *He'd* made her cry.

She hadn't shed a single tear when they'd been in the middle of the ocean. She hadn't cried when she'd heard about Jessie or Melany. She hadn't even cried when she'd found out that Robin had been taken. She'd flat-out *told* him that she hadn't cried since she was a little kid. That she'd realized it did no good and no one cared.

But *he'd* made her cry.

He could still see her standing in front of him with rivulets of tears coursing down her cheeks, dripping off her chin.

Gray scrubbed a hand over his face and tried to banish the image from his mind, but he couldn't.

How could she ask him to let her not only go back to California, but to go with her? He wouldn't be able to go on if something happened to her. Especially knowing what a sadistic son of a bitch Nightingale was.

How could he go while knowing she was purposely putting her life in danger?

But how could he not?

Gray sighed. The bottom line was that this wasn't Afghanistan. She wasn't one of those nameless women who had been used to break him. She was Allye. Tough, smart, resilient. And she'd said it several times—if he was there with her, they'd be stronger as a team. Just like they'd been in the ocean.

Knowing he was going to have to do the hardest thing he'd ever done in his life—namely, watch the woman he loved put herself in danger—Gray stood. He wasn't happy about it, but it was the right decision. She could no more sit back and allow her friends to be hurt and killed than he could.

Allye might be walking into the lion's den, but he'd make damn sure he was right there with her. He and the rest of the team would figure out something so they could keep tabs on her no matter where she went.

If Nightingale got his hands on her, which honestly seemed pretty likely, they could follow him and get to her before he did anything.

Which, he knew, was what Allye had been proposing all along. She wasn't stupid. Far from it.

As he hurried back to his car to make the long drive back down the mountain, Gray thought about the argument from a different standpoint. What if it was one of the guys who was missing? Ro or Black or Ball? Would the rest of the team sit back and do nothing if the threat of them acting would increase the likelihood of their friend being tortured? Would he refuse to go because it would remind him of that long-ago incident? Of course not. He wouldn't let one of them die because he wanted to stay safe.

But that's exactly what he'd asked Allye to do. And that wasn't fair.

He picked up his phone to call her, to apologize and tell her he'd changed his mind and they'd talk when he got home, but he didn't have any service. Swearing, he started his Audi and turned toward the exit. He'd wait until he got home. Then grovel as he asked for her forgiveness.

He should've come to his senses when he saw her tears. Should've known this wasn't something she'd propose lightly. He'd fucked up. Huge. And he needed to fix it. He just hoped Allye would forgive him.

Allye chewed on her lip as she sat stiffly in her seat on the private jet. She'd texted Rex the second Gray had left, and within twenty minutes, Ro had been at the door, ready to take her to the airport. Ball and Meat had met them there, and they'd taken off almost as soon as the plane's door had been secured.

She was scared to death to be headed back to San Francisco, but she had to go.

"Any word on Robin?" she asked Meat.

"Not yet."

"Are you sure you want to do this, love?" Ro asked.

Allye nodded but said, "No. But Rex promised that no matter what happened, you guys would have my back."

"He's right," Ball said. "Gray might have his head up his ass, but we aren't going to lead you to the wolves and leave you on your own."

"It's too close to what happened to him before," Allye said, defending Gray even though he'd broken her heart. "I don't blame him for not wanting to come."

"Well, I do," Ro complained. "Damn wanker."

Meat's laptop rang with an incoming email. He read it, then looked up at her. "Okay, here's the deal. Rex talked with someone out in California who will meet us when we land. He's going to put a tracking device just under your skin. So no matter where you go, we can find you."

Allye stared at him in confusion. "What, like a microchip in a dog?"

Meat nodded. "Pretty much."

"Seriously?" Allye asked.

"Seriously. Rex thought about giving you an external tracker. He's got a friend who's outfitted several women with them, just in case, but they've had some issues because they're removable. If Nightingale strips you all the way down, even removes your jewelry, then it won't work. So the best thing is to make you trackable in a way that can't be removed or disabled. Unless he cuts a chunk out of your skin or something."

Allye winced.

Ball leaned over and smacked Meat on the back of the head.

"Ow! What was that for?" Meat complained, rubbing the spot.

"I don't think she needed to hear that," Ball said, indicating Allye with a tilt of his head.

"It's okay," she said quickly, swallowing the bile that had risen up in her throat. "I mean, it's good I know what *could* happen, right?"

"It's not going to happen, love," Ro said calmly. "What's the plan?" he asked Meat.

"Oh, well, Black and Arrow will meet us at the plane with the guy. The chip is still in its trial phase, and he agreed to let us use it as long as he could help monitor the data. Rex thought it best to insert it in the back of her thigh. It shouldn't be obvious there, and it's not a place Nightingale would think to look. It's got a GPS transmitter, so we can track her using a handheld device. In fact, I think Rex is looking into getting some for us. Think about it. If something happens like what happened to Allye and Gray, we could go right to them in the middle of hundreds of miles of ocean."

As Meat continued to extol the virtues of the internal GPS tracker, Allye tuned him out. She gazed out the window and tried to control the shaking of her hands. She didn't know what the plan was yet, besides being injected with a microchip-like thing as if she really was an animal, but she couldn't complain about that. It made her feel better knowing they'd be able to find her no matter what.

She just wished Gray was here. This whole thing would be easier with him by her side. He probably would've made some sort of joke about the tracker and made her laugh. But she certainly wasn't laughing now.

Unbidden, a tear fell out of her eye. Then another. Before she knew it, she was crying once again. Damn it all to hell.

"Allye?" Gray called when he finally got home two hours later. It was the middle of the afternoon, and the house was eerily silent. "Allye?" he called again, flicking on a few lights. She wasn't in the kitchen or the living room. He took the stairs up to the second floor two at a time. He needed to find her. To apologize and explain where his head was at.

He opened the master bedroom door quietly, in case she was sleeping . . . and stared at the empty bed.

The sheets were still mussed from their lovemaking that morning, and seeing them made his heart hurt.

Staring at the empty room for a heartbeat, he went to the guest room she'd almost slept in that first night. If she was mad at him, she was probably sleeping in there.

He opened the door and saw that it, too, was empty.

He blinked and turned in a circle. She wasn't there. Where the hell was she?

Gray went back into the master bedroom and glanced around the space. He wasn't sure what he was looking for. Some clue as to where she might have gone, maybe. He looked in the closet—and swore long and low when he realized her suitcase was missing. Flinging open the dresser drawers, he saw that her clothes were gone as well.

"No, no, no," he muttered as he reached for his phone. He dialed her number, and it immediately went to voice mail. He left a quick message. "Kitten, it's me. Please call me back as soon as you get this. I'm sorry. I was an ass. Let me explain. I love you."

As soon as he clicked the button to hang up, Gray dialed his handler's number.

"Rex."

"Rex, it's Gray. Allye's missing."

"She's not missing," Rex said calmly.

A shiver ran up Gray's spine. "What do you mean?"

"She called me hours ago. Said she wanted to go back to California and asked for my help. I asked where *you* were, and she said you'd left. That you didn't want to go with her."

"Fuck! What did you do?" Gray accused.

"Exactly what she asked me to. I helped her."

"So help me God, Rex . . . Where is she?"

"San Francisco."

"How could you do that to her?" Gray shouted. "You know as well as I do that Nightingale will grab her before she's even there a full day!"

"I know."

Gray grit his teeth at the calmness of his handler's voice. "Do you not care?"

"Of course I fucking care," Rex ground out. "I cared about the two women he already killed. I care about the hundreds more he's most certainly kidnapped and killed in the past and will in the future, if he's not stopped."

"Allye's *mine*. You had no right!" Gray said, furious now.

"That's where you're wrong. I had every right—because *you* turned your back on her. Besides, Allye doesn't belong to anyone. She's a smart woman who's concerned about her friends. And she's fucking brave. She's scared, but she's doing it anyway. You know why?" He didn't wait for Gray to answer. "Because she trusts me, and your friends, to keep her safe. She's not stupid. She knows full well that he'll probably nab her, but she's counting on us to come and find her when he does."

Gray's heart hurt. He collapsed on the edge of the mattress, Allye's scent wafting from the sheets up to his nose as he did.

"I know why you said the things you said to her," Rex continued, his voice lowering a bit.

"She told you?"

"No. There's no way that woman would *ever* say one bad thing about you, no matter how much you hurt her. She loves you too much. She just said that because of what happened to you in the past, you couldn't go with her to San Francisco, and that she understood. But I know about Afghanistan, so I know exactly what your argument with Allye would be. Gray—this is not the same situation. Not even close."

He knew it. He'd come to the same conclusion on top of Pikes Peak. "I know, Rex. I came home to tell Allye that."

"She needs you," Rex said quietly. "She's as brave as anyone I've ever known, but she's still scared out of her mind. Having you there would go a long way toward making her able to think more clearly."

Gray sighed. "What's the plan?"

And with those three words, Gray was committed. He could no more sit at home and wait to find out what was happening in California than Allye could. He needed to get there. Now. Needed to be a part of whatever was going to happen to Allye so he could do whatever it took to bring her home, to Colorado, safely.

Nightingale smiled at the older woman in front of him. She wasn't his original target—he much preferred the younger, more beautiful women—but she'd practically walked right into his clutches.

She was quaking with fear, and he loved every second of her distress. He reached out and wrenched off the band of cloth wrapped around her head and eyes, wanting her to see who her new master was. Wanted to see the knowledge in her eyes that she would live or die based on whatever *he* wanted.

He'd dismissed the escort with a flick of his wrist earlier. Having his escorts pose as taxi drivers had been a stroke of genius. Once the women were in the customized cabs, there was no escaping. It was much less risky than snatching them off the streets, as they'd been doing. He'd gotten the idea while watching one of those crime shows one night. It was amazing the things one could learn while watching television.

He walked around his latest acquisition with a serious look on his face. He was having the time of his life, but his pets seemed to obey him better when he looked mean and wasn't smiling.

"Where is Mystic?"

"Who?" the woman asked, her voice trembling. He'd handcuffed her inside one of the vacant cages—one of the twins hadn't made it through her punishment the other night, so he had a free room. The woman was spread-eagle, with her hands cuffed to a beam above her head and her ankles shackled to chains protruding from either side of the wall.

He hadn't stripped her . . . yet. He was saving that for later. He liked to see his pets' terror increase the longer they were with him.

"Allyson Mystic." Nightingale enunciated as if she were a half-wit.

"I-I don't know. She left, took a leave of absence, and hasn't returned."

Nightingale stepped into her personal space and put his hand around her neck, lifting her chin as he did.

"I want her," he said evenly. "And if I don't get her, *you'll* pay the price. So the more you can tell me about her, the easier your time here will be. Got it?"

He loved watching her pupils dilate with fear. He couldn't wait to see Mystic's do the same thing. One blue eye and one brown, the irises almost disappearing when her pupils enlarged. He wouldn't bother trying to make this woman look like his Mystic because she was way too old to pass for her, even in the dark. But he could still have fun. She was a dancer too; maybe he'd see exactly how flexible she was. He'd start with the splits. Every dancer worth her salt could do the splits, right?

Nightingale let her neck go and walked over to where the chain attached to her right ankle was connected to the wall. It had a handy crank, and he smiled to himself as he slowly turned it.

Wiping the smile off his face, he turned to face his new pet. "Can you do the splits?"

"Wh-What?" she asked, her eyes huge in her wrinkled face.

"The splits. How flexible are you?" He cranked the wheel once more, and her foot slid out three more inches. Nightingale saw the second she realized what he was doing. The blood drained from her face, leaving her a nice shade of white.

"Please don't! I'll do whatever you want."

"What I want is Mystic."

"I don't know where she is!" the woman cried as he turned the crank another full rotation.

"Then I guess you'll be doing the splits today, won't you?" Nightingale said. "The more you can tell me what I want to know, the better off you'll be."

The woman started crying then, trying to turn her hips so she was facing the direction her leg was being pulled, but no matter how she moved, nothing stopped the relentless stretching of her leg.

Nightingale loved this part. Loved hearing their screams of pain. Loved knowing he was in charge of whatever happened to them. He turned the crank again and couldn't keep the smile from his face as she screamed. She wasn't even close to doing the splits yet. What fun!

"Sir?" a voice asked from the speaker in the corner.

Nightingale frowned. He didn't like to be interrupted. "What?" he barked.

"You asked to be notified if there were any sightings."

All irritation left. "And have there been?"

"Yes, sir. She just entered the theatre."

Nightingale secured the chain, leaving the woman standing with her legs way too far apart to be comfortable. Good. He'd let her think about what was to come. He walked up to her and leaned close, smacking her cheek. "Today's your lucky day. Looks like my Mystic has come home. Soon you'll have company."

"So you'll let me go?" the woman asked hopefully.

Nightingale laughed. "Let you go? Oh no, you're way more useful to me here. I know my Mystic is a tender soul. She won't want to see you get hurt. But you will if she doesn't obey my every command. Anything that happens to you, know that it's your precious lead dancer's fault."

The woman started blubbering again, begging to stand up straight, begging to be let go, but Nightingale had already tuned her out. He didn't want her. Didn't care about her. He had better, more important things to do. He needed to bring his unique pet home. And this was something he had to do himself. She was too valuable to trust to anyone else.

Rubbing his hands together, Nightingale left the enormous underground bunker and headed up the stairs.

He closed the innocuous door behind him, knowing no one would ever guess that below the San Rafael Exotic Animals Refuge were his greatest treasures.

Chapter Fourteen

Allye knew her breathing was too fast, but she couldn't help it. She walked faster than normal down the sidewalk toward the Dance Theatre of San Francisco. She'd come straight from the airport, and Ball had driven her as close to the theatre as he could. He'd had to drop her off a block away because of traffic, though, and every time Allye passed a guy, she wondered if he was Nightingale.

Her hair was pulled back in a ponytail, and she wore a pair of jeans and a formfitting blouse. She carried her purse and fiddled with the strap as she walked.

She knew the guys were out there, watching. Meat was in the apartment next to hers, monitoring her on his computer. Rex's contact, who'd turned out to be a veterinarian, of all things—the irony wasn't lost on her—had met the plane and come aboard and inserted the tracker into the back of her thigh.

It hadn't hurt all that much, merely like a regular shot. But she'd seen for herself the small dot on the map that had indicated it was working. Her thigh itched, but she tried to ignore it.

She was on her way to the theatre to see the other dancers for the first time since the abductions had begun. She didn't know what her reception would be. Didn't know if they were aware the kidnappings were related to her—if they'd blame her and hate her for them, or if they'd be glad to see her.

She took a deep breath and opened the door. She walked through the lobby and the door off to the side that said "Employees Only." She continued past the dressing-room doors and went straight to the common room. She took a moment to calm herself before entering.

Immediately, she was engulfed in hugs, and everyone was talking at the same time.

"Oh my God, girlfriend, welcome back!"

"We're so glad you're here."

"Did you hear about Jessie and the others?"

"I can't believe Robin is missing now."

She gave everyone hugs, then answered their questions about her absence as best she could, leaving out the fact that their friends had been kidnapped and killed because someone was obsessed with *her*.

Hours later, after she'd had her fill of everyone, it was time to go. They'd spent the afternoon talking about what was happening. It was a giant counseling session of sorts, but by the end of the day, Allye certainly didn't feel any better. Everyone had formed a kind of buddy system, which she was gratified to see. No one went anywhere by themselves. They came to work in pairs, and they left that way too.

Allye knew Ball and Arrow and the others were watching out for her, but she still felt safer walking out with a young dancer named Boyd when it was time to leave. He lived a couple of blocks from her and was happy to share a taxi.

Allye hadn't been back to her apartment yet, but was actually looking forward to it. It wasn't much, but it was her space. She'd gotten used to Gray's huge house, and thought her studio apartment was going to feel a little claustrophobic, but she supposed she had to get used to it.

She hadn't decided if she could forgive Gray yet. She had thought she'd known the kind of man he was, but now she wasn't so sure. He'd hurt her. Bad. But even though she was upset with him, she still wished he was with her. The conflicting feelings only confused her more, and she vowed to not think about it right now. She'd make a decision after

Nightingale was dead. She knew without a doubt that he would end up that way. And she was glad.

"It really is good to have you back," Boyd said as they exited the theatre and said their goodbyes to the other dancers. Some were headed to the BART, and others were walking home. She and Boyd headed to the lone taxi sitting at the curb.

"Thanks," Allye told him.

Boyd leaned over when the driver rolled down his window, and asked, "Franklin and Washington in Nob Hill?"

"Sure," the driver said. "No problem."

Allye didn't bother looking at him, other than to notice he was older than she was by a couple of decades. He had unremarkable black hair and looked to have a slight paunch. She figured it probably came from sitting all day, driving a taxi. Hard to get exercise when you were in a car.

She scooted over, and Boyd climbed in next to her.

"Long day?" the driver asked.

"Yeah," Boyd said. "But good. My friend here has been gone, and it's her first day back."

"Welcome home," the driver said, looking at her through the rear-view mirror.

The taxi had a plastic divider between the back seat and the front, probably to protect the driver from any crazy people he was transporting. There was a small sliding door that was currently open, allowing them to talk back and forth easily.

"Thanks," Allye returned.

"Where you been?"

"She was in Colorado," Boyd answered for her. He'd always been super friendly, and was very popular with the patrons at the theatre because he was so upbeat and happy. "She met a *boooooy*," he teased, smiling at Allye.

She rolled her eyes at him. "Shut up, Boyd."

He laughed.

"A man, huh? Things didn't work out?" the driver asked.

Allye shifted uncomfortably. She'd never been one to talk about herself with strangers, and the pain of her fight with Gray was still just too raw. She shrugged.

"Yeah, uprooting your entire life for someone is never a good idea. It rarely works out."

Allye pressed her lips together, not wanting to discuss it.

"But you're a pretty little thing, so I'm sure you'll find another boyfriend without too much trouble. Maybe you two are dating?" the taxi driver asked, his eyes flicking from the road to the mirror.

"Us? Naw, she's the wrong gender," Boyd teased. "I like my partners a little more manly."

Allye smiled at Boyd and tried to ignore the driver. She could feel his eyes on her through the mirror as she and Boyd talked about nothing in particular. All too soon, they pulled up in front of Boyd's apartment complex.

"I'll come by tomorrow morning, and we can ride in together," Boyd told her. "Eight o'clock work?"

Allye nodded. "That's great. Thanks, Boyd. I appreciate it."

"No problem," he said. He pulled out some cash and handed it to her to pay for his portion of the taxi. He then leaned over and gave her an air kiss. "See you later, girlfriend."

He shut the cab door behind him, and Allye watched as he put in the building's door code and entered his complex.

"Where to?"

Allye jerked in surprise, then laughed uneasily at herself for being so jumpy. "I'm only a couple of blocks away, on the other side of Lafayette Park. On the corner of Webster and California."

"Just sit back and relax, pretty Mystic. I'll have you home in no time."

She nodded and sat back, leaning her head against the headrest and closing her eyes. She was exhausted. It seemed like it had been forever since she'd had the fight with Gray, instead of that morning.

She felt the car begin moving, and sighed. She had no idea what she had to eat in her apartment after all these weeks, but she'd make do.

Allye was thinking about what she wanted for dinner when she heard an odd sound. She opened her eyes and picked up her head to see that the driver had closed the plastic partition between the seats.

He was looking at her in the mirror again . . . but this time there was something in his eyes she didn't like.

Suddenly, she realized . . . he'd called her Mystic.

How did he know her stage name? She hadn't told him, and she didn't think Boyd had mentioned it.

Just then, a plume of smoke rose from the floorboard.

She coughed and immediately went for the door handle and tugged. The door didn't open, and they continued driving down the street as if nothing was wrong.

Allye pounded on the plastic partition and tried to open it, but the handle of the little door was on the other side. Smoke was filling the back seat now, and she lifted her shirt to put it over her nose and mouth, but it was no use. She began to feel dizzy and nauseated.

Recognizing the buildings they were flying past, she knew they weren't headed toward her apartment complex anymore. They were going the wrong way.

This was it. She'd known it was inevitable that Nightingale would have her captured again, but she stupidly hadn't expected him to do it so soon.

She tried to roll the window down, but it, too, was locked. She could barely see through the thick smoke encasing the back seat now, but she looked up into the mirror and saw the man watching her once more. A sense of satisfaction was easy to read in his expression.

"Let it happen, pet. Don't fight me. You've led me on a merry chase, but now you're mine. All mine," he said as his eyes flicked between the road in front of him and the rearview mirror.

Horrified, Allye realized that the taxi driver wasn't just an escort.

It was *him*. Nightingale. He'd come for her himself this time.

Blackness began to creep in at the sides of her eyes, and she fell over onto the seat cushions, still coughing and trying to fight whatever drug he'd used on her. But it was pointless.

Her last thought before she passed out was that she hoped Rex's men really were watching her, because she was in big trouble.

Chapter Fifteen

Gray paced back and forth in front of the San Francisco International Airport. He'd had to fly commercial since the plane and pilot Rex usually used had already left with the rest of the team and Allye. Arrow was supposed to be picking him up, but he'd been waiting an hour and hadn't seen him yet.

Anxious to see Allye now that he was in California, and apologize, he resented the wait. Even worse, no one was answering his texts or phone calls—and that worried him. A fuck of a lot. Especially because Meat *always* answered. The man was glued to his cell as if it were another appendage. For him not to answer meant something was seriously wrong.

And he had a bad feeling it had to do with Allye.

After another fifteen minutes of waiting, his phone finally rang. It was Ro.

"Ro, thank fuck. Where are you guys?"

"He got her," Ro said, not beating around the bush. "We were tracking her, but then everything became a huge clusterfuck."

"What?" Gray said, outraged. "How the fuck could you guys let him get his hands on her? I thought you were all watching her?"

"We were!" Ro insisted. "Arrow was in a taxi behind the one she got into with another dancer. But apparently his driver was a stickler for following every single bloody traffic light, and Arrow fell too far behind Allye's taxi to keep his eye on them. Black was outside her apartment, posing as a homeless guy, but of course the taxi never stopped there. And Ball was following in a rental, but someone ran a red light and sideswiped him."

"And you, Ro? Where the fuck were you?"

"I was waiting outside the theatre. I was supposed to escort her back to her apartment on the cable cars, but at the last minute, she sent me a text and told me she'd be going with one of her coworkers, to try to disguise the fact that she had a bodyguard."

"Dammit!" Gray swore, running a hand over his head in agitation. "Was she going out of her way to *try* to get kidnapped?"

"Honestly? No," Ro answered as if Gray's question wasn't rhetorical. "She met my eyes before she got into the taxi, as if making sure it was okay with me. I didn't want to make a scene outside the theatre . . . but obviously I should've hauled her ass out of that taxi and taken her home myself."

"Rex told me she has a tracker, right?" Gray asked. "Why aren't you guys there taking care of that asshole and getting her back?"

"The bloody signal disappeared," Ro said. "One second it was there, the next, gone."

"Fuck!" Gray said, kicking the building he was standing next to in frustration. Rex had briefed him on the tracker Allye had inserted in the back of her leg. He wasn't happy they were experimenting on her, but on the other hand, he was glad the team had some way of following her every move. He knew as well as all of them did that simple surveillance wasn't enough. Especially not with someone like Nightingale, who'd gotten very good at flying under the radar. "Start at the beginning. What happened, exactly? How'd Nightingale get his hands on her if she was in a taxi?"

"She went to the theatre as planned and left with one of the other dancers, as I told you. They took the taxi, and after the other dancer was let out a couple of blocks from her apartment, the taxi didn't stop at her place. Meat said at first he thought maybe she was going to get something to eat, but when the vehicle went across the Golden Gate Bridge toward Sausalito, he realized something was wrong."

"Where are you?" Gray barked, heading back inside to the rental car counter. He was done waiting for someone to come get him. Besides, they were all too busy. He'd prefer they stay on the hunt for Allye, not divert to pick his ass up.

"Meat is still at Allye's apartment complex, trying to get the signal to work. The rest of us are spread out around where the signal last pinged."

"Send me the coordinates. I'll be on my way as soon as possible."

"Ten-four."

"Ro?" Gray said quickly before his friend could hang up.

"Yeah?"

"Thanks for being here for her."

"We all knew you'd show up sooner or later," Ro said, no doubt whatsoever in his tone. "You love her, and she loves you. Nothing can get in the way of that."

"I'm counting on it," Gray said. "Send the coordinates. I'll get there as soon as I can."

"Drive safe. You can't help her if you get in an accident."

"I will." Gray clicked off the phone and greeted the employee behind the counter. While she was busy getting his rental agreement ready, Gray tapped his foot impatiently, not able to keep still. He couldn't think about what was happening to Allye. Not now. He had to keep it together. She'd be okay. She had to be. Any other outcome was unacceptable.

~

Allye came awake slowly. She was confused for a moment and shook her head, trying to clear it. She started to stretch, feeling cramped, and was surprised when she couldn't fully straighten her legs.

Memory came flooding back, and her eyes popped open and looked around in alarm.

She was in a large cage, just like the man on the boat had promised she would be when she was delivered to her new "master." That seemed like a lifetime ago.

She was wearing her panties and bra, but the rest of her clothes had been taken. Her hair was loose around her head, her ponytail holder gone. The cage was in a small room with no windows. There was a concrete floor, and the walls also looked to be made out of concrete. It was chilly, and goose bumps rose on her skin.

Shifting to her knees, Allye tested the strength of the bars around her. Solid. There was a padlock on the cage door, so she couldn't get out that way. Sitting back on her ass and hugging her knees, Allye tried not to panic.

"They're coming," she told herself quietly. "They know where you are, they're coming."

The words helped calm her, if only because she fiercely hoped they were true.

How long she'd been left alone, she had no idea, but when the door to the room suddenly flew open, she jolted in fright.

Two men entered. They were wearing one-piece olive-green jumpsuits and baseball caps on their heads.

"Please help me!" she begged as they came toward her. "I'm being held without my consent."

The men ignored her and crouched on either side of her cage. They looked at each other, then one said, "On the count of three. One, two, *three.*"

Allye squealed in surprise when they lifted the cage she was in and began to carry her out of the room.

"Hey, did you hear me? I was kidnapped! Open this and let me out!"

Again, they acted as if she hadn't spoken. She held on to the bars of the cage and frantically looked around, trying to figure out where she was and what was happening.

The men carried her into another room, this one with a huge window in one wall, and roughly put the cage down. Allye's teeth rattled together as the cage vibrated with the force of the drop. The men turned to leave.

"Hey, seriously, you can't just leave me here! *Help me.* For the love of God, help me!"

One man left, but the second turned around before he exited. He looked right at her and said, "Sorry, pet. There's no help here. You belong to T.B. now. If I were you, I'd do exactly what he tells you to." Then he, too, was out the door.

Allye screamed in frustration, the sound echoing in the smaller room. She frantically pulled at the bars once more, but again they didn't budge.

At that moment, she wished she'd listened to Gray. She wanted to be back in his house. Waking him up by putting her mouth on him, knowing he'd get rough and take her exactly how he wanted . . . and exactly how she loved.

She wanted his arms around her. Wanted to be warm and safe. But no. She had to be all noble, and now here she was. She'd made her bed, now she had to lie in it.

The door opened once more, and Allye flinched. The taxi driver walked in, although now he didn't look anything like he had before. He was wearing a pristine gray suit with a red tie. His hair was combed, and he looked impeccable. But the expression on his face was one she remembered quite well. Cold and hard.

He walked over to the cage she was in and squatted beside it. "You're awake," he said.

Allye rolled her eyes. She couldn't help it. "And you're the master of understatements," she quipped.

His eyes narrowed. "Is that any way to talk to your master, Mystic?"

"You aren't my anything," she protested.

The man tsked as he shook his head. "I was so hoping you would be more cooperative."

"Let me go," she said, knowing he wouldn't, but needing to say it anyway.

"No. You might as well get comfortable, as this is your new home for the foreseeable future."

"You can't do this! I have a life, friends. You can't just kidnap me, lock me away, and tell me this is my new home."

"I just did," he said flatly.

"I don't understand," Allye said, desperate for answers. "If you could've kidnapped me in a *taxi* at any point, why put me on that stupid boat? Why go to so much trouble?"

Nightingale smirked. "I have a reputation to keep. I'm the Boss. The man behind the scenes. I only allow key personnel—those most loyal—to know which pets are my own. Where I keep them and how my operation works. Unfortunately, where you're concerned, I've learned that if I want something done right, I have to do it myself. I made an *exception* for you, Mystic. You should feel honored that I came after you, and didn't send my minions this time."

"What do you want?" Allye asked, her voice quivering.

"*You*, Mystic. And I got you. You're mine, and you can just forget about whoever you were cavorting with back in Colorado. You'll never see him again—and I'll have to punish you for *daring* to think you could be with anyone other than me."

He stood then and headed back toward the door.

"Hey," she called, "you can't just leave me here! I need to use the restroom. And I'm thirsty."

He turned at the door and shrugged. "Food and water are only for pets who behave. You, Mystic, haven't earned them yet. As far as using the bathroom? When you've earned it, I'll take you out of your crate. Until then, you can potty in the corner like the other smart animals."

Allye looked to where he indicated with his head and saw some newspapers scattered on the floor. She stared back at him in horror.

He chuckled. "God, I love seeing that look in your beautiful eyes. Has anyone told you how unique you are? It's why I had to have you, you know. With your one brown and one blue eye, and your hair . . . you're a collector's item. And now you belong to *me*. I wonder . . . are the color of your eyes genetic?"

She stared at him, not able to get one word past the lump in her throat.

"I'm betting they are. I've done some research. I guess we'll find out with our first child, won't we? Now be good. I'll be back later with a special surprise."

And with that, the man Allye knew had to be Nightingale shut the door behind him as he left, the sound of a lock clicking loudly in the bare room.

"Nooooo!" Allye wailed, sitting on her butt and kicking at the bars as hard as she could. All she managed to do was hurt the bottoms of her feet.

Interestingly enough, the tears she'd so easily shed earlier had dried up. She was more frightened than she'd ever been in her life, but the tears wouldn't come. She had the morose thought that only Gray could make her cry. Lucky him.

She huddled in the corner of her crate and rocked back and forth. "Where are you, guys? I'm here. Come and get me."

~

"The signal ended here," Black said, looking through a pair of binoculars at the entrance to the San Rafael Exotic Animals Refuge. There were a few people still wandering around even though it was getting dark and the refuge was about to close.

The park contained at least a hundred different wild animals. Lions, tigers, hippopotami, giraffes . . . the list went on and on.

Ball, Black, Ro, Gray, and Arrow were staking out the refuge from a ridge about half a mile away. They were all lying on their bellies, camouflaged by the trees surrounding them, scoping out the last place the transmitter in Allye's body had pinged.

"Isn't this place too public to hold kidnapped women?" Ball asked. "I mean, there are people with cameras everywhere."

"Look," Gray said, pointing to the right at a truck pulling into a back entrance reserved only for refuge employees. "Look at the hangtag on the mirror."

"Fuck me," Arrow said in a low voice. "That's a paw print on it, isn't it? Just like the witness said he saw on the car the night Melany was found."

"She's here," Gray said with conviction. "I can feel it."

"But why isn't the tracker transmitting?" Ro asked. "Meat said that it was pretty powerful, that there wasn't much that could interfere with it."

Gray put down his binoculars and turned to Ro. "Not much, but some things could. Like what?"

The others also put down their binoculars and concentrated on the conversation.

"Electromagnetic waves, mountains, large objects—any number of things could interfere with it. But that should only be for a short time. Not take it completely off-line like it is now," Black said.

"What if she's underground?" Gray asked slowly, picking his binoculars back up and scanning the property below them.

"Yeah, that could do it. Especially if it's something like a bunker," Ro added.

"Nightingale could've had something like that built under this place easily. And none of the guests walking overhead would have any idea it was there," Ball said.

"I've been to one of these places before," Arrow said. "There were actually underground tunnels and shit so the gamekeepers could get from one place to another, one cage to another, without endangering themselves or disturbing the animals."

"There," Gray said, and all the other men put their binoculars back up to their eyes to see where Gray was indicating. "See that gate there in the back? That's where we need to make entry. After they're closed. It looks like there's a ramp that goes underground. See? Watch that van."

They all watched as a van with the San Rafael Exotic Animals Refuge logo on the side went through an electric gate and disappeared down a ramp.

Gray inched backward until he was on the other side of the copse of trees, and stood. "Call Meat. Let him know."

"We might need to wait until—"

Gray didn't let Ball finish his sentence. "No. That psychopath has Allye. I'm not willing to wait another second longer than necessary. There's no telling what he's already done to her, or what he'll do if we wait."

Ball held up his hands in capitulation.

"Easy, Gray," Black said in a low voice. "Ball's not the one you're pissed at."

Gray took a deep breath and nodded. "I know. But I've played this game before. Nightingale's going to use her boss to make Allye do what he wants."

"Allye's smart. She knows we're coming for her. She isn't going to do anything stupid."

Gray hoped that was true. He knew how tenderhearted his Allye was. She'd put herself in danger if it meant helping someone else. Hell, she'd already done that. He just wasn't sure how far Nightingale was willing to push her.

The men climbed into the two cars they'd driven up to the lookout point. Gray barely listened as the others planned the raid. He couldn't forget the last time he'd seen Allye, with tears coursing down her cheeks. Tears she said she never shed. Tears she'd shed because of him.

Chapter Sixteen

Allye kept silent as Nightingale entered the room hours later. She was stiff and cold from sitting in one position for so long, and cold, and she badly had to pee. He calmly unlocked the door to her cage, and Allye didn't make any sudden movements. She waited to see what he wanted from her.

"Out," he ordered, snapping his fingers.

Hating him more than she'd hated anyone in her entire life, her own mother included, Allye slowly crawled out of the cage. The second she was close enough, Nightingale fastened a wide leather collar around her throat. He pulled her upright by the leather and cinched it tight. Too tight.

Forgetting all about having to pee, more concerned about breathing, she choked and brought her hands up to the strip of leather.

He smacked at them. "Lower your hands."

"Too tight," she croaked.

He tightened it further, staring down at her passively as she gasped for air. Just when she thought she was going to pass out, he loosened it.

"You have no say from here on out. None. If I want your collar tighter, then it'll be tighter. If I tell you to eat, you'll eat. If I tell you to pee, you'll pee. I *own* you, Mystic. You're mine to do whatever I want with."

She didn't respond, simply glared up at him, hoping he could read the hate in her heart.

Allye wasn't sure what he would do about her impertinence—but she hadn't expected him to laugh.

"God, I could look into those beautiful eyes all fucking day. And they're mine . . . all mine." He fastened the collar, then brought out a small padlock and clicked it into place, effectively making sure she wouldn't be able to remove or loosen the leather band of her own accord. Then he attached a leash to the ring at the front of the collar and reached up, fingering the shock of white hair on the side of her head.

"So beautiful and unique," he said, stroking her hair. "After I saw you dance that first time, I briefly debated if I wanted to have you for my own. But then I saw you at the BDSM club I go to all the time. You were like a breath of fresh air. You turned down every man's advances, and I knew then that I had to have you."

Allye gasped. She didn't remember seeing Nightingale at the club the night she'd ended up there with one of the other dancers. There was that pesky karma, having it in for her again. If she hadn't gone that night, would any of this have happened?

Nightingale's hand caressed her hair once more, and Allye wanted to jerk away from him, but with his hand on the leash, she knew she wouldn't get far. Deciding it was probably better to pretend to be docile, she did nothing.

"That's it, pet. Things will go much smoother if you do what I say, when I say." And with that, he jerked down on the leash so hard, she cried out in pain and fell to her hands and knees on the unforgiving concrete floor.

The pain in her knees made tears come to her eyes, but Allye didn't have time to recover because Nightingale was walking out of the room, still holding the leash. She had no choice but to crawl after him, as if she were an animal. It was either that or be dragged. And she had no doubt he *would* drag her if she didn't cooperate.

Vowing vengeance with every inch she had to crawl, Allye tried to look around as they left the room. They went down a hallway about as wide as she was tall, with a series of floor-to-ceiling windows spaced evenly on her right side—and she stared in horror as they passed them.

Behind each window was a room identical to her own. One held a little person, a woman who was huddled in a corner, staring at them with eyes as dead as a corpse. Another held what Allye thought was a woman, but she had tattoos on every inch of her body. When Nightingale passed, the woman leaped up from where she was lying and attacked the window, clawing at it like she really was a wild creature. The whites of her eyes seemed especially bright with the black ink that covered her entire face, including her eyelids.

Nightingale only laughed and kept dragging Allye along.

Behind the next window was a beautiful blonde woman, but she was crying hysterically.

The asshole in front of her growled at seeing her tears. He turned back and explained briefly, "She's upset because I had to put down her twin." He shrugged. "It wasn't working out, having them both. Besides, this one is much more docile. I like her better. But if she doesn't stop her blubbering, I'll give her a reason to fucking cry."

Allye briefly closed her eyes as she crawled behind the insane man holding the leash. She didn't want to see anything else. She couldn't imagine the horrors any of these women had been through, and she definitely didn't want to think about what he might have in store for *her*.

The man stopped at the next window, and Allye saw another naked woman. She was incredibly pale, and her hair was a beautiful white. She was wearing a collar much like Allye's, and was inside a cage. "That's my albino," Nightingale said conversationally. "You and her are two of my most prized possessions. So rare and interesting. She's pregnant," he informed Allye. "I can't wait to see if her baby is an albino like her. It'll be fun to train a pet from the moment she's born."

"And if it's a boy?" Allye asked quietly.

Nightingale shrugged. "Then I'll give him to the tigers for a snack. I've no use for boys."

Allye felt as if she was going to be sick. She'd only seen the four women, but knew Nightingale had probably arranged the selling of hundreds more. Maybe to people just like him, who were keeping the poor women in cages. Abusing them. Treating them like animals.

She was jerked along, and he kept talking. "Although I don't think you should be so concerned with them, Mystic. You should be worrying about yourself. If you do exactly what I tell you, then you'll be fine. Otherwise . . ." He shrugged and let his sentence trail off.

He kept walking until he reached a room at the far end of the corridor. "Are you ready, pet?" But he didn't wait for an answer, throwing open the door and entering the large auditorium-type room.

Allye's knees were thankful when the concrete floor changed to a plush red carpet. There were chairs on either side of an aisle, and what looked like a wooden stage in front of them. She kept crawling behind her kidnapper until he stopped in front of the stage. It was only about a foot higher than the floor.

"Up," he ordered, and Allye carefully stood in front of him. Her knees were red and scraped, and she was having a hard time breathing with how tight the collar was cinched around her neck, but she didn't say a word. She was biding her time. Hoping against hope that every minute she endured whatever this madman had planned was another minute she was closer to being rescued.

"I had this stage made just for you. The first time I saw you dance, I was entranced. After I saw you rebuff man after man in the BDSM club, I knew I had to have you for myself. I wanted you to dance just for me. I still remember the first piece I saw you perform onstage. The number was called 'The Bride's Sister.' Do you remember that one?"

Allye nodded. It wasn't one of her favorite shows because it involved a lot of costume changes and fast dance numbers, but she remembered it.

"Good, pet." He unclipped the leash from the collar and put his hands around her waist.

Allye flinched at his clammy touch. She didn't want him anywhere near her, let alone touching her.

He lifted her as if she weighed no more than a child. He might be older and overweight, but that didn't seem to slow him down at all. He was incredibly strong. He placed her on the edge of the stage. The surface felt abrasive, not smooth like a stage should be. She looked down and saw that it was untreated wood.

"I'm going to get splinters," she said quietly. "The wood is rough."

"I know. It'll give you incentive to dance beautifully the first time," Nightingale said as he leaned into her. "Because if it's not perfect, you'll continue to dance. I don't care if your feet are bloody nubs. You'll do it until I'm satisfied. Understand?"

Allye drew her face away, but he caught her hair in his hand and tugged her head back. It was uncomfortable and made her feel extremely vulnerable. He licked her neck from above the collar to her ear, then whispered, "Dance, pet. And it had better be good."

He dropped her hair and stepped back. Then nodded at someone off to his right.

Allye gasped when one of the men who'd moved her cage earlier stepped into the light holding on to Robin. She was naked—and had a look of such pain in her eyes, Allye recoiled in horror.

"Mystic, I think you know our guest," Nightingale said. "She's been keeping me company until you could get here. She can dance, but she's not you."

Allye slowly backed away from the monster who had kidnapped her. She looked stage right and saw nothing but concrete wall. She looked to the other side and saw the same. There was no backstage and nowhere to go. The only way out was through the door at the back of the room.

Nightingale went over to Robin and grabbed Allye's mentor and friend by the hair, dragging her to the middle of the room, right in front of the stage. The man who'd been holding her slipped up the aisle and out the door, leaving the three of them alone in the makeshift auditorium.

"Every time you mess up, she'll pay the price," Nightingale said in a voice so even, it was scary.

"Don't hurt her!" Allye begged.

"Then don't disobey me, pet," he returned, pulling out a knife and holding it to Robin's throat.

Allye's heart nearly stopped beating. Her eyes locked with Robin's, and the despair and fright she saw there almost had her going to her knees.

But then a funny thing happened. The longer she stared at the older woman, the more determination she saw in Robin's eyes. It was as if, between the two of them, they were sharing strength.

Robin was still alive. The monster hadn't killed her yet. Maybe Allye could still save her.

And for the first time, she truly understood what Gray must have felt when he'd been captured. She was helpless to do anything but exactly what Nightingale wanted.

She knew it didn't matter if she danced perfectly or if she screwed up, he was still going to hurt them both. But if she could hold on for one more minute. Then another. Then another . . . Black, Ro, Arrow, and the others would come. She had to believe that.

Trying to take a deep breath, and failing because of how tight the collar was, Allye did as she was told. She danced.

~

Gray let Arrow take the lead. He didn't want to be point because that would mean his attention would have to be on taking out anyone who got in his way, and the only thing he wanted to worry about was Allye.

Arrow and the others would subdue anyone who tried to stop them, and he'd take care of Allye. It was how it should've been from the moment she'd approached him about wanting to come back to California, but he'd been pigheaded and an ass about it.

So far, they hadn't encountered any resistance. Meat had somehow hacked into the security system around the refuge and turned off the alarms. All they'd had to do was break the lock on the back fence, and they were inside.

There were animal noises all around, but Gray barely heard them. No one knew what to expect when they breached the doors, but they were ready for anything. They'd been on enough rescue missions to know what they found would be either really good or absolutely horrifying.

Gray was betting on the latter.

The five men slipped into a dark hallway as if they were nothing but shadows. Meat's voice in their ears kept them updated on everything going on at the refuge around them via the compound's own security monitors, keeping an eye out for anyone who might come in from behind.

There wasn't even one footstep to be heard as the mercenaries made their way down the hall, toward the music they heard coming from a door at the very end.

As they passed a window, Arrow paused and stared inside. A small light was on in the ceiling, and the team could see a diminutive woman on the other side of the glass. Gray thought she was dead until she blinked. Her mouth opened, and she said something, but the glass was so thick, no one could hear her. Either that, or she wasn't making any sound.

Her tiny finger came up, and she pointed in the direction they were headed. Ball put his finger to his lips, and she nodded.

Gray dreaded seeing what was inside the next room as they approached the window. It was another woman. She was pacing back and forth angrily. The second she saw them, she pounced at the glass, and her mouth opened as if she were screaming.

"Bloody hell," Ro swore almost silently, taking an involuntarily step backward. They all saw that not only was every inch of the woman's skin tattooed, so was her tongue and inner lips.

The group kept walking and barely glanced into the last two rooms. They'd seen enough. Nightingale was going down, and these women would be freed if it was the last thing they did.

As they approached the door at the end of the hall, the music got louder.

Black put his hand on Gray's shoulder. "You in control?" he asked. "You ready to face whatever's behind that door?"

"Allye's behind that door," Gray said almost tonelessly. "I'd face down the devil himself to get to her."

"You just might have to," Ball interjected before nodding at Ro.

Instead of busting through the door as if the hounds of hell were entering, Ro reached out and silently turned the knob, then pushed against the door. It moved inward, and Gray smiled.

They'd learned during one of their very first missions together that sometimes it was more effective to sneak into where you wanted to go, and to always check to see if the door was unlocked before busting it down.

Watching Ro push the door slowly, hoping against hope it didn't squeak, Gray and the other Mountain Mercenaries entered the room, and prepared to take down the most notorious sex trader they'd ever encountered.

~

"Higher!" Nightingale barked when the pirouette Allye had just performed didn't meet his expectations.

"I'm doing the best I can," she protested, breathing hard and wincing as another splinter gouged into the ball of her foot.

Without a word, Nightingale placed the tip of the knife he was holding against Robin's arm and drew it downward, a line of red welling up in its wake.

"Don't argue with me, pet," Nightingale said. "You're killing her."

She wanting to yell at him that *she* wasn't the one killing Robin, who looked pale and weak on her knees in front of him—*he* was. But Allye kept her mouth shut and went back to her position on the stage to start where she'd left off.

She'd been dancing for a while now—she had no idea how long—but she couldn't seem to do anything right. Probably because her feet were bleeding from the coarse floor, and every time she stumbled, Nightingale hurt Robin.

Allye was in the middle of a spin when she thought she saw something in the back of the dark room. There was a spotlight on her, and the rest of the room was dark. She held her breath and continued dancing, praying that what she'd seen was help coming for her and Robin.

She'd been concentrating so hard on the back of the room, Allye had forgotten to spot as she spun. As a result, when she stopped, she was so dizzy that she staggered and fell to her knees.

Nightingale was furious. "No, pet, no! My Mystic doesn't fall over! Stupid! So *stupid*!"

Allye saw him reach for Robin again, and she'd had enough. She was done playing his games. Done being the reason he hurt her friend and mentor. She couldn't do it anymore.

"I'm done!" she said firmly. "No more."

Nightingale looked at her with such evilness and pleasure at her refusal, she shivered. "No? So you're okay with me killing her right here in front of you?"

Allye opened her mouth to respond, but Robin got there first.

"Do it, asshole," she slurred. "You're going to kill me anyway. Just do it already."

"The only one dying here tonight is *you*, Nightingale."

The deep voice with the British accent came from the darkness, and Allye had never heard anything so beautiful in all her life.

Without thinking, she ran toward the sound of the voice.

Before she'd taken more than three steps, however, Nightingale jumped on the stage and snagged her arm. She screeched and tried to yank herself out of his grip, with no luck. Nightingale jerked her toward him and wrapped an arm around her chest. He pressed the knife against her jaw above the leather collar and pulled them both upstage.

Three black shapes moved closer to the stage and surrounded it, while a fourth helped Robin stand and moved her back toward the door.

"Who are you? How'd you get in here?" Nightingale shouted, shuffling backward, practically carrying Allye with him.

"Who we are doesn't matter. All that matters is you letting her go."

Allye didn't know who spoke, but it didn't make a difference. They were here. They'd found her.

From the side, someone jumped onto the stage and held his hands up as he approached, indicating he was unarmed.

"Let her go."

Allye almost stopped breathing.

Gray. That was Gray. He was *here*!

She frantically tried to see him, but his back was to the spotlight, and all she saw was his silhouette.

"Come closer and she dies!" Nightingale said, turning to fully face the new threat, putting pressure on the bloody knife he held to her neck.

She tried not to react, but couldn't help the small whimper when the tip pressed into her skin. It was excruciatingly painful. Now *this* was exactly what Gray had tried to tell her would happen. That he wouldn't be able to bear it if she was being used to get him to do something. Just like when he was in Afghanistan.

But no. This wasn't the Middle East, and she wasn't a helpless victim. Gray wasn't tied up, and he had his badass friends at his back. Between all of them, they could surely outsmart the man holding her hostage. Couldn't they?

She couldn't see Gray's face. Couldn't tell if he was sending her any signals or not, so she'd have to be the one to send *him* some sort of signal. But what? Nightingale was holding her too tightly for her to be able to go limp and hope he dropped her. The knife he was holding to her neck was extremely sharp, and he'd easily be able to hurt her badly if Gray jumped him.

So what could she do?

"Master?" she said softly, the word seeming loud in its obscenity.

"What'd you say?" he asked, squeezing his arm around her chest tighter.

"Master," Allye repeated, "you're hurting me. I can't dance if you hurt me."

His grip loosened a fraction. "You're mine," Nightingale said. "I bought you . . . you're *mine*."

"Yours," Allye said, staring at Gray. "I'm yours to do with as you please."

"Your eyes were what drew me. I knew I had to have you," Nightingale rambled. "And your hair, so pretty, that white streak . . . I want to have babies with eyes just like yours and with that white streak in their hair."

"I want that too," Allye told him, all the while still looking in Gray's direction.

"Will you dance for me, Mystic? All I ever wanted was to collect beauty. And you're the most beautiful addition to my collection yet."

"Yes, Master," Allye dutifully told him. "I'll dance for you. I'll stay here and do whatever you want me to."

"You're lying!" he growled, tightening his hold on her and bringing the knife up to her face. He ran the flat edge up her cheek and paused with the tip just under her eye. "Maybe I'll cut out your eyes and put them in a jar. That way I can look at them whenever I want without having to deal with back talk and you betraying me. Women *always* lie. They always promise one thing and then take it away."

"I'm not lying," Allye said, knowing she'd seriously underestimated this man.

"You *are* . . . but that's okay," Nightingale said. "Because I'm going to fuck you, keep you alive long enough to have my pup, then stuff your body so I can look at your eyes anytime I want."

Allye opened her mouth to respond—but didn't get the chance.

The second Nightingale turned to face Gray—probably to taunt him some more—and moved the knife away from her face, he was ripped away from her. He was on the ground with Black and Arrow on top of him, before she could say a word. They'd moved in from behind while his attention was focused on threatening her and avoiding Gray's advance.

Then Gray was there. He wrapped his arms around her, picking her up so her feet weren't touching the rough wood planks anymore, and jumped off the stage with Allye still in his arms. He backed down the aisle until they reached Robin. Without a word, he eased Allye to the ground. He looked at the padlock on the collar around her throat, and his jaw ticked. He ran his thumb over the small scratch on her jaw from the knife Nightingale had threatened her with, then nodded at Ro, who had followed him up the aisle.

He stalked back down the aisle toward his teammates—and the loudly protesting and fighting Nightingale.

"Look away if you don't want to watch him die," Ro told Allye and Robin in a tone of voice he might have used when discussing the weather.

Allye couldn't. She wanted to see the man die. Needed to.

She couldn't hear what the men were saying, but it was obvious Black, Arrow, and Gray were getting information from him any way they could. They turned him onto his back and, using the same knife he'd used to hurt Robin and Allye, held it to his neck.

Allye finally looked away when Nightingale screamed and his feet started pounding on the rough wood of the stage.

She hoped the terrible man who had hurt so many was suffering as much as possible.

As if in confirmation, Nightingale's next scream was high-pitched and anguished.

She was about to look back when Ro said quietly, "Not yet, love."

So Allye kept her eyes on Robin. She eased over to her friend and took her hand in her own, squeezing it tightly, happy that the woman was still alive after everything she'd been through. She was relieved when Robin had the strength to return the pressure.

Nightingale screamed again, this one sounding a bit gurgled, but Allye still didn't look toward the stage. She heard him protesting one more time, pleading for his life, then he grunted.

And that was that.

"Is it over?"

"It's over," Ro confirmed.

"Are you guys going to get in trouble?"

The big Brit looked down at her and smiled then. "Trouble? Hardly. I think the city might just give us a medal."

Then Gray was there once more. His lips were drawn into a hard, thin line, and he didn't speak as he leaned over and picked her up again. Ro scooped up Robin, and they left the big, eerie room.

Allye looked over Gray's shoulder as they left. The spotlight was still shining on the stage. Nightingale's dead body lay in the middle of the wood planks, his blood staining the boards under him. His legs were spread open, his arms at his sides, and he was staring up at nothing.

Allye closed her eyes and felt only relief. It was over. Yes, there were other men to track down, and there were still hundreds of missing women Nightingale had orchestrated the sales of, but her life could return to normal.

Why she wasn't happier about that, Allye didn't know.

Yes, she did. Gray. She had no idea where they stood and what he'd want.

She laid her head on Gray's shoulder and sighed. She'd think about it later. Much later.

Chapter Seventeen

Allye lay in the hospital bed, antsy and ready to leave. They'd walked out of the bunker under the San Rafael Exotic Animals Refuge well after midnight the previous evening, into a sea of emergency lights. Rex had contacted the local police, and they'd descended in swarms.

The men Allye had seen helping Nightingale with his torture were in custody, and the women he'd been holding hostage were taken to the hospital.

Ball, Black, and Arrow had managed to sneak off without being questioned by the police, but since Ro and Gray had been carrying Robin and herself, they'd been detained.

Gray had actually kissed her on the forehead before nodding at the paramedics in the ambulance to shut the doors. She wanted to protest. Wanted to say that she wasn't going anywhere without him, but she still didn't know how he felt. He was there, yes, but he hadn't spoken more than two words to her since he'd rescued her.

He'd been so angry with her in Colorado. And she'd snuck out of his house like *she* was in the wrong. Maybe he'd just felt a sense of responsibility for her. And now that he'd rescued her—again—he was done.

The thought made the pesky tears spring to the surface once more, but Allye held them back by sheer force of will.

She'd been poked and prodded by several doctors. They'd pulled the splinters from her feet, given her an IV because she was dehydrated, and kept her overnight for observation. Now it was midmorning, and they hadn't discharged her yet. She didn't know what they were waiting for, and was contemplating getting up and simply walking out when she heard a disturbance in the hallway outside her room.

A woman was arguing with someone that she was going to see her son's fiancée, and nobody and nothing was going to stop her.

Allye grinned. She could just imagine some little old lady shaking her finger in a doctor's face and giving him hell.

She was still grinning when the door to her room opened, and a woman she'd never seen before stood there. A nurse was right behind her.

"I'm so sorry, Ms. Martin. This woman says she's related to your fiancé and won't take no for an answer. Just say the word, and I'll call security and have her removed."

Allye stared at the woman in the doorway. She was tall; she had to be almost six feet, in Allye's estimate. She was slender and wearing a knee-length skirt, a designer blouse, and three-inch Jimmy Choo shoes. She carried a Louis Vuitton bag big enough to hold plenty of clothes for Allye to survive on for a week.

"Hello, Allye," the woman said, stepping into the room with a wide grin.

"Ms. Martin, should I call security?" the nurse asked nervously.

Allye's eyes went from the woman to the nurse, and she shook her head. "No, it's fine."

"Just use the call button if you need me," the nurse said.

Before she left, Allye asked, "You were going to check on my discharge . . . Have you found the doctor yet?"

"Oh, right. I'll see what I can do," the nurse mumbled as she left the room, leaving Allye with the stranger.

The woman put her bag on the floor and stepped closer to the bed. Her silver hair was in an elaborate updo, and her brown eyes twinkled as she smiled at her. Her makeup was flawless, and she honestly looked like a model to Allye. But she was probably around sixty, so her being a model was probably unlikely.

She hovered near the side of the bed, but didn't come close enough for Allye to feel threatened in any way.

"My name is Pene Rogers, dear," the woman said. "And my son has said nothing but good things about you. I'm so glad to finally meet you, I'm only sorry it's in a situation like this."

Allye stared at the woman. *This* was Gray's mother? She'd pictured someone completely different. Not this . . . beautiful, fashionable goddess. It made Allye even more uneasy to meet her.

"Uh . . . hi. Do you know where your son is?"

She waved her hand in the air breezily. "Oh, he's taking care of something. Don't you worry. He'll be here before you know it."

That's what Allye was afraid of. "What are you doing here?"

"Gray called early last night and said he needed me. He'd left me a message that said you'd be here, so I came straight to the hospital from the airport."

Allye was confused. Early last night, she'd still been in Nightingale's clutches. How did Gray know he'd find her? Or that she'd be okay?

Pene patted her hand. "Don't think about it too hard. Grayson has always seemed to know things before they happened. Did he tell you about the time I got in a car accident and was badly wounded? He was stationed overseas and called the Red Cross before they could get in touch with him. I was fine, but he somehow knew I'd been hurt."

Allye stared at Gray's mom, not knowing exactly what to say.

But she didn't seem to notice or care. She pulled up a chair and began a mostly one-sided conversation as if it were the most natural thing in the world.

"I feel as if I already know you. I looked you up online, you know. You dance beautifully. I've read all your interviews too. I think you'll have your work cut out for you if you want Grayson to turn into a vegetarian, but it's good for him to eat healthier. He eats too much red meat as it is. But honestly, it's no wonder my son loves you so much. You're gracious, beautiful, and talented."

"Um . . . I think you have the wrong idea," Allye told her. "We had a fight. I'm not sure we're even together anymore."

Pene stared at her for a long moment, then smiled. "One thing you need to learn about Grayson. He's kind of a hothead. His father, rest his soul, was like that too. Grayson gets all worked up about something, then when he's had time to think, he comes to his senses. You just need to give him that thinking time and space. I've told him time and time again that if he doesn't get that under control, he's going to suffer the consequences. I hate to tell him 'I told you so,' but . . . if the shoe fits."

Allye couldn't help but smile.

Pene leaned in, rested her elbows on the mattress, and lowered her voice as if she were telling a secret. "I probably shouldn't bring this up, since I'm his mother and all, but Lordy, after his father and I fought, and the man came back and we had a more civilized conversation . . . the make-up sex was out of this world!"

Allye blushed hotly. Then she asked tentatively, "Your husband died?" She thought she recalled Gray saying something about it while they'd been in the ocean, but she couldn't be sure.

"Unfortunately, yes. I miss that man every minute of every day, but he gave me the best twenty years of my life. I wouldn't trade those for anything in the world. He used to say, 'Pene, my love, you only have one life, and you have to live every day as if it's your last.' And that's what we did together. He was a train engineer, and it was a freak accident. A car was stuck on the tracks, and instead of getting out of the control room like he was trained to do, away from the impact, my husband did everything he could to slow down the train before it hit the car."

"What happened?" Allye asked, horrified for the beautiful woman sitting before her.

"At impact, the car caught fire, and it spread to the control room, and he couldn't get out."

Allye couldn't help herself. She reached out and put her hand on Pene's, squeezing lightly. "I'm so sorry."

Pene nodded. "Thank you, sweetheart. Frankly, it sucked. But Grayson and his brother were there for me. What I learned through all of it is to love hard while you have the chance. Love with your whole heart, and give it your all. Make whatever sacrifices you have to in order to make your relationship work. Because, as I said, we only live once. Make it count."

Allye's eyes teared up. It seemed once the dam had been broken, there was no holding back her tears anymore.

"Lordy, don't cry, dear! Grayson will have my head if he walks in here and sees you in tears, especially since you never cry."

"He told you that?" Allye asked, holding her tears back by changing the subject.

"Oh yes. He's told me all sorts of things about you."

"I didn't know you talked that often."

"He's my child. I'd talk to him every day if he let me. But I try to control myself." The older woman winked at her.

Allye couldn't fathom that. Her own mother had never talked to her unless she had to. The foster parents she'd had weren't that way with their own children either. It was as if, once the kids turned eighteen, the parents were glad to see them head out into the world so they could have their lives back.

"You'll see when you have your own kids," Pene said, patting Allye's hand knowingly.

Gray's mom stayed with her and chatted about what Gray was like as a kid, what she did now with her volunteer groups, and even a little about Gray's younger brother, Jackson.

Allye lost all track of time, fascinated by Pene and how open and friendly she was. But soon she was nodding along to whatever Pene was saying, because she was feeling extremely tired and wasn't exactly paying attention anymore.

"I hope when you come out to Florida to visit, you'll come to one of my clogging classes. We're not as good as you, but I've told all my friends about you, and they're dying to meet you. Maybe you can talk to that dance group of yours and tell them a trip to Florida for a performance is a good idea. No, I know! I'll come up there to Denver. Girls' road trip! It'll be a ton of fun and—"

"Mom, can't you see she's exhausted? Give it up."

And with those words, Allye was suddenly wide-awake again.

Gray was standing in the doorway, leaning on it with his arms across his chest. When he saw her looking at him, he pushed upright and sauntered across the room. He kissed his mom on the cheek, then turned to her. "How you feeling, kitten?"

Hearing him say his nickname for her in that low, sexy voice made the tears spring to her eyes once more.

"Don't cry. God, don't cry," he said in a tortured tone.

He sat on the edge of her bed and gathered her into his arms, burying his face in her hair.

She barely noticed when Gray's mom slipped silently out of the room, leaving them alone.

"I'm so sorry," he said, not lifting his head. "I was a dick. I should've listened to you. I had already decided you were right and there was no way you'd hide out while other people were being hurt and killed, and was on my way back home. And for the record, I couldn't do it either."

"I shouldn't have rushed off without talking to you again," Allye replied. "I was hurt and wasn't thinking straight."

Gray pulled back. "I guess we both still have some learning to do about each other, huh?" He gently ran his thumbs under her eyes, wiping away the stray tears that dampened her cheeks. "I hate that I made you cry, when you never cry."

She gave him a small smile and held on to his wrists. "I think it's good for me."

He rolled his eyes at her, which made her smile even wider.

"Take me home?" she whispered.

"To your apartment?" he asked.

Allye shook her head. "No, home. To Colorado. I miss your house."

"*Our* house. And nothing would please me more than to take you home." He paused then, as if thinking about whether he should ask something. She saw the moment he decided to just go for it. "Will you miss it here? The dance theatre? Your friends?"

Allye immediately shook her head. "I can dance in Colorado. And my friends will still be my friends. Hopefully I'll make new ones too."

"You will," he vowed. "How could you not? You're amazing."

She smiled up at him. "How's Robin? Can I see her before we go?"

"Last I heard, she's okay. Has some pulled muscles—and before you ask, no, you don't need to know how she got those—and she had to have quite a few stitches, but her husband is here, and he told me earlier she can go home in a few days."

"I'm glad."

"You did awesome up there," Gray said. "I hated that you were in danger, but you stayed smart and did what you could to keep him off balance and distracted while the others snuck up on him."

Allye nodded sadly, then said quietly, "I'm glad he's dead. Did you see those other women in the other rooms?"

"Yeah. They're here in the hospital, too, although I did hear they had to take the one with all the tattoos to the mental ward. Nightingale really messed her up."

"He suffered, right?" Allye asked after glancing at the door to make sure it was still closed.

"Yeah, kitten. We made sure of it."

"Good."

"I love you," Gray said after a moment. "So much, you just don't know. When I first met you, I thought you were a bit too snarky for my taste. But by the time Black fished us out of the ocean, I think I knew you were it for me. Levelheaded, calm under pressure, and someone I definitely liked having at my side in an emergency."

"Really?"

"Really. I was shocked as hell when you showed up at The Pit, but relieved as well. I knew I'd been given a second chance. My dad always used to tell me to live the life you're given with no regrets. Well, I regretted letting you go and not getting your number the second I left that beach. Then there you were. In Colorado. It was a sign, and I wasn't going to let you go again."

"I'm glad you didn't. I can't promise to always be the best girlfriend, because I've never really been loved by anyone before. But I promise to try to be receptive to what you're saying and do my best to not run off without talking to you again."

Gray shook his head. "No, kitten. I'll do *my* best to listen and not fly off the handle."

"Your mom says you inherited that from your dad."

"I suppose I did," he said sheepishly.

"I'll give you space when you need it," Allye vowed. "You're allowed to process, Gray. I'll try not to push you to make a decision when it's something big and important."

"Speaking of something big and important," Gray said, running his hand over her hair once, then standing.

Allye gasped when he went down on one knee on the hospital-room floor. She stared at him with her mouth open and her eyes wide.

"Allye Martin, I love you. So much so, I can't imagine spending the rest of my life without you. Will you marry me? Sleep by my side for the rest of our lives? Have children with me that we'll love unconditionally and annoy so much they'll be happy to leave home after graduating high school, but then will miss us so much they'll show up the next night for a home-cooked meal? Will you put up with my mood swings and my job with weird hours? Will you promise, no matter what I might say or do, that you'll never leave me and will love me forever? I can't live without you, kitten. I gave you up once, and let you down in the worst way. I won't do it again."

This time, Allye's tears were joyous ones. "Yes, Gray. Of course I'll marry you. I love you so much."

Then she was in his arms, and he was holding her as if he'd never let her go.

Allye happened to look up, and she saw Gray's mom looking in the window of the small hospital room. She was crying, too, and when she saw that Allye had noticed her, she gave her a thumbs-up and a smile.

Allye closed her eyes and let Gray take her weight. How she'd gone from almost drowning in a boat in the middle of the ocean to being happier than she'd ever been in her entire life, she didn't know. But as Pene Rogers said, live life as if every day is your last. And that's just what she was going to do.

Epilogue

"Allye!" Gray called. "Let's go! We're going to be late!"

"Keep your pants on!" she yelled down the stairs. "I'm comin'."

Gray grinned and went back to pacing. It was recital afternoon at the Barbara Ellis Studio of Dance in Colorado Springs, where Allye had been teaching since they'd returned from California. She'd made the decision that she didn't want to dance herself anymore, at least not with a professional dance theatre. Part of that decision was made because she'd have to drive up to Denver at least twice a week to continue to do so, as there wasn't a professional theatre in Colorado Springs. And she'd said the other part of her decision was because she'd enjoyed teaching the class with little Rory, the girl with Down syndrome, and she wanted to do it as a career.

Barbara had gladly brought Allye on staff. This afternoon was the first recital since she'd started teaching full-time, and the class for children with disabilities was making its debut. There were eight boys and girls in the class—three with Down syndrome, two in wheelchairs, one who used a walker, and a pair of sisters with seizure disorders.

Gray thought he was more nervous than Allye. He heard her on the stairs, turned, and froze.

He couldn't believe someone as beautiful as Allye was with *him*.

She had on a fairly modest dress. It was black, with a high neck and long sleeves, but cutouts left her shoulders bare. It was formfitting and sleek, and shimmery from whatever was in the fabric. And in her heels, she was slightly taller than usual.

She did a little spin at the bottom of the stairs and asked, "Do I look okay?"

"Do you look okay?" Gray asked as he slowly walked toward her.

"Yeah. The dress is new, and one of the girls at work helped me pick it out, but I thought it might be too much. I mean, it's only an afternoon dance recital and—"

Gray didn't let her finish. He put one hand behind her neck and pulled her to him so hard, she let out a small "umph" as she hit his chest. Then his lips were on hers, and he was kissing her as if he'd never get enough.

She didn't push him away. In fact, one hand went around the back of *his* neck, and her fingernails dug into his skin as she held him and kissed back. Their heads tilted one way, then the other, as their breathing sped up.

Gray pulled back when he knew he was one second away from spinning her around, hiking up her skirt, and taking her right there on the stairs.

He could tell she knew how on edge he was. Her eyes sparkled with lust, and she had a rosy flush to her cheeks. She licked her lips slowly, and he almost decided the hell with being on time.

"I guess I look okay," she teased.

"You look good enough to eat," he retorted. "And I'm fucking starving."

She rolled her eyes at him, and Gray felt his cock get even harder. God, he couldn't get enough of her sass. The thought that he'd almost lost her hit him at the weirdest times, and this was one of them.

"Don't," she said, leaning forward and kissing him softly. "I'm here, and I'm fine."

"I love you," he told her.

"And I love you too," she returned immediately. "But we really do need to get going. The kids are gonna flip if I'm late."

"No, they aren't," Gray told her. "They'll greet you just like they always do, with big hugs."

"True," Allye admitted. She brought one hand up to his face and palmed his cheek. "How'd I get so lucky?"

"That's my line," Gray said.

They smiled at each other, and he finally broke their embrace, turning her and giving her a little push toward the garage and then a smack on the butt. "Get going, woman, your minions await."

Giggling, she led the way to the garage.

Hours later, after Allye's special-needs kids stole the show by being the most enthusiastic group of kids ever to dance, even though they definitely weren't the most coordinated; and after Barbara Ellis announced that the name of the school was being changed to the Barbara Ellis and Allyson Mystic Studio of Dance; and after his mom surprised them by showing up at the recital with two of her friends; and after Ro, Ball, Black, Meat, and Arrow *also* surprised them by showing up with enough flowers for every little girl and boy to receive one, making Allye cry in the process; and after Allye said hello to every parent who showed up to watch the performances, Gray finally pulled into the garage back at their house.

He hit the button to close the garage door and shut off the engine.

"Stay there," he ordered as he climbed out.

Allye stayed sitting, a small smile on her face as she humored him.

Gray stalked around the car to the passenger side and opened the door. The first thing he saw was the overhead light glinting off the engagement ring on her finger. He'd wanted to get her something big and gaudy, but defied tradition and let her pick out what she liked instead. The last thing he wanted to do was buy her something she wasn't going to love. But he'd arranged it so that, when they went to the jewelers, the man didn't tell her anything about prices. Gray had wanted Allye to design exactly what she wanted, price be damned.

She'd ended up with a ring Gray never would've picked out for her, but one he knew was perfect. Her eyes had lit up the first time she'd seen it, and he knew he'd move heaven and earth to see that kind of amazement and joy in her eyes every day for the rest of their lives.

It was platinum, with two small, square diamonds on either side of a bigger emerald-cut stone. Total carats were only about two. He would've gone with a four- or five-carat ring that no one would be able to mistake for anything other than what it was, a claiming, but he loved what she'd created for herself simply because *she* loved it so much.

Reaching down, Gray helped Allye out of the car, then closed the door behind her. He crowded her back toward the vehicle, and his hands went to her hips and started inching up her dress. "I couldn't think about anything other than doing this the entire time today."

She smiled at him and played with the buttons on his white dress shirt as he slowly slid her dress over her hips. "Yeah?"

"Yeah," he told her, then shifted her over two feet or so and abruptly spun her around so she was facing the hood of the still-warm car. He pushed on her back, and she eagerly bent over, spreading her legs without him having to tell her to.

His hand went between her legs, and he found she was soaking wet for him. "You're awfully wet, kitten."

"I fantasized about this all the way home. About you taking me in this dress, without bothering to take it off first."

"You did, huh?" Gray asked as he roughly fingered her, making sure she was slick and could take him without pain.

"Uh-huh."

"What else did you think about?" he asked as his free hand went to the button and zipper on his pants.

"Us in the shower. In the—" Her words cut off as Gray pulled her panties to the side and thrust into her without warning.

"This?" he asked. "Did you think about this?"

"Yes . . . oh God, yes." Allye leaned over farther, offering herself up to him, the heels putting her at just the right height for him to thrust into her without having to bend his knees.

Gray knew he was acting crazy, but seeing how wonderful she was with all the kids at the recital just made him love her all the more. And that made him want to show her exactly how much she meant to him. He'd controlled himself all afternoon. Hadn't snuck her away for a quickie in one of the empty workout rooms. He needed this. Needed *her*.

Their skin slapped together as he thrust in and out, her dress thrown up over her back, and he held on to it with one hand as the other kept hold of her hip. His pants and briefs had been shoved down only as far as they needed to be to get his cock out and inside her.

Gray looked down where they were joined, and he felt himself spurt a bit of precome as he saw how slick his bare cock was with her juices. He wasn't wearing a condom, and he couldn't even be bothered to worry about it. If he got her pregnant, so be it. He was going to marry her as soon as she was ready, and with or without child, she was his.

"Please," Allye moaned as her hands scrambled on the hood for purchase.

"You want to come, kitten?" he asked, not slowing his thrusts.

"Yes."

"Then make yourself come," he ordered.

One of her hands immediately disappeared under her, and Gray could feel her fingers along his length as he pulled out. She didn't comment on his lack of condom but immediately used their slickness to wet her fingers before bringing them to her clit. He pressed back inside her even as she stuck her butt out farther and urgently stroked, bringing herself to orgasm within seconds.

"Gray, I . . ."

"Yes, kitten. Let go. I got ya."

And she did. Her legs shook, and her body clenched down on his cock as he drove it in and out of her a little slower as she orgasmed. Just as she finished, Gray felt his own release shoot up from his balls and out his cock.

The feeling of coming deep inside her was like nothing he'd ever experienced before. He hadn't thought making love without a condom would feel all that different, but he was wrong. So very wrong. The warmth around his dick increased tenfold, and he could already imagine the thousands, millions, of sperm from his come swimming their way up her channel to her womb.

He smiled and shifted so he was pressed even tighter to her ass, not wanting even one drop to escape before it had a chance to do its thing.

Allye sighed under him and shifted. Gray knew he needed to move, but he really didn't want to. Making a mental note to fuck her again as soon as possible, in a bed next time so he could fall asleep with his cock still inside her, Gray eased out of her body.

He watched in fascination as his come immediately began to leak from inside her.

"Gray?" she asked, turning her head to look at him. "I need to get inside and clean up."

Knowing she was right, Gray pulled his underwear and pants up, but didn't button them. He then turned Allye, not bothering to pull down her dress, and picked her up. He carried her into the house and up the stairs.

He put her on her feet in the bathroom and kneeled down to unbuckle her high heels. He felt her fingers in his hair as he concentrated on the complicated fastenings. Some people might think doing this for her wasn't manly, but as far as he was concerned, taking care of her in this little way was one of the many manly things he did for her on a daily basis. And he wanted to do it. Wanted to make her happy.

Comfortable. Wanted to make sure she was fed, and was never thirsty. It was his honor, and he'd happily spend the rest of his life taking off her shoes for her at the end of every day.

"Shower?" he asked as he stood and turned her around to unzip her dress.

"Bath, I think," she answered.

Running his hand down her spine, he pushed the dress over her hips, and it fell in a puddle at their feet. Looking down, Gray saw the small scar on the back of her leg where the doctor had removed the tracking device. He'd wanted to leave it in, but Allye had refused, saying she wasn't ever going to put herself in a situation like the one she'd been in back in California, and thus the tracker wasn't necessary.

Gray wanted to protest that with his job as a Mountain Mercenary, she could always be at risk from someone wanting revenge against him or Rex, but in the end, he didn't want to upset her. Meat was working on improving the design anyway so it wasn't as painful to remove and was more effective no matter where the wearer was . . . like underground in a concrete bunker.

He kissed her shoulder and leaned over to turn on the water in the tub. "Take your time, kitten. I'll start dinner. Veggie lasagna all right?"

Allye turned then and looped her arms around his neck. "Perfect. I love you, Gray. Thank you for coming today. It meant a lot."

"Anytime. Anything that's important to you is important to me."

"Are we going to see your mom tomorrow?"

He wrinkled his nose. "Yeah. She said she's coming over around eleven. And bringing her friends. Is that all right?"

"Absolutely. I love your mom."

Gray couldn't help the silly grin he knew was on his face. For a woman who'd once said that no moms ever liked her, she sure was being proven wrong now. And that reminded him. "Shall we talk about karma again?" he asked.

She rolled her eyes. "No."

"Sure? I mean, I'm willing to give you all sorts of examples of how karma has worked out for you."

"Go," she ordered, turning him toward the door and giving him a small push.

Gray went, but he spun around before he left. "I love you, kitten."

Her face went soft. "I love you too. Now get."

He got.

Ronan Cross, known as Ro to his friends, was concentrating on the suspension of the late-model Ford pickup he was working on when he smelled the most delicious thing he'd ever smelled in his life.

He was used to the smell of oil, body odor, or gasoline when he was at work in his small garage. But the smell of lilacs was as out of place as a plate of bacon at a vegetarian retreat.

He climbed out from under the truck and stared at the woman standing in the bay, looking nervous and unsure. She was tall for a woman, maybe half a foot shorter than his six-three. But she had the kind of curves Ro was partial to. Marilyn Monroe curves, he liked to call them. Wide hips, big tits, a waist he could grab on to, and legs that would likely smother him if he ever got between them.

She was wearing a short skirt, one that she felt awkward in, if the way she kept tugging at the hem was any indication. Her blouse was low cut and wasn't the right style for her body type at all. It was a size too small, and the buttons strained to stay closed, leaving small gaps down the front of her body.

Her hair was black and fell past her shoulders. It was absolutely straight, as if she'd taken an iron to it. The strands almost looked as if they had blue highlights when she shifted in the sunlight, and her eyes were an odd shade of purple. She had to be wearing contacts to make them that color, but Ro didn't care. Her makeup was heavy, her lipstick dark.

It had been so long since he'd had the desire to take a woman home, he was surprised at the immediate thought of how those painted lips would look while wrapped around his cock.

He was being rude, staring at her like he was, but Ro couldn't seem to bring himself out of the weird trance he'd gone into the second he'd smelled whatever lotion or perfume she was wearing.

Finally, she broke the tense silence by asking, "Do you have a phone I can use?"

Ro blinked. He couldn't remember the last time anyone had asked to use his phone. Almost everyone had cell phones these days.

And the more he thought about it, the more uneasy he got. He looked past the woman, out to the area in front of his shop, and didn't see a car.

Walking slowly so he didn't spook her, Ro went past the woman and looked around. His shop was located off the beaten path, and there was only a small sign at the end of his driveway indicating there was even a business. There was no sign of a vehicle, and he had no idea how the woman had found him, much less gotten there without a car.

"Where's your car, love?" he asked.

She blinked, looked surprised, then blurted out, "You're English."

"Was, yeah," he said. "Now I'm American. Your car?"

"Oh. Uh . . . I-I don't have one," she stammered.

"How'd you get here, then?" Ro asked, taking a step toward her, not missing the way she took an equal step backward, away from him. Her eyes wouldn't meet his, and he knew she was about to lie.

"A friend dropped me off, but it's the wrong address. I accidentally left my purse in her car and need to call her to come pick me back up."

Ro eyed her for a long minute. It was true that she wasn't carrying a purse, and the shoes on her feet weren't appropriate for walking long distances. But she was lying to him about the friend. He knew she was.

If he'd seen her on the street in downtown Colorado Springs, he would've immediately thought she was a prostitute, but she wasn't downtown. She was standing in the middle of his out-of-the-way garage, shifting uncomfortably and not meeting his eyes. She was no whore. He'd bet his life on it.

"I have a phone you can use," he said softly, not wanting to scare her.

"Thank you," she said, breathing a sigh of relief. She almost looked like she was going to cry for a moment, but she turned her head away and gazed around his shop.

Ro grabbed a rag from a shelf and tried to rub some of the grease off his hands. He reached into his back pocket and took out his cell phone. It was warm from his body heat. He unlocked it and held it out to the woman in front of him.

"Here you go."

"Thanks." She held the phone as if she wasn't sure what to do next.

"Go on, love. I unlocked it for you. Just hit the little phone icon, and call whoever you wish."

She nodded and looked at the phone in her hand for a moment before seeming to make a decision. Then she slowly dialed a number and looked down at the floor while she waited for someone to answer.

Ro knew the polite thing to do would be to give her space. But call him curious, he couldn't leave without knowing more about her situation, because it wasn't sitting well with him at all. People just didn't show up at his place by accident.

"Hi, Abbie? It's me, Chloe. I need a ride." There was a pause while she listened to whoever was on the other end of the line. "I know." Another pause. "I didn't mean to. Will you come and get me or what?" A longer pause, as if the mysterious Abbie was really speaking her mind. "I *know*," she repeated, with a bit of resentment. "Will you come get me or not?"

She looked up at Ro then and said, "I need the address."

Ro gave it to her willingly and watched as she repeated it to whoever Abbie was, and then thanked her before hanging up.

She gave him a weak smile and held out his phone to him. He took it and made sure to brush her fingers with his own as he did. The blush on her face was adorably cute and made her outfit seem all the more out of place.

"You want something to drink while you're waiting?" he asked.

"Oh no, thank you. I don't want to be a bother. I'll just go wait out there," she said, gesturing to the open bay door with her thumb.

"It's not a bother," Ro insisted.

"Just go back to work doing . . . whatever. I'm good. I appreciate the use of your phone." And with that, she turned to walk out.

Ro could've let her go, if that was that. He might've been intrigued and might've wondered what was up with the pretty woman who'd randomly wandered into his auto-body shop out of the blue.

But the second she turned and he saw the huge bruise on her back, it sealed both their fates.

The blouse she had on was white and sheer. He could easily see the outline of the black bra she had on underneath—and the black-and-blue mark on her back was just as noticeable.

He moved before his brain had even fully registered what he was seeing. He stopped her with a hand around her biceps. "You're hurt," he said in a low, pissed-off tone.

She looked up at him in surprise. When she saw where his gaze was, she tried to twist her arm out of his grip. "I'm fine."

"Show me."

"What?"

"Show me," Ro repeated.

"I don't think—"

"I'm not going to hurt you," he said evenly. "I just want to make sure you don't need medical attention."

"I don't," she insisted. She'd stopped trying to get away from him and stood stock-still.

"Please. I won't touch you, I just want to see how badly you're injured."

The woman frowned. "You're not going to let this go, are you?"

"No."

"Why?"

"Because I have a feeling you didn't get that from falling into something. Show me, and I'll let it drop."

He didn't think she was going to, but after a short stare-down, she defiantly lifted her shirt in the back just enough for him to see the mark on her right side.

It was above where her kidneys were. It had to have hurt like a son of a bitch, had to *still* hurt, and Ro knew there was only one thing that made a mark that size and shape. A fist.

She dropped her shirt, but he didn't release her arm. "What's your name?" he asked, steel in his tone.

"Why?" she asked, trying to get him to let go once more. Her other hand came up, and she tried to pry his fingers off her arm. "You're hurting me. Let go."

"I'm not hurting you," Ro replied, knowing his grip was tight, but not bruisingly so. If he was going to help this woman, he needed to know her name. "What's your name?"

"What's yours?" she sassed back.

"Ronan Cross. You can call me Ro. Your turn."

She stared at him for a beat, then said softly, "Chloe Harris."

The name sounded familiar for some reason, but it took him a second to put two and two together. "Fuck. Tell me you're not married to Leon Harris."

Leon Harris was one of the heads of the local branch of La Cosa Nostra, the Mafia, which was headquartered up in Denver. Rex knew about the group, of course, but stayed out of their way because they mainly dealt with counterfeiting, insider trading, extortion, and other corrupt practices—not crimes against women. The group was made up of several major families in the Denver area and a few lower-level families. They all worked together and had one another's backs.

They weren't Mafia like the old-school gangster films romanticized. But they were just as dangerous. Recently, they'd branched out and invited a few old and connected families in Colorado Springs to join their ranks. The Harris family being one of them.

Ro recalled seeing the patriarch, Leon Harris, on television once. He had hair as black as midnight and was tall. Chloe reminded him an awful lot of that asshole.

"I'm not married to Leon Harris," Chloe recited dutifully.

"Thank fuck," Ro breathed out in relief.

"He's my brother," she said quietly.

Ro just stared at her. "He do this to you?" he asked, indicating the bruise on her back.

"Look, it's none of your business," she said, struggling against his hold once again.

Ro let her go. It wasn't as if she were going anywhere. The mysterious Abbie wasn't there yet, and she couldn't exactly go walking off when there wasn't anywhere to go.

"Talk to me," Ro growled.

Chloe crossed her arms, making the gaps in her blouse close slightly, and shook her head. "I don't know you. All I wanted was to use your phone."

"And all I want, love, is to make sure you're safe, happy, and healthy. And by the looks of that bruise, and the fact you're standing in my shop with no car anywhere, you aren't any of the three."

They had another slight staring contest then, with Ro glaring at her with his own arms crossed, and her glaring right back. She licked her lips and finally looked away from him uneasily.

"I'm not going to hurt you," Ro said. "My mum would kick my arse if I ever did anything to hurt a woman."

"I'm okay. I'm moving out soon."

"Christ," Ro said. "You live in the same house as him?"

"He's my brother," Chloe said. "So yeah, I do."

Ro reached into his back pocket. The chain attached to his belt loop jingled when he pulled out his wallet. He extracted a business card. It had his logo and Ro's AUTO BODY across the top. He held it out to her.

She looked at the card like it was a snake that would bite her if she reached for it.

Stepping toward her, Ro picked up her hand and put the card in her palm, wrapping her fingers around it. "That's my card. You need anything, and I mean *anything*, you call me. I'll help you out no matter what time it is. Got it?"

"Why?" she whispered, not looking down at the card.

"Because you need it. And you smell better than anyone I've ever smelled in my life."

She blinked at that, then smiled. "You're offering to help me because of the way I smell?"

"Look around, love. You think anything in this place smells good? It doesn't. So yeah, when a breath of fresh air comes into my shop, smelling and looking like you, with a bloody bruise on her back that I know was put there by a man? You better believe I'm offering to help her."

"Oh, well . . . thank you."

"Don't thank me unless you intend to use that," Ro said, motioning to the card with a nod.

"I don't think I'll need it, but I'll call if something comes up."

Ro knew it was the best he was going to get right then.

He saw a car pull into his driveway and approach them. It was a Mercedes. This year's model, if he wasn't mistaken. The woman scowled at him and Chloe as she stopped. She didn't bother to get out.

"That's Abbie. I need to go," she said as she stepped backward, away from him.

He saw her tuck his business card into a small pocket on the front of her shirt, while her back was still toward the woman who'd arrived to pick her up.

"Thank you," she said softly, then turned to walk to the Mercedes.

Ro kept his eyes on the driver, just as she kept her eyes on him. The second that Chloe entered the car, the woman turned and began to berate her. Ro could tell she was yelling at Chloe by the way she gestured to him with her hand and the way her brows were drawn down in anger or consternation.

The woman shook her head as if in disgust, then looked behind her, slowly backing out of his driveway rather than taking the time to turn around.

Ro memorized the license-plate number on the Mercedes, then brought his gaze up to Chloe. She wasn't looking at him. Her head was bowed, and she stared at her lap as Abbie backed the car away from the house and shop.

He still didn't know how Chloe had ended up at his shop, but he'd find out. Making a mental note to call Rex as soon as possible, Ro took a few steps until he was standing at the outer edge of the shop floor.

He was still standing there long after the car had disappeared from view.

Chloe was a mystery. She looked to be around his age, midthirties. He knew Leon Harris had just turned thirty because he'd had a huge shindig downtown and had invited a bunch of local foster kids. It had all been for show, but it had caught the media's attention, and they'd done a short segment on it for the local news.

Why was Chloe living with her younger brother? Why was she letting someone beat on her? And why was she wearing clothes that were made for a younger, thinner, more . . . *worldly* woman? All questions Ro didn't have answers to . . . yet.

He recalled the way she'd tucked his card into her pocket. Away from prying eyes? He hoped so. Come hell or high water, she'd be hearing from him again.

Turning back toward the truck, Ro inhaled deeply, still able to smell the slight scent of lilac in the air. Oh yeah, Chloe Harris hadn't seen the last of him.

Acknowledgments

This is the place in a book where an author thanks all the people who have helped her with this story.

I literally couldn't ever thank everyone who has helped me. From my amazing editors to my husband, who puts up with click-click-clicking on the laptop all the time. From my friends who help me brainstorm, to my dogs, who don't care *what* I do as long as they can sleep on the couch next to me.

But I'd be remiss if I didn't thank *you*, dear reader, for picking up this book and reading my words. There are better books out there, I'm sure. But I hope reading this story, which came straight from my imagination, gives you a few hours of entertainment. And besides, reading anything is always better than doing things like taking out the trash or cleaning the house, right?

Acknowledgments

[illegible]

About the Author

Photo © 2015 A&C Photography

Susan Stoker is a *New York Times*, *USA Today*, and *Wall Street Journal* bestselling author whose series include Badge of Honor: Texas Heroes, SEAL of Protection, and Delta Force Heroes. Married to a retired Army noncommissioned officer, Stoker has lived all over the country—from Missouri to California to Colorado to Texas—and currently lives under the big skies of Tennessee. A true believer in happily ever after, Stoker enjoys writing novels in which romance turns to love. To learn more about the author and her work, visit her website, www.stokeraces.com, or find her on Facebook at www.facebook.com/authorsusanstoker.

Connect with Susan Online

Susan's Facebook Profile and Page

www.facebook.com/authorsstoker

www.facebook.com/authorsusanstoker

Follow Susan on Twitter

www.twitter.com/Susan_Stoker

Find Susan's Books on Goodreads

www.goodreads.com/SusanStoker

E-mail

Susan@StokerAces.com

Website

www.StokerAces.com